ALWAYS AND FOREVER

RUGBY BROTHERS, BOOK 3

TIARA INSERTO

OVLE PUBLISHING

For L.O.V.E

"I did then what I knew how to do. Now that I know better, I do better." - Maya Angelou

DIGITAL ISBN:978-1-949823-06-6

PRINT ISBN: 978-1-949823-07-3

Cover design by LLewellen Designs

CHAPTER ONE

AHIPARA, NEW ZEALAND

MANO SAT UP SUDDENLY. THE SHEET THAT COVERED HIS TORSO FELL at the abrupt movement. He was breathing hard, but the filtered light streaming through broken blinds revealed nothing out of the ordinary. He glanced at the small electric clock on the side table. It was barely past dawn. A slight movement drew his attention to the body next to him. Long black hair cascaded past shoulders that revealed a small tattoo of a heart with an arrow.

Mano closed his eyes, his arm reaching for his neck to massage tense muscles that were always there. He searched his memory as to how he ended up back here, in his bedroom, with someone he didn't recognize.

Nothing.

A blank.

Too many days were starting like this one.

He moved slowly out of bed, hoping the stranger with the gentle curves would stay asleep. He wasn't ready to face eyes tinged with anger or disappointment. Probably both. He saw those emotions in his own reflection every morning. He didn't need the added weight of someone else's feelings on his shoulders.

He spied clothes on the floor, put them on, then quietly moved out of the bedroom. He walked barefoot into the living room, surveying the minimally furnished bach. It was small but well-built with dark wood floors which contrasted with clean, beige walls. Large windows were shuttered. When they were opened, the small living area would be flooded with natural light, even on the cloudiest of days.

He walked into the small galley kitchen, opened the fridge, and reached for a beer. He swallowed the cold liquid quickly. His eyes turned toward the bedroom. It was still quiet. It would have been easy to have forgotten he had company. He'd let her sleep, the stranger in his bed.

Outside, the brightness of the day surprised him. He raised his hands instinctively, hearing the waves rather than seeing them. He knew he had sunnies somewhere in the house. It'd been a while since he needed them. Nothing enticed him to step out of his house during the day, other than to do a quick run to the shops for the essentials. Turning into a night owl had been easy; he would sleep in the darkened house until the sounds of the day ceased.

But the sun felt good today.

He raised his face to the warmth and inhaled deeply. The sea had called him; it was the one place Margot didn't exist in his memory. She had preferred the coolness of the mountains or the earthy feel of the forests. Her aversion to the water and beach was one reason why he hadn't taken the job with Uncle Malcolm. As much as he loved being on the boats, he'd wanted Margot to feel happy about their life together.

So much for that.

He took another drink from the bottle but started to cough when his eyes settled on the two approaching figures coming up from the beach. He squinted to make sure his eyes weren't deceiving him. How the hell did they find him?

Still too distant to distinguish the faces clearly, Mano nevertheless recognized the movements of the two men walking steadily toward him. Sensing and anticipating how they used their bodies were what had made the three of them part of such a successful team not so long ago. Much of his adult life was spent alongside Mitch Molloy and Connor Dane. They were men he admired, loved, and respected. Men he hadn't planned on seeing again for a very long time.

He was tempted to go back inside, seal it, and pretend he didn't know they were there. But the sleeping stranger in his bed complicated things. The last thing he wanted was to be in a locked house with a woman who didn't know what was going on.

He watched Mitch and Connor take the hill with practiced ease and agility. One of the reasons the bach was an attractive purchase was the steep hill that acted as a natural deterrent to anyone exploring the public beach. Obviously, such rules didn't apply to two retired rugby players who, at the peaks of their careers, were considered the best in the world.

A shot of adrenaline went through his body when they both stopped simultaneously.

They had seen him.

Their pace quickened, and Mano fought the urge to run inside. He gripped the bottle tighter. He'd never run away from a fight before.

Seconds later, Connor and Mitch stood near meters from him. Connor's eyes reflected his relief before a smile spread across his face. Mitch, true to character, kept his emotions checked. Mano lifted the bottle to his lips, his gaze still on the two men who returned his study of them. Though both men had been retired for several years, neither was out of shape. *Bet they could still give the younger fellas a good run for their money,* thought Mano as he carefully placed the bottle on the top of the wooden railing.

"You're a hard man to find, Mano," Connor said.

Mano leaned onto the railing. Despite being a good two

meters higher than where Connor and Mitch stood, he could sense the strange mix of anxiety, nervousness, and maybe a little anger directed at him. Mitch had his arms folded across his broad chest while Connor stood askance, his hands resting on his waist.

Mano met Mitch's eyes first, dark and unyielding; they didn't give him any insight into what was going through his former captain's mind. Mano raised his chin defiantly, then gulped the clear amber liquid while ignoring what flowed out the corners of his mouth. He wiped his mouth with the back of his hand and returned the bottle to the railing.

Mitch's lips thinned. His eyes grew darker as they narrowed. Mano knew that look: it was a mask of self-control that Mitch effectively used on every game day. He didn't want them here, but Mano couldn't quite bury the twinge of remorse at his disregard for his friend's concern.

Connor placed his hand on Mitch's arm, pulling him back slightly. He stepped forward with a cautious smile. "You've done well to make yourself disappear. I don't think anyone would have thought you'd have headed to Ahipara. What brought you here?"

"Always wanted to surf."

Mitch and Connor glanced at each other. They knew he was lying. But the truth was, he didn't know either. One minute, he was at the airport, ready to board the plane back to France. The next, he was at the car dealership buying a navy blue ute he didn't need.

Then he drove and drove, only pulling over to the side of the road when fatigue caused him to swerve in and out of lanes. Did he even eat? Unexpectedly, he found himself at the graveside of his former teammate and friend, Jay Morrison. Jay had taught him so much about dealing with his feelings. And it was there he allowed himself to cry for the first time since Margot walked out on him.

When there were no more tears to shed, his anger at her took over. He headed to the first pub he saw and drank himself into oblivion. If it made the news, he didn't know or care. He suspected his fame had something to do with him waking up the next morning, alone, on a makeshift cot in an empty pub. He left cash on the cot before leaving, driving aimlessly until he saw a "For Sale" sign on a wooden gate. He offered above asking, in cash, and with no conditions so that he could move in right away. The owner was more than happy with those terms.

When was that?

He didn't know.

Didn't care.

The gritty sound of the sliding door drew the attention of his "visitors."

"Mano?" Her voice was unexpectedly soft.

He turned to face her, unable to command a smile to his face. He hoped he could hide his indifference to her presence. "Are you okay?"

She nodded, now dressed in a plain t-shirt and jeans. Her long hair was now pulled back into a tight ponytail. She wore glasses that framed large brown eyes. "I had a shower. Hope you don't mind, but I grabbed a bottle of water from the fridge."

"Are you hungry?"

She shook her head with a smile. "I better be going. Thanks for last night."

"Do you need a lift?"

"I drove us back here, remember? You left your ute at the pub." Her voice trailed off when she looked past Mano. Her eyes widened slightly when she saw who was standing beyond the deck. He recognized the look. She knew who they were, but he wasn't going to bother being nice and offer introductions. He was done being nice.

But she surprised him by being distracted for only a few seconds. Instead, she took a step toward him and gave him a soft kiss on his cheek. "Don't worry. I know what last night was about. We both needed to forget things for a bit. I came with my eyes wide open. You didn't lie about what to expect this morning. I'm grateful for that. Not enough honest men about, you know."

He didn't watch her leave. He couldn't because his eyes started to fill tears. Tears he thought he had finished shedding at Jay's grave. As soon as he heard the door close, he hunched over the railing.

"Mate?"

He didn't want to see the pity that laced Connor's voice, but he couldn't stop the torrent of rage that started churning from within. He squeezed the bottle in his hand tighter, his eyes trained on the scattered designs of soil, sand, and rock. To look up would bring his two best friends into the hell he was living.

"Go away," he growled.

Mitch's large body loomed in front of him. "No."

Pain burned up his arm as he made contact with Mitch's jaw; fury overwhelmed any other emotion that could have existed.

"Mano!" Connor's shout sounded far away as he felt Mitch deflect his next punch, pushing him backward.

He threw blindly, rage dictating his swings. "Leave me alone!"

"That will never happen!" Mitch yelled as he lunged.

The wooden deck shook, but the fall didn't release Mitch's hold on him. Mano continued to kick and punch, but his actions were rendered ineffective with Connor now helping Mitch restrain him. He fought harder, but they were stronger. He released his frustrations in screams that were drowned out by waves crashing on the beach below.

Anger yielded quickly to despair. But the fuel for desperation never lasted long under the weight of sorrow.

Then there was no more to give. No more energy to fight.

"We're not leaving, mate," Mitch said quietly.

Mano had spent a lifetime training himself to control his feelings, his actions, his reactions. That was his father's rule. *Manage it, or it will manage you, son.* It was a mantra that rang in his head long after his father's passing, one he had brought with him to every facet of his life.

But he couldn't "manage it," this violent tornado of emotions that threatened to pull him into a hole so deep he wasn't sure he wanted out. He didn't want to "manage" it. He was tired of "managing."

He turned slowly and placed his forehead flat on the deck. The crashing waves didn't mask the heavy breathing from Connor and Mitch. They continued to watch him, ready to pounce if the situation called for it. It was tempting; he wanted the beating. Instead, Mano pushed his torso up, pausing on all fours when an unexpected shot of pain came up the left side of his body.

"You all right?" Connor asked.

He pushed through the pain and stood up. Without glancing backward, he walked through the back door and straight to his bedroom.

* * *

Mano opened his eyes to scabbed knees.

He rolled onto his back and covered his face with his arm. He felt his bed give way. "Who gave you permission to come into my bedroom?" His throat felt tight and dry.

"Mate, you need to keep hydrated." Connor's voice was quiet but firm.

"Not thirsty."

"Drink the damn water, Mano." The second voice, coming from the doorway, was less patient. "I've known you for nearly twenty years, and you've never drunk more than one of anything. Seeing you with a bottle of beer at nine in the morning and finding nothing but empty liquor bottles in the rubbish...."

"You're not in charge of me, Molloy. Get the hell out of my house. No one asked you to come up here."

"You're not yourself, mate," Connor said.

"And given the circumstances…" Mitch interrupted.

Mano's abrupt movement surprised Connor, water splashing out of the glass at his sudden step backward. But Mitch didn't flinch at Mano's proximity. Instead, he stood taller, folded his arms, and stared lazily back. "You heard Con. Drink some water, Mano. You don't look good."

Mano inched his face close enough to feel Mitch's breath. "Go home to your wife and daughter. I don't want you here."

Mitch's sneer reignited Mano's anger, but when he tried to swing, his fist was held back.

"Steady, mate," Connor whispered. "You know you're not really angry at us."

He broke free of Connor's hold. "I can be angry at anyone I want! Maybe it's you I need to hit instead of Mitch."

"No, not really. You got a couple in already, and I have a photoshoot next week. Makeup can only hide so much."

Mitch snorted, and just like that, Mano's anger waned. He stared back and forth between the two before sitting on his bed again, head in his hands. He felt a gentle but heavy touch on his shoulder.

"We're here for you, mate," Connor said. "We've been looking for you for a week. When your uncle is worried enough to call Neela, we knew this was serious."

Mano raised his head slightly. "Uncle Malcolm called Neela?" He shook his head. "No way. Uncle Malcolm wouldn't call Neela."

"Oh, but he did," Connor said as he showed Mano his phone.

Neela: Dad called. Hasn't heard from Mano. Neither have I. You? We're worried.

Mano pushed the phone away.

"Everyone's worried about you," Connor continued. "Even Barnsey tried to get RugNZ involved. You're not the sort to just disappear. Neela and Blake drove down to Dunedin looking for you."

Mano frowned. "Why Dunedin?"

"Neela said you liked the fishing down there."

"I mentioned that once, like ten years ago."

"Apparently, your cousin remembers everything you've ever said to her."

Mitch pulled the stool from the corner and sat in front of Mano. "We're not going anywhere until we know you're good."

Mano squeezed his eyes shut. "I don't know if I'll ever be good again. Nothing makes sense anymore. It was the last thing I ever expected her to do."

"She spent the last two years fighting cancer, Mano," Connor said. "There's no right or wrong way to deal with what she went through. She loves you. We all see that."

Mano scoffed. "She loves me? But she doesn't want me in her life? What am I supposed to do? Wait? Go? What? Tell me, Con? What does a man do when the woman he thought he'd spend the rest of his life with leaves?"

Connor didn't have answers to those questions. No one did. But voicing them for the first time added a finality to his situation. Pained eyes stared back at him. He turned away, his gaze landing on a rug that had seen better days. He blinked when the bedroom window rattled as a sudden gust of wind blew outside.

For two years, he had prayed daily for a miracle for his beloved, that she would survive this disease that had claimed so many. When she went into remission, he never knew such relief and such hope. Except he'd failed to include in his prayers a place for him in her future.

Mano pushed past Mitch and walked toward the living room. He stood in front of the large window that overlooked the deck, revealing a view that should have calmed him with its uninterrupted beauty. Even on its busiest day, with the strongest winds attracting the most skilled surfers from all over, parts of the beach remained untouched.

"She wrote me a note," he began. He didn't have to turn to know Mitch was probably leaning against the kitchen counter while Connor would prefer the small sofa. "At least she wrote it instead of typing it. Two lines that could have been for anybody. That's all I got from her. We shared everything, and when she ends it, all I get is a 'Thank you' and 'Go live your life.'"

He pursed his lips; the now-familiar pounding in his head had returned. Incessant; merciless. It began as soon as he read Margot's words and returned whenever he took the time to think. The only thing that softened its presence was drink. Lots of it. His mother would have been disappointed; his father would have understood.

"Go live your life." His voice was louder than expected. "What the hell does that even mean? She was my life. She knew that."

"Mate…"

He cursed loudly before walking to the fridge. He reached for a glass bottle and flicked open the cover with his teeth. "I'm going for a walk. Don't worry. I'll be back. You should go. Just shut the door. Lots of sandflies this time of year."

He half expected at least one of them to follow him. Their presence would've fed his anger. He felt their eyes on him as he walked barefoot toward the beach, sudden swirls of wind throwing sand in his eyes.

Mano caught a flash of red in the water. He recognized the surfboard from last week, distinctive in color and a contrast to the blue of the ocean it pierced through. The lone surfer took the wave with the ease and grace of someone who had been doing it for years. Shouts echoed through the wind. He scanned the water and picked up another group of surfers not too far away, a younger group, eager in their efforts to pick up the next wave.

He pulled on his hood, took another swig of his drink, but changed his direction from the water's edge to away…just away.

When he returned a couple of hours later, he noticed sleeping pads on the living room floor. The smell of real food lingered.

Connor was at the kitchen counter, his laptop open. He looked up when Mano entered.

"He's here, mate. Do you want to say 'hi'?"

Mano shook his head, but Connor had already turned the screen toward him. "He's been waiting for a long time to talk to you," Connor said quietly.

Mano gave Connor his beer bottle then inhaled deeply. He pulled a smile from somewhere. "Hi, Fred. How's my godson doing?"

"Uncle Mano! I've missed you!" Big blue eyes shone through the computer screen. "Did Dad tell you? I told him not to, but Mummy says he can't keep a secret ever!"

"Your dad hasn't told me anything."

"I could get down Jayne's ramp on my skateboard today! I did it! And she didn't even have to hold my hands! On my own, Uncle Mano!"

A little flame of joy burned through the heaviness of his heart. This time, the smile was genuine. "I'm proud of you, mate! You should be too!"

"I am!" Fred's head disappeared every other second as he jumped up and down. "I did it! Jayne was so happy for me that she started to cry! I've never ever seen her cry before!"

Mano looked at Jayne's father. Mitch didn't hide his smile as he continued to stir whatever it was he was cooking on the stovetop.

"Uncle Mano? When are you coming back?"

Mitch stopped stirring. Connor's body stiffened. Neither looked at him, but they wanted to know the answer as well.

Mano sighed. "I'm not sure, mate. You know I'm always thinking of you."

"Don't be away too long, okay? I've said the prayers you taught me every night this week."

"You're a good fella, Fred Dane." He bit back what he wanted to add. *Prayers don't work, mate.* But Fred's toothy grin stopped him, and Mano could only return the smile. "I'll see you when I can, right? Take care of your little bro. And give your mum a big hug for me."

"I will. I love you, uncle."

Mano's throat tightened; oxygen didn't reach his lungs. "I love you too, mate," he forced out.

He turned the screen back to Connor and walked straight into his bedroom, shutting the door. He leaned against the door, his breathing shallow, the pounding in his head more relentless than ever.

Dammit.

* * *

They wouldn't leave.

He yelled; they yelled back. He tried to start a fight, but together, they were stronger. When he had nothing left inside, they held him. They took turns to slowly feed his soul…then his body.

After a fortnight, Connor flew home for the weekend; Mitch went home the next. But they both came back.

They started running one morning, a slow, steady pace on the beach. His body must have remembered what it was like to be in shape because the following morning, he was ready to repeat the exercise.

Then they started to incorporate sprints, pushing him by example. Longer runs; faster runs; sit-ups; push-ups. They helped strangers pull their kayaks, surfboards, and boats out of the water. The memories of his shared youth with Jay came back, and their late friend's name came up on cold nights by an outdoor fire.

"I'm not him, you know," Mano said. "I just want to be alone."

"Don't believe you, yet," Mitch said, his eyes steady on the flames. "Jay never said when it was bad. We just learned to trust the signs."

"And you think I'm…"

Connor shook his head. "We know you're in shock with Margot leaving."

"People end relationships all the time." Mano threw a twig into the fire. "Go home. Your families need you."

"*You* are family," Connor responded without hesitation.

"You can't stay here forever," Mano said. "You have real lives to go back to. Mine is here now."

Connor shook his head. "We won't stay here forever. When you're back in a good place, we'll go."

"And who decides that, eh?"

"Mate, we know you better than you know yourself."

Mitch's quiet voice spoke next. "After Jay died, Con and I made a promise never to ignore our instincts when it came to our friends. Being here is where we're supposed to be, brother. Nothing you say will convince us otherwise."

Later that night, alone in bed, darkness masking anything he could focus on, Mano recognized he had reached a set of crossroads in his life. He had spent most of his life moving with whatever opportunity presented itself to achieve his goals. Until now, there were only two he had focused on.

Playing for the national team was a straight road, though a longer and bumpier one than he could have ever imagined. The path to marrying Margot was supposed to be shorter and smoother. But the unexpected dead end of that journey had thrown him into disarray.

Where to now?

If his rugby brothers hadn't shown up when they did, he might have continued in his attempts to drive through the dead end instead of turning around.

But which road he was to take next remained a decision he had yet to make.

He woke up the next morning, still unsure of what lay ahead. But for the first time since their arrival, he took charge of breakfast. The sound of the blender woke up Mitch and Connor.

"You all right, mate?" Mitch asked.

Mano studied the mixture before deciding to pulse the liquid further. "Yes. Just thought we could use one of your brother's famous green protein shakes before we head out this morning."

He caught the look Connor threw at Mitch.

Hope.

"Con? I don't think you've tried one of Tim Molloy's protein recipes," Mano said.

"I'll give anything a go at least once," Connor replied.

They ran ten kilometers after breakfast, up and down the beach. While he was the youngest of the three men and still — technically— playing professionally, his month of careless living hadn't done him any favors.

They kept running in the morning. Usually, in silence. They'd then leave him to his thoughts for the rest of the day, but he was never alone. Slowly, he recognized that their quiet presence allowed him to start waking up from the nightmare of his life. The darkness he had sought previously seemed less inviting, but at night, the voice of his lost love continued to haunt his dreams.

One afternoon, after a swim in the ocean, a rugby ball conveniently rolled at their feet. They stared at it; looks exchanged before Mitch picked it up. The owner, a young fella, grinned unapologetically at the three men. With his wet suit unzipped and lying low on his hips, he raised his hands to catch Mitch's toss but didn't stop moving until he reached them.

"Fancy a bit of a game? Us against you three." He nodded his head to the group of young men behind him.

"Not quite the fair odds, is it?" Mitch asked. "There's six of you."

"Seven," interjected another broad-shouldered man who walked up and stood behind his friend. Bronzed and muscled with dirty-blond hair, he grinned. "We think it's pretty fair given none of us have won the World Championship."

"We're old," Connor said, earning a side-glance from Mitch.

"We've been watching the three of you on the beach these last couple of weeks, bro," said the first man. "Old or not, I bet it'd be fun."

"We've got a few bottles from the best breweries in the area up for grabs," the second man tempted.

Connor snorted. Mano shook his head slightly but knew whatever Mitch decided, Connor and he would stand behind their friend. It was how it'd always been.

Mitch tossed the ball back at the first man. "A six-pack and whatever else you brought for the barbie. We've seen you lot around as well. You come prepared."

The surfers didn't tell the rugby players they'd played high school rugby; four had played in state championships. It was supposed to have been touch rugby, but after an "accidental" hit to Mitch's face, the competitiveness that took Mitch, Connor, and Mano to the top level of their sport ignited. No one hurt their captain. Ever.

A couple of hours later, they laughed unashamedly as they carried the chilly bin back to Mano's bach, bruised physically but high with victory.

The careful diet observed over the last few weeks was forgotten that night. They took a step back in time, to a shared period of their lives before global accolades and the frenzied interests in their personal lives. Before the trophies and medals, they were just mates. Impromptu barbecues were the norm.

Connor whistled when he surveyed their winnings. "For a group of surfers, they eat well. King shrimp and steak?"

"You know whose face you pushed into the sand, don't you?" Mitch asked, tossing Connor a can of beer.

"Should I?"

Mano grinned. "That was Ryan Monroe. He's in the current top five of world surfing."

"Well, he plays rugby like shit. Your cousin could take him down without breaking a sweat," Connor said.

"That she could," Mano agreed.

The fire hissed and flamed as they placed the meat and prawns on the grill.

"We're leaving tomorrow, mate," Mitch said.

Mano raised his eyebrows. "Just like that?"

"What do you want? A speech? You're good."

Mano poked at one of the steaks to turn it over. "You trust me again, eh?"

"Mate, I not only trust you with my life but my daughter's."

Mano paused his grilling. "You can't say stuff like that to me," he forced out.

Mitch grinned then took a long drink. "Why not? It's the truth. Besides my own family, you and Con are the two men I'd trust with everything I have. I might put Stanton on that list as well only because my wife adores him. But he's right at the bottom of it."

Mano's lips lifted slightly. "Now that he's married to my cousin, I guess I should say something to defend his honor."

The three men exchanged glances then shook their heads in unison.

An hour later, Mano broke the satisfying sound of silence. "How did you find me?"

"You know Stanton's brother can hack into anything, right?" Connor said.

"I shouldn't ask anymore, should I?"

Mitch shook his head. "Tim managed to get into your room to find your bank records. He owes you a lock, by the way."

Mano raised his eyebrows at the idea of Mitch's geeky, bespectacled younger brother with the genius IQ—who rented a room in his townhouse—doing anything remotely illegal.

"Yeah," Mitch agreed. "I couldn't believe it myself. I think he broke three knives doing it. But we were all pretty frantic."

"Once Tim found your bank records, Stanton's brother managed to figure out that you'd bought this place," Connor finished.

Mano leaned back in his chair. "In theory, I could have all of you arrested for trying to find me."

"Yes," Mitch said.

"Good to know I have something to hold over all of you for the rest of your life."

"Uh...we...also heard the message Margot left on the answering machine," Connor said softly.

Mano folded his arms across his chest. "In the three years we were together, she never once used that number. I guess she wanted to make sure everyone who lived there knew she was leaving me."

"Mano..."

Mano waved his hand dismissively at Mitch's interruption. "It's all right. I understand why you did what you did."

"The club in France will still offer you a contract through the year. They will impose penalties for disappearing," Connor said.

"Was that you or Mitch?"

"Stanton. Finally put his law degree to good use," Mitch answered.

"I'm done with France. The reason I went no longer applies."

Mano was surprised he didn't feel any anger when he said it out loud. Whatever Margot did now was no longer his business, but his feelings for her parents didn't end just because his relationship with their daughter had. Antoinette and Michael were good people. They'd welcomed him openly and willingly, never once asking for more than he offered.

They had initially tried to refuse his offer to pay for Margot's private treatment. In the end, pride took a back seat to the fear of loss. Antoinette was also practical enough to recognize that Michael's continuing needs as Alzheimer's began to set in was going to be an additional drain on their family finances.

No, he'd never regret the season in France. As hurt as he was, he wouldn't regret loving Margot either.

"You plan on staying here?" Mitch asked.

"Why not? I have a house."

An odd composition of incredulity and "Are you stupid?" were on the faces of his two friends.

Mano licked his fingers before reaching for the kitchen towel that doubled as his serviette. "I don't need much."

"If you're doing this to hide from the world, you're not being who you are. You're still young. There's someone else out there for you."

He turned sharply and faced Connor. "There won't be anyone else. She was going to be the only one I'd ever have in my life. Could you honestly see yourself loving anyone other than Cat?" He nodded in Mitch's direction. "And he was pretty much a goner as soon as he laid eyes on Liana. Ever seen him do that before?"

"The difference is that they still want us," Mitch said. "Margot left you."

A bolt of anger shot through Mano's body. A few weeks ago, he wouldn't have given a second thought to hitting Mitch. But fact was fact, so he kept his fists by his side. This time. "Doesn't stop how I still feel about her."

But Mitch didn't back down. "I've never lied to you. The man I know would face the life he was meant to live, whatever it is. You hiding out here? Picking up a game of footy on the beach with surfers? This isn't you, mate."

"What does that mean anyway? 'The life I'm meant to live'? Maybe it's meant to be here, away from everything I've ever known, away from the memories I had made with her. Talk to me again about living the life I'm meant to live when Liana isn't in your life anymore, Mitch, because I can tell you, it's hell!"

Mano ignored the look Connor threw at Mitch. They sat quietly until the last embers died, no more words exchanged.

The next morning, before Mitch and Connor headed home, they had a final run up and down the sand dunes. He welcomed the burn in his thighs after a sleepless night. He liked being physically strong again, but instinctively, he also knew he was not entirely out of the emotional hole he had fallen in.

After they packed the car, Connor held on especially tight in their embrace. "Hang in there, my brother. It's not just Fred who wants to see you home, yeah?"

"I know. Thanks, mate. You didn't have to come...."

Connor broke their hug and placed his hands on Mano's shoulders. "I did. I had to be here. If the situation were reversed, you would have been here as well. Thicker than blood, eh?" He stared squarely at Mano. "Please call Spurgeon. He's waiting. You will, won't you? We all need help once in a while. Can't be strong all the time."

Mitch handed Mano a paper. "An athletic director at an American college had reached out to Liana a couple of months ago. He'd asked her if I knew of anyone who'd be interested in a consulting position with them for a few months. Pro rugby is expanding over there, and the college wants to build a stronger program to give its students a chance at playing in the professional league. I checked with Liana last night, and the position is still open."

Mano stared at the paper, frowning. "America?"

"Northern California. Liana says the director is a good bloke. And the college is known for producing top athletes that compete internationally. The rugby head coach used to play for the American national team."

Mano frowned. "Do we know him?"

"The records said we've played against him once. But I don't remember him personally."

Mano nodded as Mitch reached for a hug. They were both aware of what remained unspoken. They were more than friends. He knew Connor and Mitch would do anything for him, as he would for them.

"Thicker than blood," Mano muttered.

"Always."

"And call Spurgeon!" Connor yelled from the car.

After they disappeared from his sight, Mano walked back into the house, hands in the pockets of his hoodie. The emptiness didn't bother him. He looked toward the kitchen: not a thing out of place. Few people would have associated such an immaculate setting to three rugby players living together for weeks.

There was no suggestion of bacchanalia-type festivities; no alcohol bottles or cans scattered on the floor; not one broken window. Instead, the aluminum sink shone; the fridge was full of fruit, vegetables, yogurt, and skimmed milk. The kitchen counter smelled of lemon spray. The floors were swept, and fluffed cushions decorated the sofa. Mano shook his head, a smile resting on his lips. *Connor.*

They would have stayed if they thought he was in any more danger. Now it was up to him to move his life forward. To keep going. It had been nearly two months since Margot left. He had accepted the reality of a life without her almost immediately. What he hadn't been able to do was decide how to live it.

He looked at the folded sheet of paper, still in his hand, and opened it.

Alistair Montgomery
Athletics Director
St. Anne's College
Seven Hills, California
(555) 555-3214

He had always liked California.

CHAPTER TWO

SIX MONTHS LATER. SEVEN HILLS, CA.

SHE WAS PUSHING IT BUT SILENTLY PRAYED THAT HER FATHER wouldn't notice the slight delay in getting back.

One more lap...just one more won't hurt....

She could feel her kick being less potent as she turned the wall, her arms less precise as they cut through the water. Just an extra ten minutes longer than her regular Saturday morning, but she wanted to push herself further today. In a schedule that was detailed to the minute, this was a slight indulgence.

When her hands touched the wall, she blew out of her mouth before dunking herself in and out of the water in a ritual she first started when she was seven. *Ten dunks. Blow as many bubbles as you can....* She could still hear the voice of her first swim coach decades later. Those early lessons lasted a lifetime. It was fortunate her first coach was someone who knew what she was talking about.

Eden surveyed the indoor pool. She had been the first one in at five this morning. Two hours later, all ten lanes were used. She spotted the bright pink cap of Linda Wellens, her teammate, and captain of the local Masters team. Ten years older, Linda was one of the first people to encourage her to return to competing but at the Masters level. Eden smiled at the memory; who knew the words of a stranger could plant a seed to an idea that wouldn't go away?

Eden was just about to pull herself out of her lane when Linda called out, "Do you have a minute?"

Eden swam to the rope. "Everything okay?"

Linda rested her goggles on her forehead. "Why is it that —as we become older— the first thing we ask of each other is whether everything is okay?"

"What do you mean?"

"In your twenties, did you automatically think something could be wrong when someone stops you and asks for some of your time?"

Eden laughed, pulling off her swim cap. She leaned her head back to wet her head. "No. Okay, let's try again. What can I do for you?"

"Rumor has it that Jordan Kennedy has asked you to work out with his team."

Eden frowned. "He just texted me last night. How did you know?"

Linda flashed a wide smile. "I didn't. But someone who knew someone had asked. I couldn't confirm anything but can now. Well? Are you going to do it?"

Eden chewed on the bottom of her lip. "I don't know. It's a pretty elite team. Nearly everyone has swum at Nationals before."

"Of course it'll be elite. It's Jordan Kennedy. Everyone knows he has ambitions to get the Berkeley club swimmers on top of as many podiums as possible at Nationals. Has a mission, that kid. I like it. That it's not over after swimming at college."

"He's been very successful."

"You should do it."

Eden grimaced. "I don't know."

"You can hold your own with any of them. Seems pretty straightforward to me."

"There's some etiquette involved here with my former swim club."

"I hadn't realized they had asked you too."

Eden sighed. "They didn't."

Linda's eyes showed her understanding. "Doesn't matter. You broke the over-30s record in the 50 meters three weeks ago. Right now, you're one point two seconds away from qualifying for Nationals in that event. And you're just under two seconds away for qualifying in the 100 meters. Don't you want to know if you can still compete against some of the fastest swimmers in the world?"

"Don't *you* think it's a bit weird for you to know my times so well?"

Linda's laugh echoed through the pool room. "Sweetheart, when more than half your life is spent in the pool thinking in nanoseconds, it's just second nature to remember things like that. One point two seconds away from qualifying for Nationals, Eden. One point two."

"I have to think about it."

Linda pulled her goggles down. "If it were me making those times, I wouldn't be here talking to some old lady about it. I'd be swimming with a future National champion with broad shoulders and tight Speedos.

Before Eden could say anything, Linda disappeared from her view, the latter's silhouette moving stealth-like underwater before emerging a good ten meters away. Not that she had anything to say in response to Linda's statements.

One point two seconds to cut. Doable over a decade ago when her body was younger, and swimming was all she had to focus on. But now? Hitting the pool five days a week was a victory in itself.

Eden glanced at the large clock on the wall. She had eight minutes to rinse off, put on some dry clothes, and get into the car. Then hopefully, assuming no surprises on the drive back to the apartment, her dad would be on his way back to the city seventeen minutes after she drove out of the parking lot.

She changed out of her swimsuit and into a pair of sweatpants and a long-sleeved shirt with practiced efficiency. She didn't mind being damp on the drive back, the driver's seat already covered with a towel.

Light traffic on the weekend wasn't unusual, but the streets were far from empty. The line at the drive-through coffee stand was already five cars long. While the local schools hadn't officially started, there were plenty of year-round sports that kept all the drive-throughs busy on the weekends.

Seven Hills attracted active families. Nestled in the East Bay Hills half an hour outside of San Francisco, it was originally a ranching community that was quickly forgotten by those attracted to the busier, more cosmopolitan neighborhoods closer to the city. Back in the day, one drove by Seven Hills to get somewhere else. It hadn't even warranted a mention in the local traffic reports.

Then Sister Mary Francis of St. Anne's College for Women emerged from the convent in the hills to begin fundraising for Freshman Joan Myers, who was just under a second away from setting the fastest hundred meters time in track and field in 1950. But Joan's dreams of Games glory weren't supported at home when her mother insisted that her daughter's future was better served in the classroom than on the track.

Fortunately, Sister Mary Francis was not just Joan Myers' advisor and confidant. Before she took her vows, Sister Mary Francis was Lucy Barnet, fencer, who represented Wales in the Commonwealth Games. She recognized the competitive fire in young Miss Myers' spirit, and thus began St. Anne's transition from a college primarily focused on academics to an institution of higher learning which had produced over a dozen world champions and Games medalists in various sports.

And now, Eden played a part in adding to St. Anne's celebrated history, though not as an athlete, but in administration. Eden smiled. It was a dream job in many ways. It paid the bills; she loved getting to know the students, and she had access to top-notch training facilities.

Not bad for a college-dropout.

Precisely seven minutes and fifty seconds later—she scraped through a yellow light—Eden pulled into her parking spot, glancing up toward her apartment as she exited the car. The elderly figure on the small balcony held up his cup, his smile welcoming her home. She waved and watched him reenter her apartment. Whether she was thirteen or thirty-three, it felt nice knowing her dad was on the lookout to ensure she got home safe.

She didn't pass anyone as she took the four flights of stairs up to her apartment. That was expected to change in the next week when the new school year began.

Eden had been lucky to have nabbed the small two-bedroom apartment close to the campus. There was no doubt that her boss's references made the difference. Everyone wanted to be in the good books with St. Anne's Director of Athletics. She had looked for a year, commuting for over an hour from the city until she secured the apartment. Like much of the Bay Area, afford-able rentals were hard to come by, especially as a single parent with a limited income.

"Dad?" She placed her keys in the bowl on the wooden console then threw her shoes in the basket by the door.

"Kitchen!"

She could still smell the slight scent of cinnamon in the air. Her stomach growled. One of the good things about being a swimmer-in-training was a four-thousand-calorie-a-day diet. She smiled at the silver-haired man handwashing the last of the dishes from breakfast.

"Pancakes?" She bent slightly to kiss Robert Pak on the cheek.

"Oven."

"You know we have a dishwasher for that," she said as she peered into the still-warm oven.

"Yeah, but I started with the pans and kept going. Aidan's in the shower. Just woke up. He did say 'good morning' first, so keep that in mind before you lose your temper with him."

Eden made a face. "He starts it."

"And you have a choice whether to engage with him or not."

"I don't remember either you or Pop 'engaging' with me when I gave you some lip back in the day."

"Ahh...but that was us. You're supposed to do better than your parents. That boy is growing like a weed."

"Half an inch since you saw him."

"Got his dad's genes."

"I'm not too shabby for an Asian."

"Half Asian, dear. Your mother's genes are your saving grace. She was the swimmer. Otherwise, you'd be as short as me." Robert wiped his hands on a kitchen towel then folded it neatly next to the sink. He looked around. "Okay. I think I'm done. I'll see you in a month?"

"Yes, but it's dinner, remember? With Pop? For your anniversary?"

Robert's eyes widened. "I forgot!"

Eden laughed. "Oh, Dad!"

"Well, we've been together for so long... It's all starting to feel the same."

"That's not the happily-ever-after story your daughter wants to hear. And it's a big deal. Thirty years. That's worth celebrating for anyone, not least a nurse and a retired fire-fighter."

"Okay. But no gifts," Robert warned as he picked up his backpack from the small round dining table. "You know how Pop feels about gifts. I, on the other hand, won't make too big of a deal if you sneak something in a brown paper bag for me to take home."

"You're getting a nice new set of Tupperware," Eden teased. "Though I haven't heard from Aunt Letty yet."

"I'll give her a call. And don't worry about Aidan. He's a good boy. Just finding himself. It's normal for thirteen-year-olds to push back a little. You're doing a good job. You know that, right?"

She sighed. "Sometimes, I just don't know anymore."

"No parent knows everything. It's normal not to know." Robert put his arm around Eden's waist as she draped her arm over his shoulders. They walked toward the front door. "Aidan says you're heading to the airport?"

Eden checked her watch. "I'm impressed. It took you over ten minutes to bring it up. I assume your grandson said who it is we're meeting at the airport?"

Robert clicked his tongue. "I can't believe you kept it a secret."

"I wasn't supposed to pick him up. He's a big enough super-star in the world of rugby that Alistair wanted to greet him in person. I take it you know who he is?"

Robert feigned a hurt look. "What kind of rugby fan would I be if I didn't know who Mano Palua is? There's only a handful of people in the world who can claim a world championship; the man has two!"

Eden laughed. "Aidan said the exact same thing. You're a terrible influence on him."

"How did Alistair get one of the all-time greats to come out to St. Anne's? And why isn't this all over the website?"

"Mr. Palua didn't want anything announced until he arrived. Alistair had a tough time with that one, but I guess this guy must be a bigger deal than I thought if Alistair conceded on that point."

"Mano Palua is more than a big deal. He's part of rugby history." Robert tilted his head slightly. "Sounds like St. Anne's is finally getting serious about the sport. You have a ton of talent there."

"Yes. But it's always been about funding. Whatever anyone says about Alistair, no one will argue against his networking skills. He made a new friend who likes rugby a lot. Then there's the professional league expanding. Alistair knows a trend when he sees one."

"How much is 'a lot'?"

"I know nothing, heard nothing, and saw nothing. But it's a lot of zeros in the donation to the program."

Robert whistled. "Is Mano Palua coming with family?"

"I don't think so. Well, not flying with him anyway. Alistair only mentioned him, and Mr. Palua didn't say anything about traveling with anyone else in his email."

"You've been writing to him?"

"Just one email, Dad! Had to introduce myself, so he knows not to expect a tall, balding guy at the airport."

"I don't mind being late for work."

"No, but your patients and the other people on your team would. Go already! You can fangirl about him at one of our matches."

"Well, if he doesn't know anyone else and is traveling alone, he can join us for dinner next month."

"Dad! It's supposed to be a family thing. We can't invite a stranger to your anniversary."

"You know I have a soft spot for new people in our country."

"You have a soft spot for rugby. Period. It's why you visit us more often during the season, isn't it?"

"It brings me back to my halcyon days on the East Coast when I was young and active. Just me and your dad. The two Pak brothers! The only Koreans in Bergen County playing rugby. We were small, but our little legs carried us far!"

"Oh, Dad!"

"Invite him. If I could have a ten-minute conversation with an All Black, you'll never have to buy me another present again. But, you know, no pressure."

Eden groaned. "I thought it was the child who was supposed to push for unreasonable requests." She glanced at the wall clock in the hallway. "You'd better get going. I know it's Saturday, but you never know what traffic is like going over the bridge. And thanks for staying over, Dad."

Robert hesitated, his eyes on the brass doorknob. "I wish I could help out more with Aidan, but with Pop's mom the way she is…"

Eden tightened her arm across her father's shoulder and kissed the top of his head. She'd been taller than him since she was thirteen. "I know. It's okay. You and Pop need to look after Grandma Mattie. Pop's her favorite and probably the only one who can get her to follow the doctor's orders."

Robert grinned. "You're right there. Oh wait, I just remembered. Does this rugby guy need a car? After Mattie's stroke, we're selling it."

"I'll ask. Will you send me the information?"

After locking the door, Eden walked down the hallway and knocked on Aidan's door. Aidan's angst at transferring to a new middle school was somewhat appeased when he realized he could get his own room. The door had remained mostly shut ever since the last box was unpacked. However, she drew the line at it being locked. He tested her rule right away and came back to his door off its hinges. He hadn't broken that rule since.

"You okay in there, bud?" she asked through the door.

"Yeah."

"We leave in an hour for the airport, okay? And don't forget a sweater. It's always cold at the airport." Eden waited. "Aidan?"

"Yes! I heard you. One hour! Sweater! Geez…"

Eden closed her eyes and counted to ten. Didn't work. She still wanted to scream back but took a deep breath and counted to twenty. "I'm taking a shower if you need anything."

She turned her head to listen.

Nothing.

At least she knew his attitude wasn't directed only at her. Brandon had actually called her the day after one of Aidan's weekend stays with him, sharing how Aidan had been exceptionally rude to both him and Lisa. As soon as she heard his comments, her heart began to race. Eden automatically braced herself for any criticism her ex-boyfriend could throw at her about her parenting skills. But she underestimated Brandon.

Instead of judgment, he wanted to work with her on a plan. Would she stay for dinner when Aidan next stayed for the weekend? Maybe between Brandon, Lisa, and herself, they could come up with some ideas on how to remain "consistent" with parenting their son.

"Is this really your idea, Brandon?" she had asked. Sure enough, he admitted it was his wife's idea. While a good father, he was never one to initiate anything. Then he married Lisa, and things started to change—for the better. Eden didn't know which soap opera this scenario would be believable in, but she was sure Brandon's new wife had a lot to do with his more involved parenting.

Aidan was already in the living room when she emerged from her bedroom, now changed and free from any scent of chlorine. Saturdays were "whatever-you-want-to-do" mornings. Usually, that translated to whatever was on TV. Right now, it seemed to be some type of anime series. She rustled Aidan's hair then found a bowl of cut fruit in the fridge—*thanks, Dad!* — poured herself a tall glass of orange juice, and started on the still-warm stack of whole wheat pancakes. She sat facing the small balcony which overlooked the trail that meandered into a small grove of redwood trees. The trail was popular with both runners and cyclists, especially on a bright late summer morning such as this one.

The scheduled trip to the airport meant missing a late afternoon workout at the gym; however, that also meant she saved babysitting money, money that was always needed for something else.

She hadn't lied to her dad; she was still doing okay. Brandon was always on time with his child support, so all of Aidan's basic needs were met. But living from paycheck to paycheck was a lifestyle she didn't like. And now, there were the additional costs of a masseuse, a nutritionist, and possibly the need for other specialists that the modern athlete might use to give her the extra edge in competition. Luckily, St. Anne's allowed her to access them at more affordable rates.

The reduced work hours she had asked Alistair for would start making a real dent in her budget if she didn't qualify by the end of the year. Odd to think her dreams were based on how much money she had in her savings account; however, knowing she had a roof over her son's head and that food was available in the fridge was non-negotiable.

Her recent successes at the meets reignited the need to know if she were good enough and if she could compete at the highest level. The desire to try was so strong that it helped manage the fear of living with financial uncertainty on most days.

Most days.

She glanced at Aidan, his light brown hair falling over the face that was the spitting image of her ex-boyfriend. So much for her DNA entering the mix, she mused. When she shared her desire to go back to competitive swimming last year with her son, his reaction was lukewarm at best. Their verbal sparring had increased over the summer. Suddenly, everything she'd ask him to do needed an explanation. While he had yet to complain about her increased pool and gym times, she would find herself facing looks of apathy or boredom.

What happened to the little boy who would look at her with such joy? She could do no wrong in his eyes back then. Those days were over.

* * *

"Is that him?"

"No, bud. You've seen his picture. He has shoulder-length hair. Here, this is one of him in civilian clothes," she said, handing him the photo she had printed late last night.

While her son and father may know who Mano Palua was,

she wasn't sure if she could pick him out of a crowd, especially in a big one like today's. She had been tempted to put up a sign, but she felt self-conscious enough as it was, picking up a stranger. There was quite a selection of pictures of Mano, mainly of him in uniform or on the field. There was also a handful of photos in more casual settings.

Taken from afar, he was usually with three or four men. A couple of others were with the same beautiful woman, suggesting interest in him went beyond the sport. There was also a small blurb in what she thought was a New Zealand gossip magazine speculating the end of a serious relationship.

Eden looked at the clock. It'd been an hour since Mano's flight had landed, but with three other planes arriving at the same time, she suspected the delay was at immigration. She looked around at the busy Arrival Hall, enjoying the scenes of people greeting loved ones. An older woman bestowed many kisses on a baby who was now in her arms. A woman in army fatigues rushed by them and threw herself into the arms of a man. Were they long separations? Eden wondered. Did it matter?

Eden smiled at the well-dressed gentleman with flowers in his hand. He looked eagerly at the TV screens above them, installed to show the live feed of passengers who had already cleared Customs and Immigration. Their presence didn't stop the crowd gathering at the barriers which were yards away from the glass doors. Anticipation among the waiting rose slightly each time the opaque doors slid open, satisfying a handful of people at a time.

"Mom, I think our rugby player has arrived."

Eden followed Aidan's raised hand, now pointing at the stocky figure dressed in black sweats and a pullover. With his dreadlocks tied back, Mano's cheekbones were especially prominent. His profile was one that time would have little impact on. He looked as if he was carved out of granite.

She lifted her hand in greeting. Mano nodded, hooded eyes

catching hers immediately. She inhaled sharply at being the subject of such intensity, even from a distance.

He moved toward her with long, confident strides and carried a backpack over one shoulder while pulling a suitcase. Despite the eagerness of the crowd to reunite with other emerging passengers, Eden noticed everyone gave him a wide berth. It wasn't just his size—he was about six feet tall, and loose clothes didn't hide his physique—he walked with a self-assurance that dared anyone to cross his path.

"Do they all have necks that big?" Aidan whispered.

"You've met some of the rugby players at the college."

"None of them look like him."

Eden chewed on her lip. He was right. Mano Palua didn't look like any rugby player she had ever seen either. He wasn't *that* tall, but he was sure big. She swallowed. "You ready, bud? Let's welcome him to California."

She knew he was in his mid-30s and was playing competitively until earlier this year. Her trained eye recognized he moved as if still in shape; his build reflected a disciplined lifestyle.

"Eden?"

She took his offered hand. It was rough, and his grip was firm. "Hi! Welcome! Good flight? Alistair sends his apologies again...." Her voice faltered. She noticed a bead of sweat around his forehead. Despite being tan, there was a hint of paleness underneath. "Are you okay?"

He nodded. "Just a long flight."

"Mom?"

"Oh! Yes...uh...this is my son, Aidan. Aidan, Mr. Palua."

"Please, call me Mano."

"How do you do, sir?"

Sir? Eden stared. Did her thirteen-year-old just exhibit some...*manners*? She risked a sideways glance. Then again, Mano Palua would fall under the category of someone who commanded manners without needing to ask for it.

"Pleased to meet you, Aidan."

"My granddad says you're a world champion. I've never met a world champion before, though my father medaled in the Games once. Like before I was born."

"A Games medal means he was a champion."

"Do you have to be as big as you to become a rugby champion?"

"Aidan!" Eden covered her son's mouth. "Sorry! He's like me. A bit of a motormouth. You know. Stuff comes out." Aidan pushed her hand away, his glare saying more than words could at that moment. Eden laughed nervously. "What he meant was…"

Mano's face remained impassive, unreadable. *Granite.* Dark eyes stared at Aidan. "You'll find players of any height on a rugby team."

Her son continued to surprise her when he offered to help with Mano's luggage. If the larger, obviously stronger man found the offer amusing, he didn't let on. Aidan stayed by Mano's side as they walked to the parking garage. She could just hear him ask Mano more rugby-related questions. She wondered if her dad had coached Aidan on any of these questions.

Mano, to Eden's relief, was patient with Aidan's unexpected inquisition. Or so she hoped. She should step in and limit Aidan's questions, but it had been so long since her son did anything other than door-slamming and eye-rolling in her presence that she welcomed this glimpse into the young man he was growing into.

"I'm over there, in the black Forester," she said, leading the group to the far right of the parking area.

She popped open the trunk for Mano to put his bags in. He slid silently into the passenger seat. She turned on the radio instinctively after starting the car. Fifteen minutes later, when the San Francisco skyline started to appear, Eden pointed to some of the more iconic buildings of the city. "And if you like baseball, or even if you don't, on our right, you'll just be able to see the stadium for the San Francisco team. It's one of the better-designed stadiums in the whole country. We like it there, don't we, Aidan?"

Aidan grunted.

She looked in her rearview mirror; her son glared back.

"And now we're on the lower span of the Oakland Bay Bridge," she continued, keeping her voice as neutral as possible. "It's not as famous as the Golden Gate, but this is the bridge that takes us home."

Music didn't seem to fill the car as she had hoped. She cleared her throat. "Once we pass Treasure Island—which used to be a naval base—we'll be on the newest part of the bridge."

Mano concentrated on the passing scenery through his window. "Is your name really Eden Pak?"

His voice was so unexpected that she glanced at him. But his face remained averted. "Yes," she said. "Eden was my maternal grandmother's middle name, and Pak is my father's family name. It's Korean."

He grunted.

"Why?"

"It's the name of the largest stadium in my country."

"Like a sports stadium?"

"Yeah. I've had some of my best memories playing in that stadium."

"Why didn't you ask about it when I emailed you?"

"I didn't want to be rude and ask such personal questions until we met."

She nodded at the logic. "Pak's quite a common Korean name."

He paused. "Liana Murphy sends her regards. She said you were a big help when she visited the campus."

Eden smiled. "She's great. I must admit I hadn't realized how famous she was. I don't follow soccer at all. Are you good friends with her?"

"Yes. Her husband, Mitch Molloy, and I played together for most of our careers."

Half an hour later, she exited the freeway and drove toward the eastern end of Seven Hills. When she turned into a familiar cul-de-sac, Aidan spoke for the first time since the airport.

"Hey! Mrs. Yuan's car is in the driveway. Can I go over?"

"Only if it's for a quick hello. We're not staying long, bud. We need to get Mr. Palua into the house first and make sure he has everything he needs. Like good hosts."

"And how long is that going to take?"

"Aidan!"

She saw it for the first time then: a shadow of a smile on a face that revealed nothing. She had to remind herself not to stare. Not just a man of few words but also a man of few expressions. What would it take for a full smile?

Eden fished for the house keys that she had picked up from the office yesterday. She wiped her feet on the outdoor mat before unlocking the door to enter the small ranch house.

"Okay, we're in. Mr. Palua is *in* the house," Aidan said. "Can I go to Matthew's house now?"

She sighed. "Yes, but if no one is there, come straight back, understand?"

He rushed outside before she finished her sentence. She stood on the porch watching Aidan ring the bright orange door. It opened to an excited Matthew who dragged her son into the house quickly. Patricia Yuan stepped out and waved to Eden, who returned the gesture immediately.

"If you ever need anything, the Yuans are wonderful people," Eden said, closing the door behind her. "I can introduce you to them, though I think Patty will do the honors herself. She's one of those people who makes it a point to know her neighbors."

She suddenly realized that she was alone in the living room. She glanced around. This was one of the smaller ranch houses in the neighborhood. *Probably one of the original ones,* thought Eden, taking in the minimal furnishings scattered through the house.

It had its original wooden floors, and a sizeable, neutral-colored seagrass carpet covered the sitting area where an L-shape couch was placed right under the large windows. The blinds were still closed, but once opened, they would let in plenty of light. A brick fireplace with a large mantle centered the room. It'd be the perfect place for Christmas stockings and a wreath, she mused. That was the one thing she wished she had in her apartment. She had fond memories of growing up with a fire in winter, her two dads always lighting one once the weather turned.

She walked through the small dining area toward the kitchen. Clear glass panels revealed plates, cups, and glasses. A coffeemaker matched the chrome toaster, which sat on the otherwise empty counter. The only nod to color was in the bright red electric kettle. A back door at the far end of the kitchen was opened. She poked her head through it and spotted Mano walking toward the edge of the large backyard. He'd finished the last of his bottled water.

She hesitated, wondering if he needed to be alone. She must have made a sound as he turned suddenly.

His face reflected his surprise as if he'd forgotten he was not by himself. Then there was a brief second of vulnerability before his eyes rolled back, and he promptly fell facedown with a thud.

CHAPTER THREE

"Oh my god! Oh my god…don't be dead…don't be dead…Phone…phone… Where's my phone? Mano? Mr. Palua? Mano?"

Her hand was cool against his skin. Or was he hot? She reached under him, and he felt the strain in her body as she turned him to lie on his back. He heard his own moan as well as a clear sigh of relief from Eden. "You're alive! Thank God! Oh geez… Mano? Stay with me! Don't black out! I need to get my phone. I think I left it in the kitchen! I have to call an ambulance."

"No." Was that whisper of a voice his?

He heard her run to the deck and, in seconds, felt her gently elevate his legs and rest them on something hard. "Can you open your eyes?"

His eyelids felt like lead, but he managed to part them enough to see dark eyes peer back, relief in them instantaneous.

"I'm going to the kitchen. Don't move. But stay conscious!"

He wasn't sure who was more surprised to see his hand on her wrist. "No."

"Mano, you just fainted."

"I didn't faint." The pounding in his head intensified, but he managed to keep his eyes focused on Eden.

"Uh...okay... You didn't faint. You just collapsed so hard the squirrels jumped from one tree to another."

He moved slightly, willing his limbs to obey his silent instructions. He knew his body. It wasn't responding as it should. He pushed against the ground.

"Slowly," Eden whispered. He felt her arm reach around him, simultaneously supporting and pushing him up. She glanced over him clinically, a studied scan he was used to when medics would check him after a bad tackle.

"I'm fine." He winced internally at the abruptness of his words.

She arched an eyebrow, obviously not impressed with his rant. "We'll see. Stay here. Let me get you some water. Promise you won't move, or I swear I'll call the ambulance."

A soft wind rustled the branches of the eucalyptus trees around them, its faint scent wafting around the otherwise quiet garden. He rested his elbows on his knees and bowed his head. He couldn't stop his eyes from closing, but as soon as he heard Eden's footsteps on the wooden deck, he opened them again.

He took the offered glass of water and drank it under her watchful gaze. Her phone buzzed, taking her attention off him momentarily.

"My dad's a nurse," she explained. "He asked if you've been sick or exposed to sick people in the last few days."

He shook his head, then regretted the action immediately. The silent pounding went to the front of his head.

"Did you drink a lot on the plane?"

"I slept." Mano fought to keep his voice even. No need for her to know how much effort there was in talking. "I've traveled a lot for work, Eden. I know the importance of being hydrated on long-haul flights."

"Is that a no?" She typed quickly into her phone. "I told him you didn't drink much on the plane, *may* have lost consciousness for a second, and landed on your head."

"I'm fine."

"You fell face-first into the ground." She pointed at a flat patch of grass to their right. "Right there. You can even see your face print in the grass."

Despite the pressure in his head, Mano couldn't resist looking to where Eden pointed. "That's an exaggeration."

"Okay, Mr. Rugby-Champion, let's get you into the house. I want to check your temperature. Do you need help getting up?"

It was the last thing he wanted to do, but he understood what she was trying to gauge. He took a deep breath then slowly rose. She stood close, her body ready to step in to shoulder his weight. He'd probably crush most people, but Mano suspected Eden Pak knew how to use the full strength of her body.

He walked cautiously but independently to the deck. Once there, he grabbed the wooden railing and turned his body against it. He inhaled deeply, grateful that the world had stopped spinning.

Eden stood next to him, also leaning against the railing, her eyes continuing their assessment. "Alistair said you chose this place?"

An innocuous question, but Mano wasn't fooled. She wanted to see if he was thinking straight. "Yeah. The backyard is bigger than I thought."

"Is that a good thing?"

"It's a very good thing."

He turned away from her study of him.

"Listen, let me get Matthew's mom. Patty used to be a doctor—"

"No," he growled. "I'll be fine."

"Mano?"

"Yeah?"

"Were you always this stubborn with your doctors?"

"I didn't have a choice when I played professionally."

"Now?"

"I'm not playing professionally."

"Well, I think you need to go to bed because you look like you're going to faint again any minute."

"I don't faint." But the ground had started to move again.

* * *

When he opened his eyes, it was dark and silent. Luminous numbers on the small radio clock on his side table flashed. It was early in the evening. He sat up slowly, his body aching at different points. The pounding in his head was gone, but there was a heaviness in his bones that warned him that he wasn't in top shape.

He surveyed what would be his bedroom for the next year. It was simply furnished: a small desk sat in the corner, a large bureau against the wall faced the queen bed he was on. Plantation shutters allowed just a hint of light into the room.

Vague images of Eden helping him change into a clean shirt surfaced. She had checked his temperature with a thermometer of unknown origins. Raised eyebrows at the reading suggested he was hotter than he felt. Under his direction, she found the bottle of paracetamol in his suitcase. Before he let sleep claim him, he wondered at the depth of concern in her face. He was a stranger. But she cared.

He frowned at the smell of lasagna lingering in the air. He opened the door and walked barefoot to the living room. Eden lowered a magazine at his entrance, and a full, familiar smile greeted him. He knew that smile. It was on her profile picture on the college website whose link she had sent to him just a day ago. *So you'll know who I am,* she had typed.

"You look way better." She stood to pick up the thermometer from the round coffee table.

"No. I'm good." He was sure he wasn't supposed to hear her next words.

"Worse than Aidan…" Her eyes widened when she realized she had spoken aloud, her fingers rising to her lips.

Despite feeling like he just played a match against the Wallabies, he felt the side of his mouth turn slightly. An interesting shade of pink formed at the base of Eden's neck. He turned to face the large window which overlooked the street. "Where is Aidan?"

"He's staying over at Matthew's place tonight. Matthew's mom gave me some extra lasagna. Interested? Food will do you good."

It'd been almost twelve hours since he last ate something, but he felt far from hungry. Still, he recognized the value of getting some calories in his body. His nod elicited an immediate smile.

"Good!" she said. "It's a mild night. Let's eat outside. Why don't you wash up and I'll see you in the back?"

When he came out of the bathroom, he found Eden bent over the oven door. Now without the sweater she'd worn to the airport, her simple cotton shirt and jeans showed off a trim athletic figure.

She glanced over her shoulder. "Will you grab the plates?"

He took the bright yellow plates that had two sets of cutlery and cloth napkins on them and followed her to the deck. The small metal table had a pitcher of water and glasses waiting.

"Sit," she instructed. "I just have to bring out the salad. I did a quick run to the grocery store while you were sleeping. I picked up some things to see you through the next few days."

"You didn't have—"

"There was nothing in the house, and you're not in any condition to go shopping today."

"I'm fine."

"You're welcome." Her smile softened her words.

He swallowed and tempered his irritation. "Thank you."

A warm breeze rustled the line of trees to the right of the garden. Was that an oak? He'd have to do a little research on what exactly was in his backyard.

"You chose a pretty nice place to live, Mano," Eden said when she came back.

"It doesn't feel like you're only half an hour from the city," he said as he joined her at the table.

She served the lasagna onto two plates. "No, Seven Hills has still managed to retain its charm that way. The hills make it diffi-cult for new buildings, so even though we need more housing in the area, there just isn't a lot of buildable land out here." She pointed past the grove of trees to the right. "I live just past these trees."

"There are houses behind here?"

"Just as the road turns, there's an entrance to a path which will lead you to a trail that goes through most of Seven Hills. My apartment complex is about a ten-minute walk from here. The trail's used a lot, especially by the kids to get to the middle and high schools. This house is in a good location: quiet but still pretty central. If you're a runner, you could get to the sports field at St. Anne's in about twenty minutes, I think."

He stretched when he finished the last of his meal, surprised at his appetite, given the lack of energy. He started to get up to help clear the table, but she held up her hand. "No, you rest."

"I can help."

"Mano, I don't know you very well, but if you collapse on my watch, morally, I have a responsibility for your well-being for at least twelve hours unless you fall under the care of a quali-fied medical professional."

He frowned. "I don't think I know this 'code of morality' you're talking about."

Her natural smile reappeared, making her look at least a decade younger. "Ah, well…. You'll just have to believe me."

He picked up the pitcher and glasses anyway and followed her into the kitchen. He checked the refrigerator: yogurt, a tray of eggs, low-fat milk, cheese, butter, fruit, sandwich meats, salad. "How much do I owe you?"

She waved with the back of her hand as she loaded the dishwasher. "Call it a welcome-to-California present."

"I can't—"

"I hope you like blue because I realized you didn't have bedsheets in the house, so I stopped by Target as well. They're in the dryer. You can pay me back for that if it makes you feel better. I put the receipt on the notice board."

"Thank you."

"I can't take any credit for thinking about bedsheets. My dad reminded me to check." She wiped her hands on the kitchen towel. "Anyway, I'd better go. Now that I've seen you again after your nap, I can rest easy."

Unexpectedly, she placed her hand on his cheek then his forehead. He moved slightly but didn't escape her touch. He was suddenly aware he couldn't remember the last time someone touched him on his face.

She smiled again. "No fever. Good. You have my number; call me if you need anything. I put Patty's number on your notice board as well. I told her you were jetlagged and recovering from a cold. She'll probably come by to check on you tomorrow."

"Patty?"

"Sorry. Matthew's mom. Patricia Yuan, but she goes by 'Patty.' Matt's Aidan's best friend. Patty's incredible. Some people say she's intense, but she's nice."

"Intense?"

Eden tilted her head thoughtfully. "In a good way. Highly energetic? Spirited? Actively animated? Anyway, you can judge for yourself."

"I can't wait," Mano muttered under his breath.

"Patty knows everyone and everything about everyone. If you have a question about anything, Patty's your lady."

He watched Eden check her pockets before looking satisfied that she had everything.

"Get some rest, okay?"

"Eden…uh… Thanks. I owe you."

"Nonsense. We're colleagues. We look out for one another at St. Anne's." Her eyes met his, and a frisson of awareness simmered from within. He dismissed it immediately. She cleared her throat then held out her hand. "Well…uh… I guess I'll let you settle in properly. Let me know if you need anything."

He took the offered hand, caught the slight widening in her eyes, but didn't let go. She, too, felt it, this current between them. He turned her hand slightly, her firm grip not unexpected. "Thank you."

The tinge of pink had returned to the base of her neck. When she pulled back, he released his hold, the sudden break in physical contact a relief.

Or so he told himself.

"I'd better go," she repeated as she headed to the door. "Going to swing by the Yuans' to say good night. To Aidan. You know…just down the street."

He nodded, not assisting or hampering her departure, etiquette having him wait for her as she put on her shoes then closed the door behind her.

He headed straight to the shower. Damn headache had come back. Falling flat on his face wasn't how he expected to start his stay in California. He had been working almost nonstop the past few months, accepting any job that landed his way: promos, analysis, making public appearances. He did, however, hold on to his last shred of dignity by turning down a celebrity dance show, much to Connor's disappointment.

Being busy kept his mind off his loneliness. Exhaustion was his preferred companion. But maybe he should have eaten on the plane…or at least have drunk some water.

He looked for tea but only found ground coffee. There were lemons in the fruit basket, and he satisfied the need for something warm with honey and lemon mixed with hot water. Moving to the large window, he counted five houses. Each boasted immaculately kept front lawns and gardens. Though still bright, his rental's porchlight and garden lights were on. *Probably on a timer somewhere,* he thought absentmindedly. In the absence of streetlights, they'd keep the cul-de-sac from being shrouded in complete darkness when night came.

Laughter took his attention to the house three doors down with the bright orange door. He recognized Eden's figure as she emerged from the shadows of the house, voices breaking the silence of his new neighborhood. Bending over slightly, she spoke to her son. Whatever she said must have been the right thing, as there was a broad smile on Aidan's face. It was the first one he had seen the boy show his mother since they'd met at the airport. She laughed easily with the shorter, attractive woman who was also standing at the doorway, the latter's arm draped over a bespectacled boy.

Suddenly, Aidan spotted him through the window and waved.

He froze, now wishing he had kept his living room shrouded in darkness. Aidan was persistent. His aggressive hand movements demanded a response from Mano. He didn't owe the boy anything, yet his arm rose in acknowledgment.

He clenched his jaw when everyone at the doorstep turned to identify what – or who – was the object of Aidan's attention. Four sets of eyes were now focused on him, their study as intense as any opponent he had faced on the pitch. He returned their scrutiny, his eyes resting on the petite woman whose face took on a determined look.

Dammit!

Eden shook her head, but the woman—Patty, he assumed— began to walk down her driveway toward him, an eager Aidan matching her stride, his arms gesticulating to unknown words. Mano didn't think twice; he reached for the cord to the blinds and shut the view of the approaching entourage. Seconds later, loud staccato knocks indicated Patty Yuan et al. didn't get the hint.

He could return to his bedroom, but he understood some evils were best faced immediately.

"Hi! I'm Patricia Yuan, but call me Patty. And this is Matthew. Eden said you're feeling better. That's good!"

Mano took Patty's hand before offering his own to Matthew. Wide-eyed, the youngster seemed reluctant to take Mano's hand until his mother nudged him. Eden shrugged her shoulders slightly, as if in an apology.

"My husband is out of town, but I'll send him over to say hi when he returns. He needs a new friend," said Patty. "Do you golf? Yes? Great! Charles spends way too much time on his own."

"Thanks, but..."

"Oh, no thanks necessary. It's how we do things around here. Just jump right in! Best way to get involved in the community!"

"Thanks, but..."

"Eden said you're here alone? Well, we'll just have to be your family while you live here. You'll love Mrs. Henderson next door. She likes to give everyone a day to settle in, but she'll be around tomorrow for sure with banana bread. Don't refuse it. She'll never forgive you, and then we'll all pay for it. You'll see teenagers come in and out of her house during the week. Don't worry about them. She watches her granddaughter after school and keeps an open-door policy for a lot of Carolyn's friends. Some of the neighbors don't like it, but there's your pool of cheap labor, right there! Babysitting, yard work, odds, and ends!"

"Thanks, but—"

Patty poked her head through the door. "You're lucky to get this rental. Lara took good care of this house. It's been in her family for years. But you also better live up to her reputation come October."

"October?"

"Halloween, of course!"

Mano blinked. "Wait. What?"

Matthew and Aidan nodded excitedly. "We can help," Aidan said. "It was so cool last year, wasn't it, Matt?'

"Lara had a ghost float above her shed. It was awesome!" Matthew said.

"A ghost?" Mano asked.

Patty smiled. "Yes! It's a tradition in the neighborhood: start trick-or-treating at Lara's House of Horrors. But it's never really too scary for the little ones. I think we had a couple of hundred kids down our street last year, didn't we, Matthew?"

Matthew nodded.

Did he hear that correctly? "Two hundred?"

"Yeah, I know. It was a small showing because it rained. Lara lets the kids go through the side gate and straight into the back-yard. I wonder if she left any of the decorations in the garage. I'll email her and find out for you. It's hysterical to hear the kids scream throughout the night!"

"That sounds…" He struggled to find a word that wouldn't offend nor lie.

"I have pictures from last year. Charles will help. It'll be fine," Patty reassured him.

Eden cleared her throat, her eyes sparkling in amusement. "Patty, I think we should leave Mano alone for now. He's only been in our country for a few hours."

Patty waved her hand. "Of course! Of course! Sorry! We just get so excited when new people come into our little neigh-borhood!"

He took a deep breath. Patty was certainly…enthusiastic. "Thank you. If you'll excuse me, I still have to unpack."

"Of course! Of course! You should get some rest too. Fainting—"

"I don't faint…" He glanced sharply at a wide-eyed Eden.

"—isn't good," Patty finished, ignoring Mano's interruption completely. "I used to practice. Don't anymore. But if you need anything, Lara has our street's phone list in her kitchen. I made sure she left it there. You never know!"

The loud buzzing from his mobile surprised them all. Patty eyed it then faced Mano. "Don't you want to get it? Could be important."

He narrowed his eyes; Patty smiled brightly. Eden cleared her throat again. "You are absolutely right, Patty. Why don't we all leave Mano alone? He doesn't want a bunch of strangers listening in, right?"

Patty nodded. "But you must come over soon, Mano! I make—"

He nodded and shut the door before Patty could get another word in. Big strides took him to the coffee table where his phone rested, its incessant buzzing only adding to the headache. "What?!"

Connor's laugh sounded like he was only minutes away instead of several time zones. "Easy, mate! I just wanted to know how you are!"

Mano sat on a barstool. "I've only been gone a day. You and Mitch need to trust me again."

"How are you feeling?"

Mano frowned. "Why do you ask?"

"Fred came down with a cold after your visit. Still coughing through the night. Since you spent so much time with him...."

"Well, that might explain it," Mano muttered. "I got a little light-headed but otherwise feel fine. How's Fred doing?"

"Better today. What time is it over there?"

"Just past eight."

"Was Alistair there to meet you?"

"No. He was held up, so he sent his assistant. She's been... uh...helpful. Do you know two hundred kids might show up at my house for Halloween?"

"Wait. Back up. She?"

"Eden. Eden Pak."

"Is that really her name?"

"Yeah, it is."

"That's a bit unreal, isn't it? Is she nice?"

Mano heard what Connor was really asking. "Knock it off."

"Mate, you haven't looked at a woman in six months."

"I'm here to work."

"Promise me something: don't hide. Remember what Spurgeon said. Meet people. Start with this Eden Pak. Her name is already perfect for you—your favorite place to play..."

"That's hardly a reason to choose friends, Con."

Connor ignored the interruption. "Smile. You've got a nice one. Never mind what the sponsors said in the past. It's a good smile. Sometimes it's a little strained, but it's not as scary as most people say. Be...you know...friendly."

Mano brought his free hand to his hair, pulling at it lightly as he walked into his bedroom. He faced a framed print of 'Moulin Rouge: La Goulue' hanging over the bureau in his bedroom. It was the same painting he used to see every Thursday in the local patisserie while he played in France. And as they did a year ago, his eyes were drawn to the swirling petticoat of the dancer taunting him in the same fashion as Connor's words. *Meet people.* He looked out his bedroom window to the swaying branches of the trees. "That's easy for you. You like people."

"You need to have at least one friend, Mano."

"You sound like mum."

"One friend," Connor insisted. "Even you can do that."

"Only one? Don't you have faith in my friend-making abilities?"

"Not much. You haven't made a new friend in years."

He now leaned against the wall. "You're right. I should make new friends. The ones I have told me to leave the country."

"Done with love, my brother," said Connor, laughing again. "You sound good otherwise."

"Hope you think that in a week."

"Yeah, me too."

Mano wasn't supposed to hear that, so quiet was Connor's voice. He sighed. "I'm all right, mate. I was never in any danger." He saw Connor in his mind as the silence stretched between them: his friend would have one hand behind his neck, his head bowed by the weight of fear.

Connor cleared his throat. "Okay, so tell me about the two hundred kids that are supposed to show up at your house? Cat is going to love this!"

Mano didn't miss the touch of worry still present in his friend's voice. No surprise. He had given everyone a scare when he'd disappeared months ago. There was a part of him that was still tempted to return to the bach by the beach, but it was the discussion with his accountant—and not Dr. Spurgeon— that the reality of his situation hit him. He couldn't last more than a few years without an income, even with the simplest of lifestyles.

Ironic. Money, a commodity he was determined never to be a significant factor for most of his life, was now the primary reason for many decisions over the last couple of years.

Being practical was annoying.

He had been careful with his finances, surrounding himself with good role models in his sport and learning from those who weren't as successful. Too many professional athletes struggle after their playing years.

Helping with Margot's extra treatments, Michael's living expenses at the care facility, and then his impulse buy with the bach made a more significant impact on his savings than he'd realized. He wasn't in trouble, but it was a bit of a shock to see the numbers in black and white.

Still, even the new contract from the rugby club in France wasn't enough to change his mind. While he knew he could never walk entirely away from the sport he loved, he was ready to stay off the pitch. His body was holding up, but it was taking longer to recover. Seeing his former flatmate's career end abruptly with one hit was a reminder he had been luckier than most.

His retirement from rugby warranted some mention in the news. After all, he was captain of the national team for a handful of games. But after a day's worth of attention, his name disappeared from the media. He'd never generated the same kind of interest as his two more charismatic and media-friendly predecessors, Mitch Molloy and Connor Dane. He preferred it that way.

It was the one thing about his success on the rugby pitch he tolerated but never enjoyed: continually being in the public eye. Spurgeon, fortunately, gave him the right tools to deal with the attention. Mano found that as long as he was prepared, facing questions and the constant scrutiny was manageable.

Time in California may not have been his idea initially, but the longer he thought about the prospect, the more attractive it became. No one knew him in this country. His sport was a side note in America, at best. Maybe he'd get some attention from the expat community who brought their passion for rugby with them from foreign lands, but he could be a "nobody" for a while in America.

Maybe, when the year was up, he could return home and start a life without fanfare or attention. He would be old news by then. Public interest would have moved on to the latest stars of the sport. Maybe Uncle Malcolm would still have that job for him to work on the boats. Perhaps, by then, he'd understand how to live a life without her.

He continued to combat the pounding headache with warm water and lemon, finally finishing his first day in California in his new backyard. Twilight deepened the colors of an unfamiliar sky. At least this part of the rental lived up to its promise. It was private and quiet. His phone sounded.

Eden: Will you text me back, so I know you haven't fainted again? I'll call the ambulance if I don't hear from you in ten mins.

Mano frowned. It'd been a few hours since Eden had left. He turned the hand that held the phone, his eyes lingering on the spot her thumb had rested when they had shaken hands. She had smelled of gardenias.

One friend… No, not her. Even if she smelled good.

He reread Eden's message. He wanted to ignore it but thought Eden was a woman who'd keep her word.

53

Mano: I don't faint.

CHAPTER FOUR

WITH AIDAN STAYING OVERNIGHT AT MATTHEW'S, EDEN ARRIVED AT the pool exactly at five past five the next morning. The near-empty parking lot confirmed she would be the first. The only other car—a strikingly bright blue two-door sedan—was a familiar sight.

Aimee, a St. Anne's student, was on duty at the check-in counter. Hair pulled back haphazardly, shadows under her eyes, she nevertheless gave Eden a wide smile when the latter passed her member's card through the scanner.

"Looks like you had a good night, Aimee."

Aimee grinned sheepishly. "I'm almost looking forward to classes starting again. Socializing is hard work. I wasn't expecting you this morning. Rumor has it you'll be swimming with the Berkeley club soon."

Eden angled her head. "Well, I'll always be a Beaver."

Aimee laughed then groaned, closing her eyes briefly. "I don't understand how something that seemed so fun at the time could hurt so much in the morning."

"Hydrate."

Besides working at the university rec center, Aimee was one

of Eden's army of babysitters. Despite her initial appearance, the captain of the fencing team took her sport seriously. Once the school year began, Aimee's social life would be significantly reduced, and she would be laser-sharp in her attitude toward academics and breaking the west coast college drought of collegiate titles in her sport.

Eden's shoes squeaked on the newly cleaned floors, the medical scent of pine still lingering. She pushed through the glass door and walked toward the benches. After shedding her clothes, she showered while the low hum of the air filtration system kept her actions from being the only noise in the otherwise silent hall.

At the pool's edge, she knelt and dipped her goggles into the water, watching the soft waves move past the lines of buoys before they ceased to have any power. The water was clear and at a constant temperature of 80°F. Eden tucked her hair underneath her swim cap, rolled her shoulders, then began her usual warm-ups: swinging her arms loosely, across her back and front, then a slow progression of stretches.

She dove into the middle lane and let her muscles do the work she had spent years perfecting. This was the only place she could quiet her mind; the world above the watermark ceased for an hour or two. She had tried to leave it once. As a new mother, unsure how she and Brandon would juggle parenting with work, school, and his ambitions for the Summer Games, she fed an unconscious fear that she would never return as a competitive athlete.

The unplanned C-section, a longer than expected recovery, out-of-whack hormones, then recognizing she was no longer privy to an insider's community of coaches and trainers made it easier to stay away from the one place she had felt most like herself.

Two years after Aidan's birth, her dads pushed her back into the pool. Just as they had done when she was five years old, on her first day of swim lessons. Aidan needed to learn to swim, they argued. Brandon could take him, she argued back. In the end, the half-hour sessions in the "Parent and Me" class at the local Y were the gentle reintroduction she needed.

The pool welcomed her back. Her body knew it was home, so easily she moved through the water. She was guided by instinct in that first swim back, even when her stamina was no longer what it was. After that, it was just a matter of managing schedules to squeeze in that one day a week at the pool. Then it was two days. Then she gave up cable TV to pay for babysitting so she could make it three days a week.

A slight shift in the currents suggested another body had entered the pool. When she turned at the wall, a figure appeared in the lane next to her. Then she sensed another body in the far lane. Then another.

The Beavers were coming out, even on a Sunday morning.

But it wasn't a Beaver who greeted her after she finished swimming her final set of laps.

"Eden?"

"Jordan? What are you doing here?"

She'd had minimal contact with St. Anne's most recent Summer Games' champion. He started working as a TA at the college around the same time as she, but their paths rarely crossed since he wasn't a student-athlete.

Besides being a popular addition to the faculty—his classes usually achieved full enrollment before the other instructors'—he stayed in the public eye with occasional commentary on the local TV stations whenever the competitive swim season came around.

"Taking advantage of faculty privileges," he said as he closed the short gap between them, muscled arms hung over the divider. Brown eyes, no longer shielded by goggles, studied her intently. "But I won't lie, I had hoped I'd catch you. You haven't replied to my messages."

"I'm still thinking about your offer."

"I hope you'll join us. Really."

"It's just...well...I used to swim on the women's team at Cal and—"

Jordan held up his hand. "Hey, I totally get it. And if they want you back, I won't be offended. Makes sense to swim where you have history. But Brady's new there. Good coach, but he may not remember you. You know we at St. Anne's look out for one another. Just want you to know you have a place with me... with us...with this team."

Eden gave a little laugh. "What a coincidence. I said something similar to our new rugby consultant yesterday."

Jordan smiled. "It's a good philosophy to follow. Sports can be lonely. But, hey, no pressure, Eden. The offer is there. I think we're all excited we could have another National swimmer among us."

A shiver went up her spine. Could that be her again? A National swimmer?

"I promise," Eden said. "Tomorrow. Give me one more day to think about it. Driving out to Berkeley is a big commitment. Twice a day is workable during the summer, but once school starts...."

"We can carpool in the morning. I don't live far from here. And with Kenny now officially retired, I can confirm that Tommy Jones is coming back."

Eden's eyes widened. This was news. "Tommy's back?"

"You knew him from your college days, right?"

"Yeah. Brandon would say he wouldn't have made it to the Summer Games without Tommy Jones' coaching. You've done your homework, Jordan."

"Well, I know my sport; I know its history. Especially locally. Brandon O'Callaghan's name still carries some weight. He must give you some tips here and there."

Eden shook her head. "Swimming doesn't come up much

between us now that we have a thirteen-year-old. Aidan takes priority in our conversations."

"Of course." Jordan glanced around the pool. "Tommy still talks about Brandon's reaction time off the block."

Eden laughed. "Like a bolt of lightning?"

"Yes!" Jordan's face was thoughtful. "Tommy has your name in his notebook."

Eden blinked. "No way. Seriously?"

Jordan smiled. "Yes. It's there. Saw it myself when we caught up last week. I only got my name in it when I broke the State's record in the IM."

"The race you medaled in."

"You know what it means when your name gets into his book, right? He thinks you have a shot." Jordan swam to the ladder, turning to her before climbing it. "Tomorrow?"

"Tomorrow," she repeated. "I'll decide by tomorrow."

"I look forward to hearing from you," Jordan said.

"Hey, Jordan!" Eden turned to find Linda Wellens' grinning face under her bright pink cap from the other lane.

Eden rolled her eyes. She sensed trouble.

"Hi Linda," Jordan said.

"Come back, will you? It's always good to have some young blood in this pool once in a while."

"Watch who you're calling 'old,' Wellens!" a voice came from the other side of the pool.

"Saw you sucking it in when you noticed Jordan was here, Bob!" Linda yelled back.

Jordan laughed. "Of course. But will you still welcome me back if I take your star swimmer to Berkeley?"

Linda glanced at Eden before looking past her again. "Help her qualify for Nationals, and the Beavers will always welcome you two back."

"You got yourself a deal, Linda," Jordan said. "Tomorrow, Eden. I now have your team captain's blessing to take you away. No excuses. See you soon, I hope."

Eden gave Jordan a quick nod. Linda continued to hang on the buoys, her gaze following Jordan as he left the pool, a slight smile on her lips. Eden silently counted to ten. "Linda! You're up to something. But what? And I'm not sure how I feel that you're so willing to get rid of me."

Linda adjusted the straps from her goggles. "In the two years since Jordan Kennedy moved to the Bay Area, he has recruited some of the top swimmers for the Berkeley club. That kid has ambitions. The Beavers are a safe environment for you, but you need more. One point two seconds is not impossible to drop, but it can be long enough never to realize a dream." Linda returned her gaze to Eden. "Besides, he's hot."

"Linda!"

"He is. I may be sixty, but a hot body is a hot body. And you haven't gone out on a date for as long as I've known you."

A few days ago, Eden might have paid more attention to how attractive Jordan was. Instead, lips that wouldn't smile burned in her memory. "Uncomfortable topic, Linda."

"No crime in looking, Eden," Linda said. "Hot or not, call him tomorrow, please. You'll always have a spot here with the Beavers. We love you, but as the saying goes, if you love them, set them free. Time for you to go." Linda smiled again before going under and pushing off from the wall.

Eden was technically done with her morning swim, but the anxiety in her body remained. She had decisions to make. Her time at the last meet was thrilling, but it now brought consequences she hadn't expected.

She, too, kicked off against the wall and returned to a rhythm that would see her through the next ten minutes. But her mind, usually silent in her morning swim, wouldn't rest. She knew Linda was right. Swimming with the Beavers had gotten her further than she had expected. But there was no one else that could push her. And now Tommy Jones and his famous notebook were back in the Bay Area.

Tommy knew her. He knew how she swam. More importantly, he had a hand in taking another thirty-something to the podium at last year's Nationals.

She looked up at the wall clock and mentally calculated she had eight minutes to shower and change. If she didn't bump into anyone, she'd be at Patty Yuan's door in twenty minutes—plenty of time to then walk with Aidan to Sunday Mass.

She miscalculated by three minutes. Not her fault, she rationalized. Sunday drivers in the suburbs were terrible.

As the familiar chimes of the Yuan's doorbell reverberated indoors, Eden glanced toward Mano's house. She hadn't appreciated the house very much until now. It was merely the house at the end of the street. Sometimes, its owner—and now Mano's landlady—would sit outside, usually with Mrs. Henderson on her porch. Pride in ownership was evident. A new coat of paint in a dark gray hue kept the house looking classy instead of old. Its lawns were neat with lavender guiding the path that led to the front door. Eden grinned.

The blinds were down.

The man learned quickly. She'd send him a text after Mass, just to see how he was doing. At least she knew he remained alert last night.

"Good morning!" Patty greeted her as she opened the door. "He's on his way down. I can't guarantee they had their eight hours of sleep, though they were quiet after nine o'clock."

"You sound suspicious."

"I told Charles we need a program that can selectively switch off access to the Wi-Fi, but he's dragging on it. Thinks I worry too much."

The thumping of the stairs revealed a sleepy-eyed teenager, shirt untucked with a loose tie around his neck. "Am I serving for Father Brian or Father Paul?" Aidan asked, pulling his backpack over his shoulder.

Eden's hand was pushed away when she tried to reach for Aidan's tie. "Father Brian."

"Then I won't need the tie."

"Your grandmother wants you to wear a tie."

"How would she know? She's miles away."

"You'll know you didn't live up to your word, Aidan O'Callaghan. And I won't lie for you."

She ignored her son's glare as she consciously smiled extra wide for the sake of her friend. "Thank you for letting Aidan stay over. We'll have to have Matthew over soon."

"He'd love that." Patty turned her head slightly, careful to make eye contact with Aidan. "You know you are always welcome here, right? You're such a good friend to Matt."

Aidan nodded, then his eyes grew wide. "Excuse me. Hey! Mano! Mano! Wait up!"

Both women watched Aidan as he ran toward the road, literally stopping Mano in his tracks. "Oh...hello," murmured Patty. "I thought you said he wasn't feeling well yesterday. He seems pretty healthy today."

"Patty..."

"Oh, to be a gray shirt on that man...."

Don't stare! He's a colleague! Turn around!

Mano's hair was pulled up into a man bun, emphasizing the thickness of his neck and muscled shoulders. He crossed his arms as he spoke to Aidan, biceps straining the sleeves of an athletic shirt that clung to his body. Damp patches suggested a workout worthy of a top athlete.

Eden cleared her throat. "Aidan! We have to go!"

"Five minutes, Mom. Please!"

Patty grinned. "Better go get him. I know Father Brian. He may not care about ties, but he won't be happy if you're late."

Eden pulled at her earlobe as she walked toward Aidan and Mano. Neither her son nor the rugby player bothered to look her way until she was right next to them.

"What do you say, Mr. Palua?"

Mano's dark eyes were suddenly on Eden, and she swallowed nervously. "Hi!"

Aidan raised his eyebrows, surprise etched on his face. No doubt at the unusual high pitch of her voice, thought Eden.

"Good morning," Mano said. "Aidan said you're off to church."

"Yes. He's an altar server at St. Anne's chapel once a month. It's something all the O'Callaghan boys do apparently," Eden explained. "His dad was an altar server; his grandfather was an altar server. I think an O'Callaghan even worked in the Vatican."

"Mom, no one asked."

This time, it was she who was guilty of staring at someone's smile. Well, almost a smile. On a face of granite.

"Mom? Can I?" Aidan asked impatiently.

"Can you what?" Eden asked.

"Weren't you listening?" Aidan huffed. "Mano... I mean, Mr. Palua said he'd help me with rugby if it's okay with you."

"I didn't think you were serious about rugby. I mean, it's just something you did with Granddad once in a while."

"Oh geez, Mom!" Aidan shook his head and started walking away, frustration evident in his gait.

"Hey!" Eden blew out of her mouth. "Sorry about that. He's a little...uh...explosive these days."

"How old is he?"

"Thirteen."

"Sounds about right."

"Yeah, that's what my dads say. But..."

"When I was that age, Mum used to say I'd get mad if the cat purred too loudly."

"What did she do when you got angry?"

"Signed me up for more rugby."

Eden laughed, her eyes returning to Mano's lips.

"I used to," he said.

"Huh?"

"You just said I should smile more often."

Eden's eyes widened as she felt the familiar wave of heat

flood her face. She groaned. "I'm sorry! I do that sometimes, say things out loud before I think it through. It was so bad as a teenager, one of my dads had me go through a neuropsych evaluation. But nothing. I'm normal other than I just blurt things out! No filter."

Aidan's loud yell followed by him gesturing to an imaginary wristwatch interrupted Eden's unexpected confession. She inhaled deeply and shrugged. "Sorry. It's just me."

Mano frowned. "If what you say is true, nothing wrong with that." He nodded in Aidan's direction. "Your son asked if he could have a handful of coaching sessions with me in exchange for putting up the Halloween decorations."

"Seriously?"

"I don't know anything about Halloween, and Mrs. Henderson stopped by this morning...." He paused as if considering the weight of his next words. "She said to expect three hundred children. That's more than what Patty said. That can't be right. Three hundred?"

Eden nodded. "If it's not raining, I wouldn't be surprised by that number. Seven Hills attracts young families. Young families love Halloween."

Mano's jaw seemed to clench tighter. "If Aidan has your permission, I will have Mondays off."

"Are you sure?"

Mano's voice was firm. "I don't do Halloween, but I respect traditions. If it's what's expected, I'd better do something about it. A few coaching sessions seem a fair trade for help."

An hour later, Eden's suspicion that Father Brian was going to recycle a homily was confirmed when Eula Lathrop, three pews up, gave her husband a nudge followed by a look of approval. Eula liked this one, which usually meant it would start with an anecdote from Father Brian's childhood in Dublin that would eventually tie into the gospel for the day.

Usually, she liked Father Brian's homilies, but the dark, deep-set eyes of a stranger intrigued her. There was a story behind them. She could sense it. Maybe Mano Palua was a deadbeat dad who wanted to run away from his obligations. Or he was thrown out of his country for wild behavior. She didn't know much about rugby beyond what happened on the field. Her dad used to take her out to Golden Gate Park to watch the local club team play every weekend. She knew the rules and the positions but nothing more.

Robert Pak was in heaven when Aidan started to show more than a casual interest in the sport. They'd often watch games online; squeals of disbelief and unexpected language would come from the dining table where the laptop would be propped up. As an athlete, she understood what could come with the responsibility and honor of representing one's country. Some like Brandon thrived on it and were able to create a life beyond sport; others sunk under the expectations of glory.

All could be revealed if she'd clicked on the many links that came up when she'd first searched for Mano's picture. Given how big the sport was in New Zealand and his success in it, there was bound to be a great deal of information about Mano. Except it didn't feel right nosing into someone's life like that. It was the one thing that weighed on Brandon's mind as he continued to make headway in the world of sports broadcasting: the possible loss of privacy.

Eden looked toward the back of Aidan's head, now seated on the front pew as Father Brian continued to discuss the virtues of forgiveness. That was one thing she never doubted about her ex-boyfriend: that he'd be a good father. Surprisingly, they didn't disagree much when it came to Aidan's welfare. She frowned.

So far.

Aidan's decision to quit swimming didn't go over too well with Brandon. She appeased his frustration that at least their son was interested in other sports. Then Aidan dropped out of base-ball and refused to try cross-country. Brandon insisted Aidan take up a sport. Their son refused. She tried to ease the tension between father and son by suggesting that, maybe, Aidan needed to explore the arts, to take a break from sports. Aidan balked at her idea of picking up a musical instrument then drew stick figures on any dry surface to prove his point that he would not benefit from an art class.

That's why this morning's question about working out with Mano was more than a surprise.

It was a whisper of hope that her son would do more than play video games as an extracurricular activity.

Eden uncrossed and crossed her legs, adjusting her body slightly against the hard surface of the polished wooden seat. She arched her neck slightly, partly to loosen it but mainly to enjoy the sun hitting the rose window of the chapel: petals of blues, greens, gold, and red in an abstract combination glowed.

"Let us recite the Creed."

Eden stood up with the congregation and bowed her head respectfully. Ten years of taking Aidan to Mass had made her actions automatic. Her dad, a self-proclaimed agnostic with a collection of self-help books that rivaled any library, wasn't pleased about her decision. "Never trust anyone who says they speak for any god," he had muttered.

It was Aidan's great-grandmother's wish that Aidan attended Mass every Sunday, a promise Margaret O'Callaghan extracted from Eden on her deathbed. At first, it was a chore. She didn't grow up religious, but after nearly a decade of attending Mass, it wasn't any different from something she *had* to do rather than something she wanted to do.

She could have argued that Aidan didn't need all this cere-mony, that this weekly attendance in a system she didn't believe in was unnecessary. It was, however, an important part of Aidan's family and, therefore, part of his heritage. She couldn't deny him that. What had been tedious and foreign was now comforting in its consistency. There was a reason for everything; a message behind every action; a purpose behind each word. Nothing was said or done by accident.

When Communion was distributed, she excused herself out of the chapel. She'd wait for Aidan to change out of his robes then, together, they'd swing by the college cafeteria for Sunday brunch. A few people began to trickle out of the chapel after her. Then the sound of the pipe organ—used only for this Mass—marked the end of the service. The heavy dark doors opened, Aidan coming out first with the crucifix in hand.

He saw her immediately. "Won't be long."

Father Brian nodded as he walked toward her. "First time I've seen you since the Masters meet. I understand 'congratulations' are in order. A new record in the 50. Impressive!"

"I hadn't realized you followed swimming, Father."

Father Brian shook hands with another member of the congregation. "I swam in college. But if you must know, I'm only on top of things because Linda Wellens is my cousin. She wrote a request for you to drop one point two seconds in our prayer book. I had to call her up to explain that it wasn't quite what the purpose of the book is."

"Linda Wellens is your cousin?"

Father Brian nodded as he continued to shake hands with parishioners. "Oh, yes. She's quite a nuisance, really. Always asking for one intercession or another. Who does she think I am? God?" he winked.

Eden laughed. "I hadn't realized how much of a fan I had in Linda."

Father Brian waved at a family walking past them. "As a child, she was our leader. Everything that Linda has achieved, she's done on her own. The only thing she couldn't do was get to the top ranks of swimming. Time's not kind to athletes, especially those who don't fulfill their dreams. Ah, Aidan, my boy! What's the plan for today? Swift? Kipling? London? Twain?"

"What?" Aidan frowned.

Eden exchanged a grin with Father Brian. "We're keeping it simple today. School starts in a week, and we need to get organized. Right?"

Aidan grunted, earning a chuckle from Father Brian. "You're going to have a fine year. Eighth grade already. Can't believe it. Last year of middle school. What are you most looking forward to?"

"They have a rugby club this year," Aidan said. "And I'm going to try out."

CHAPTER FIVE

MANO WATCHED DAWN BREAK OVER THE LINE OF TREES BEHIND THE house. He was sitting on the deck in the backyard, having put on a fleece as his one concession to the unexpected chilly summer morning. A cup of hot tea warmed his hands. It was an unfamiliar brand; never tried tea with "a hint of ginseng" before. Connor would be impressed.

He had been up for a couple of hours, unused to a quiet that was different from the townhouse he owned—but shared with roommates—in Christchurch. It wasn't that the house was completely absent from noise; there was an achingly slow leak in the bathroom he would need to fix, and the house creaked occasionally. Neither was anything that should keep him up through the night or wake him before the sun rose. But they weren't sounds he was used to.

A squirrel popped its head out of the tree before it ran deftly across the fence. Was it the same one that jumped from tree to tree in the bush area behind the fence? It had enthralled him yesterday morning. He'd have to take a video of it and send it back to Fred Dane. That kid would go crazy about it.

He had spent yesterday afternoon walking through the neighborhood. He knew he'd be close to the college campus, but the ability to walk to the center of town was a pleasant surprise. He managed to bring home a couple of bags of groceries, though Eden did a good job of filling the pantry and refrigerator with enough to see him through his first week.

He hadn't expected to see her yesterday morning. She looked fresh with her hair damp from a shower. Also unexpected was the enthusiastic greeting Aidan had thrown on him. He liked that boy with the big brown eyes, who saw everything. Mum would have said he had an old soul, and that "old soul" wanted to try his hand at rugby.

Aidan didn't even bother with a greeting after running over from Eden's side yesterday.

"Matt and I talked about it last night," he had huffed. "And we both agree you being here is an answer to our prayers."

"Mate, I don't think so."

"No, listen. Last week, Matt and I were discussing whether or not we should go out for rugby. My granddad has always tried to get me interested in the sport. We've passed the ball around. And when the school said it's going to start a club this year...."

"Mate, do you want to try this for yourself or for your grandfather?'"

"Does it matter?"

Mano had glanced up to see Eden studying them at this point with sharp, assessing eyes, but she hung back. He turned back to Aidan. "It needs to come from within, this desire to play."

Aidan stood straighter. "It does. Granddad was just the introduction. This is my choice. Coming to you and asking for help? My choice."

He should have said "no." This wasn't part of his plan. But something in Aidan's eyes spoke to him. It was honest and a little desperate. Aidan reminded him of himself at that age and recognized the boy was looking for something to excel in, especially as the son of a swimming champion.

Mano put his lips to the still-warm mug, grimacing slightly as the unfamiliar flavor hit his taste buds. He only agreed to toss the ball back and forth, if time allowed, and only if their parents approved.

It'd be something he'd do back home for his friends.

Make new friends.

He shook his head slightly. Connor's voice was in his head again. He'd been trying to shut out so many things from within —thoughts, emotions, memories—that he'd forgotten to hear his own voice anymore. But whether he was listening to Connor's advice or trusting his own gut, the offer to Aidan came from a real desire to feed the enthusiasm for a sport he loved. At the very least, he was sure he could find out what type of training the school's rugby program offered. He made a mental note to ask Alistair about it when they met later that morning.

The athletics director had called last night to welcome him. He had also received an email from the Men's Rugby coach, now back from the team retreat. Mano read and reread the email sent by Brett McKenzie. He came to the conclusion that he may not have as enthusiastic a reception as Alistair would lead him to believe.

Two hours later, dressed in shorts and a collared blue polo, he left the house. He caught sight of Mrs. Henderson next door through the large window. Seated in an armchair, mug in one hand, and in a striking pink dressing gown, she gave him a wave and thumbs-up as he passed her house.

He held his hand up automatically though reluctantly. She had swung by last night with banana bread and an offer to join her book club. He took the bread but declined the book club offer. She didn't seem put off with his rejection and told him they were reading Maya Angelou this month. "Her words are one of the voices of our country," Mrs. Henderson stated solemnly.

Damn rental should have a warning sign: Not For Introverts.

Unlike yesterday, the trail that morning was busier with different types of people. Walkers, cyclists, and joggers passed him, but he recognized others were moving with a determination fueled by necessity rather than choice.

St. Anne's College officially welcomed back its staff today.

He studied the schedule Alistair had emailed him. His morning was to be spent familiarizing himself with his colleagues and the campus. Then there was a general meeting for the entire athletic department scheduled for the afternoon. When not working with the rugby players, he seemed to be in a lot of meetings.

Mano stifled his distaste. He knew the higher one went up the "rugby ladder," the more backroom work had to be done. There was play time, then there was plan time. He disliked sitting in rooms. He belonged out on the field. His predecessors on the national team were able to handle the balance better. His own captaining style was different. He'd rather just work with the players. Fortunately, the management knew how to work with each captain's strengths, and the honor to lead was never a burden.

Clear signage made it easy to find the athletic department. Finding the head of St. Anne's entire athletics department on his desk, retrieving darts from the ceiling, was, however, the last thing he'd thought would happen on his first day. Neither was the inability to breathe when Eden gave him a smile.

Dressed casually in slacks and a polo shirt, she had turned just as he looked through the open door of Alistair Montgomery's office.

"Hey! Welcome! You found us! How are you?" Eden said. He caught the small dimple at the corner of her mouth. Why hadn't he noticed it before? The haircut intrigued him: a buzz cut on one side that was softened by the long top that flipped casually over. It could have looked severe on somebody else. On Eden, it only highlighted her face and a long, slender neck. She was so different from Margot who was petite and wore her straight brown hair loose, parted in the middle.

He froze at the unexpected comparison. Thankfully, Eden seem preoccupied with collecting more darts. "Ignore him, Mano. I told him to take it down weeks ago."

"I did," said the giant as he pulled the last three darts. "These are a different batch."

"You have a target on the wall," Eden said, putting the darts in a box on the desk.

"I don't look at the wall when I'm thinking." For his height, Alistair Montgomery jumped off his desk with surprising ease and dexterity. He gave Mano a sheepish look as he stepped forward, arm extended. "Sorry. I really did forget these were up here. Eden's giving me a hard time because the provost is stopping by with a potential donor. Anyway, good to meet you at last, Mano. Welcome! Over jet lag yet?"

Mano returned the firm handshake. "Almost." He took in the brightly lit room, high windows letting in plenty of sunshine. It was simply furnished; the large desk that had held Alistair's weight took up most of the room. A row of filing cabinets and shelves were behind him. Adjacent, a wall of framed newspaper cuttings highlighted current and past success stories from St. Anne's athletics department: track and field; swimming; basketball; lacrosse.

"No, nothing from rugby yet," Alistair said. "And that's why we're excited you're here."

"Thank you for the opportunity to be part of the program." A quick glance at Eden confirmed the feeling that she was still looking at him. She turned away when their eyes met, reaching for a stack of folders on the desk, a soft stain of pink visible at the base of her neck.

She cleared her throat. "I'll leave you two. Mano, when you're done, there's some paperwork that needs to be completed. It's a little crazy with the whole staff here today for the first time since summer break. If I'm not here, Sarah—the other admin—can also help you. She's really nice."

Mano pursed his lips and nodded while silently questioning the sudden uptick of his heart rate at her study of him.

"Hey, Eden," Alistair interrupted. "Just before you go. One

more time: are you sure? I haven't officially turned in your request or my approval."

Eden exhaled. A flash of nervousness washed over her face before being replaced by the large smile that had nearly paralyzed him minutes ago. "I'm sure. Sarah said she'd welcome the extra hours. As long as you're good with it too."

"On paper, I'm good. I'm covered by two capable assistants. And it's just for one semester, right?"

"Yes. And thanks. I really appreciate the support," Eden said quickly as if to prevent the conversation from continuing. "Mano? Good to see you again." She shut the door quietly behind her, but Alistair continued to stare at it for a few seconds.

"Sometimes, it's just not clear what's the best thing to do," Alistair muttered.

"Pardon?"

"Sorry," Alistair said, unwrapping his legs and moving to his side of the desk. "I'm trying not to think ahead of myself, that's all. I hate surprises, but isn't life just full of them? Anyway, I can't thank you enough for accepting our offer. You'll add some extra credibility to the program. Some of the boosters will be interested in meeting you."

"You've mentioned that in your email to me. That's not a problem. I'm used to representing the sport off the field. All I ask is that I'm given ample time to prepare for these meetings."

"Of course. And you're okay with the list of interviews with the press we've set up? Great. Eden will have those dates for you. I hope you understand why we're going to take advantage of your credentials."

Mano nodded. "Your email was clear. I appreciate that. And I'll do what I can."

"I owe Liana Murphy."

Mano allowed himself half a smile. "She said she trusts you."

"She did?" Alistair sighed. "I'll always think of her as the one who got away."

Mano's smile disappeared. "She's happily married."

Alistair waved his hand. "No, not in that way. I've met Mitch Molloy. He'd have my head. I was hoping I'd have her join us as the head of the soccer program. I'll keep trying though. Just let her know how much you love living in California, and maybe, eventually, I'll win her over!"

Mano asked Alistair about rugby's history in the American college system. He knew firsthand how vital traditions and history were in his sport. If none existed, then it had to be built. He also noticed that Alistair was very selective with what he said of Brett McKenzie.

"He has been key in the development of both Men's and Women's Rugby at the club level for the last five years," Alistair continued. "I'm sure you both will get along."

Mano nodded but refrained from adding his thoughts. Until he met the man, he'd reserve his opinion about how well they'd work together.

"Have you seen much of the campus? No? I'll have Eden show you to your office. She's a good tour guide. Charms everyone. I think one of our top basketball recruits decided on St. Anne's because of her."

They reentered the front office to see Eden talking to a young woman with bright purple hair and a tall student with a pair of trainers slung over his shoulder.

"Hey, Derek," Alistair said. "Could you give me five minutes? I just have to make a phone call. Eden? Do you have time now to show Mano where he's going to work?"

Eden nodded. "Mano, may I introduce you to assistant-extra-ordinaire, Sarah, and this is Derek Wilson. Derek is the starting center of our basketball team."

Sarah waved her greetings while Derek broke into a grin. "Hey! You're the new rugby coach everyone's talking about. Nice to meet you, man! There's a picture of you in my dorm room. My roommate, Carter, will be playing for you this season. He's a big fan, man. Said he met you when you were in England for some championship or something."

Or something? The World Championship, mate… Years of controlling his expression in front of the media was proving to be useful as a private citizen. "I'm here mainly as a consultant. Not as a coach. But I look forward to meeting your roommate. Carter, is it?"

Derek nodded his head vigorously. "Yeah, Carter Holmes. Big dude who runs like the wind. Man, I told him he could have been playing football at some top ten college or something. The dude has some speed! But he's obsessed with rugby and wants to play for our country. Didn't even know we had a national rugby team. What are they called? Vultures?"

"Eagles."

"Yeah! That's it, man! Eagles!" Behind Derek, Mano saw Eden and Sarah exchange glances of amusement. But the basketball player remained focused on him. "You used to play for your country, right? Do you guys have a name for your national team?"

"Yeah."

"Like Kangaroos or something?"

Mano tensed. "What makes you say that?"

"Isn't that the national animal of Australia?"

"Oh, Derek," Eden said, shaking her head.

"What?" Derek asked. "I'm pretty sure it's a kangaroo. It's on their planes, isn't it?"

"The red kangaroo is the national animal of Australia. But I'm not from Australia. I'm from New Zealand."

Derek's eyes widened. "Dude, sorry! We have a lot of Australians play tennis here, and you sound just like them."

"Bet I'm going to hear that a lot," Mano muttered.

Eden threw back her head with laughter and surprised Mano by putting her arm through his. "You need to work on your geography, Derek. That was terrible. Anyway, I'll show Mr. Palua to his office."

He had to fight the urge to reach for her hand when she pulled away, the sudden loss of her touch felt acutely. He stared ahead, mildly hearing her. She was stopped every few minutes, a student or another staff member asking a question or offering a greeting. She never forgot to introduce him to faces and names he wouldn't remember. His attention was still on the place where she first touched him today.

"Are you feeling okay?" Eden asked.

He gave her a side-glance as they walked down the long hall, anonymous voices echoing. "I'm fine. Why?"

"You seemed preoccupied."

She didn't pursue the matter further, knocking on the door before waiting for a response. Two men looked up immediately.

"Eden!"

"Hey, stranger!"

The shorter, stockier man turned to him. "I don't need an introduction. It's just an honor, Mr. Palua. I'm Jackson Fleming. Assistant coach to Brett."

"Please, call me Mano. We're colleagues." He turned to the older man who now stood next to Jackson.

"And I'm Harry Winters. I coach the women's team. Saw you play in Chicago last year. I'm looking forward to picking your brains. In exchange for a home-cooked meal, perhaps?"

"Of course. No home-cooked meal necessary."

"Nonsense," Harry said. "My wife will be thrilled. She couldn't believe it when I said you'd be here. Apparently—and I don't quite believe her—you walked right past her in Chicago, but she was too nervous to say 'hi.'"

Eden handed Mano a file with an apologetic face. "Some new paperwork that the college is requiring. I'll need to get these back from you by today. Sorry. It is a bit of a rush. Give the office a call if you have any questions about them. And I'll see all three of you at the department meeting later. Don't be late!"

Jackson sat on the corner of his desk. "Sarah said you're cutting your work hours. Dare I think it's because you're going to give it a go?"

Harry crossed his arms. "Give what a go?"

"Don't you read the faculty newsletters? Alistair's efficient assistant broke the Masters record in the 50 Free. Just a couple of seconds off the qualifying times for Nationals."

Harry whistled. "Eden Pak! That's fantastic! Congratulations! Are you sticking with the Beavers?"

"Well...."

"You're seconds away," Jackson repeated. "You gotta go for it, Eden. Beavers are great, but you'll need to up your game to not just qualify for but to reach the finals. Is it going to be Berkeley or Oakland?"

"Berkeley or Oakland?" Harry looked at Jackson, frowning. "I don't get the question."

"Besides the university teams, Berkeley and Oakland have two swim clubs that send swimmers to Nationals every year. Swimmers who get on the podium."

"Why do you know so much about swimming, Jackson?" Harry said.

Eden rolled her eyes. "You really don't read the faculty newsletters, do you, Harry? Jackson's family are local legends in the swim community. All four of his sisters had county records. Their house has ribbons everywhere...."

"But none of them were able to beat Eden Pak." Jackson grinned. "The summer you dominated I heard your name so often it haunted me. Now that we're working together, I can see that my sisters totally exaggerated about you. You're not the cold, calculating swim-machine they said you were!"

Mano lost himself in Eden's laugh: full, free, and fearless. Her eyes sparkled as she swatted Jackson's arm with the other file in her hand.

"You're the one exaggerating!" she said.

Jackson smiled. "They're keeping up with your times, you know. Mia's even talking about getting on a Masters team now."

"Well, if she does, I look forward to lining up against her again." Eden offered Mano one last smile before leaving him to his new colleagues.

"She's very nice," Jackson said with a twinkle in his eye. "Still single."

Harry stifled a cough. "Uh, so Brett has you working at the corner desk. You'll find a couple of binders already on there. They're summaries of our last season for both the men's and women's teams."

Mano appreciated the change in subject. Getting his mind back to the world he knew so well was a welcome-relief from the unexpected distraction of Eden. Fortunately, Harry's lack of interest in the comings and goings of his fellow faculty members didn't translate to Mano. Harry dominated the conversation for the next hour, quizzing Mano about his experiences as a rugby player.

The rest of the morning went by fast as he finished the requested paperwork, set up his faculty accounts—sending a quick email to Connor and Mitch in the process—and finally meeting Brett McKenzie, the head coach of men's rugby.

He was tall with a shaved head; Mano pegged him for a lock in his playing days. While not unfriendly, Brett viewed Mano suspiciously. "Pleased to meet you, Mano. Must say I was surprised when Alistair said we had someone with your professional history coming to our little college."

Do you see me as prey or predator? Mano cracked his neck, stopping that sneer that threatened to erupt from his lips. "It's good —"

Brett continued as if he didn't hear Mano. "A former captain of New Zealand rugby? Here at St. Anne's? Wow. What a surprise."

Behind him, Harry shook his head in disapproval.

Mano inched his chin up slightly, meeting Brett's gaze. He wasn't going to be interrupted again. "I'm honored to be here. Just let me know what I can do."

Brett nodded slowly. "I will." He glanced over Mano's shoulder. "Jackson, will you show Mano around? I'll catch up with you guys at the department meeting." He held up a folder.

"Eden's going to have my head if I don't get these forms done before it."

Jackson gave Mano an apologetic look but ignored the subject of the head coach as he led Mano out of the building. Mano blinked when they emerged from the cool white adobe halls. The fog that shrouded the campus when he arrived earlier had evaporated, replaced by sunshine and a cloudless blue sky. The quiet, empty campus he had walked through on Sunday was now bustling with energy: people were walking in all directions; cars maneuvered through tight parking lots; the presence of trucks, buses, and other service vehicles added to organized chaos.

"It'll settle down after the first month," Jackson said. "The first few days are always a little crazy. New students, new staff, new rules. Kinda fun! From here, you can see our field. Your binder will have all our pitch assignments for the year, including practices and home matches."

From a distance, he could just see two players on the pitch Jackson had pointed to. A ball sailed up in the air, its trajectory falling short of a goalpost he knew instinctively would measure the same as those found in any field back home. His throat caught. If he weren't here today, he'd probably be in Connor's backyard tossing the ball around with Fred.

Liar. You'd be locked in your room tearing up whatever photos you have left of Margot.

He remained silent as Jackson recited facts and anecdotes with practiced ease that suggested this wasn't the first time he was told to show people around campus. For what constituted a small campus by American standards, it was a minor labyrinth of buildings and open spaces. Turning a corner revealed an unexpected quadrangle where a few people were lying out in the sun. They turned another corner and were greeted with wall-to-wall plastic bottle containers.

Jackson grimaced. "Oh yeah, forgot this was going to be here. We have installation art pop up every semester, and I didn't check...."

"Let me guess," Mano interjected, "the faculty news."

Jackson grinned. "It's all in there!"

They finished the informal tour with a stop in the locker rooms where he met the affable equipment manager who hailed from Frimley, Surrey.

"Just like Jonny Wilkinson," said Tom Morris with a wink.

"Yeah." Mano nodded. "Know Jonny quite well. Last time we were on the pitch together, Connor Dane broke his record."

"Was Connor watching when Jonny got it back in South Africa?"

Mano smiled. Tom Morris knew his rugby. "Pleased to meet you, sir."

"Likewise, Mr. Palua. I've watched you play for years. People talk about Molloy, Dane, Stanton. But you're solid. No team wins without people who play consistently like you. Nothing fancy; just solid rugby. That's the best kind of rugby, in my opinion."

It'd been a long time since he reacted to flattery. His career was dotted with accolades and criticism. It was healthier to ignore what others thought of his game. But, occasionally, like today, when it came from someone who knew the sport, it humbled him. "My friends call me Mano, Mr. Morris."

Tom Morris said the department meeting was the only time in the year they'd see everyone in the Athletics Department. Once the academic year began, it was full steam ahead to keep training on course while managing the "student" part of student-athletes.

"St. Anne's is really tough about our kids doing well here at college," Tom said. "It's no secret that while sports bring in the boosters and investors, the nuns of St. Anne's will pull the plug on any or all the programs if we don't pay equal attention to education. It's how we lost the swim program, but we've kept the pool. Everyone has access to it, if you ever fancy a swim. Always heated."

"The nuns?"

"Oh yeah. Didn't you see the convent up on the hill yet?

Very nice, if I do say so myself. St. Anne's used to be a convent. Then a fire tore through Seven Hills, sparing only the chapel. To have the funds, they started a small college to help pull in some money. It started as a women's college, and the girls who went here were among the first women athletes anywhere."

"I thought some president in the '70s...."

"Oh, yeah. Him. Yeah, he took it to the next level and added new programs. St. Anne's now has athletes competing in thirty inter-collegiate sports. But the nuns started it. Don't mess with the nuns. Even the Jesuits are afraid of them. A good bunch of them still teach. One of them, Sister Michael, is a professor of Theology and coaches volleyball."

"Interesting combination of expertise."

Tom grinned. "Welcome to California!"

Mano caught Eden sneaking into the half-filled auditorium just as Alistair took to the podium.

Despite the unconventional manner in which they had met this morning, it was clear Alistair knew his stuff. Handouts were in bullet points. He provided links to resources for major topics he addressed. When introducing all the new members of the department, he did so in alphabetical order and with no more than five lines of bio per introduction.

There was structure in Alistair's presentation. He didn't veer from his scrip: a joke, a visual presentation, statistics, an anecdote of a student-athlete or coach, followed by another visual. While far from rapt, his new colleagues were taking the requisite notes. Harry asked a question. A few others took snapshots of the visuals with their phones. They were engaged though not inspired.

They were all there to work. No bright-eyed, inexperienced coach-trainer in this room.

Mano let his gaze return to Eden. She sat in the front row, her back to him. But he recognized her neck now. She'd reached for her earlobe often, a nervous action, he guessed. She greeted everyone by name, and judging by the hugs and smiles exchanged, she was popular with the staff.

"I don't usually do this, but we're very fortunate this year to have two professionals be part of the St. Anne's family for at least part of the year. They bring with them an extraordinary amount of experience and insight into being and working with the world's top athletes. Since they're both here, let me introduce you to them," Alistair said.

Mano stiffened.

"We have a highly respected sports psychologist joining our team. Dr. Chen, where are you? Welcome! She's worked with athletes from the college-level to the pros, all over the world. Most recently, she just completed a one-year contract travelling with a couple of the tennis pros ranked in the Top 10. If you Google her, I'm sure you'll see a photo of her in the players box at Roland Garros. Please encourage your athletes to take advantage of Dr. Chen while she's here."

Applause came up on cue.

Mano tightened his grips on the arms of his seat. A rush of adrenaline swept through his body, blocking out sound and image. He shut his eyes, trying to make sense of the pounding that was relentless in his head. Alistair's voice drilled through the haze that had engulfed him so suddenly.

"…he's one of the legends of rugby with too many accolades for me to list. We are truly honored he has agreed to spend the next few months with us. From New Zealand, former captain of the national rugby team and two times world champion, Mano Palua."

He managed a nod, but his body wouldn't move. He raised his hand to acknowledge the welcome, but sharp eyes from the front row weren't fooled. She studied him from across the room, concern somehow being shown without a word or a touch.

How did she know he wasn't all right?

As soon as Alistair made his final comments, signaling the end of the meeting, Eden moved swiftly through the crowd.

"Hey," she whispered, putting a cool bottle of water in his hand. She reached across him, giving a playful slap on Tom Harris' arm. "You, Mr. Harris, have yet to turn in your claims from your summer expenses. I need them pronto."

"Didn't I? Couldn't you just print—"

"No," Eden said firmly. "You know Alistair likes a personal spreadsheet to ensure the numbers reconcile. Will you drop it off at my desk by the end of the day? I need to go over more forms with Mano."

She continued to stand next to his seat, in the aisle, and seemed to be redirecting people away. With shaking hands, he unscrewed the bottle and downed the water. The pounding receded to a buzzing that eventually disappeared with the emptying auditorium. He bent over, resting his elbows on his knees, then massaged his temples.

Not too long ago, when frazzled thoughts accompanied anxious questions, he would turn to prayer. No longer. He stayed away from what was once a regular part of his life. He wasn't ready to return to that, aware of how angry he was at God. He accepted that Margot didn't want him in her life, but the desire to blame someone, anyone, continued to burn from within.

The pain kept him from being numb.

"Mano? Are you okay?"

"Yeah." *No.*

"You looked a little dehydrated."

"I'm fine."

"Maybe you should—"

"I'm fine."

"I have some aspirin in the office—"

"Do you have to be everyone's mother? I'm fine!"

His rebuke echoed through the auditorium. It silenced whatever conversations there were. All eyes were on them; hers were on his. But the concern that was there a few seconds ago was replaced with sadness…and a touch of pain.

Her slight touch on his shoulder sent a shiver down his back. "I'm glad you're fine," she said softly then moved away.

He leaned back in the chair, aware that no one wanted to approach him now.

It wasn't as satisfying a feeling as he thought it'd be.

CHAPTER SIX

Eden scrunched her face at the spreadsheet in front of her. She tried to combat the growing trepidation from within with disgust but failed. She was scared. Her new reality would be determined by whatever numbers popped up after she pressed the "calculate" button.

She groaned when she saw the total, highlighted in blue, as if the cool colors could mask the precariousness of her situation. She wasn't in danger of being homeless but....

It had made sense three weeks ago. But that same spreadsheet didn't anticipate a cracked windshield, Aidan's bike being stolen, or hiring extra babysitting with both her dads doing double duty taking care of Grandma Mattie.

"No more surprises, please." She clicked onto a different tab and studied the calendar she'd created when SwimUSA released the cut times for Nationals. She now had concrete goals to aim for. They had lowered the qualifying times further, so it wasn't one point two seconds she had to drop for the 50 meters free but two point one. The cut time for the 100m was three seconds faster than her current PB. Not impossible.

But she wasn't twenty anymore.

Eden pushed away from her dining table. Supporting the

back of her neck with one hand, she grabbed the still-warm mug of almond milk and headed to the balcony. The fog had moved in early in the afternoon, cooling the night significantly. No staring at the sky and counting the stars tonight. Just a dark blanket of black above her.

Not that the absence of stars was noticed. Her mind returned to the calendar, wondering which meet would give her the best chance. Neither were ideal: San Luis Obispo was only five weeks away. She'd developed an efficient taper of two weeks prior to the last meet. It was Brandon's turn to watch Aiden that weekend. Because of the proximity of the meet, a healthy number of swimmers from both Berkeley and the Beavers were pooling resources to rent houses for the meet.

San Luis Obispo made sense financially.

She just wasn't sure if she could get her body ready in time to drop her time.

The next meet she could see herself preparing for was in Mesa. Next year. That meant her budget would need to stretch even longer without a fulltime job. But Mesa would give her more time to prepare; perhaps optimize her diet further; there'd be opportunity redesign her training in the gym and in the pool. And she could explore using a longer time for tapering, which Jordan suggested might work in her favor. She sighed.

It had been a month since she gave notice to cut hours at work.

I can make this work; I know I can!

But she was restless. She glanced at the wall clock. It was just past nine. She went inside and knocked gently on Aidan's door. "Bud? I'm just going for a walk, okay? I'll have my phone."

A muffled response indicated he had heard her.

She grabbed her jacket, phone, keys, and a small flashlight, then ran down the stairwell with a sudden burst of energy fueled by an unknown source of emotion. Frustration? Anxiety? Fear?

She zipped her jacket up and pulled on the hoodie when she

reached the ground floor. Once outside of the security gate, she decided to follow the trail that led to the college. Newly installed solar lighting kept the path from being too dark, and she knew Campus Safety had started bike patrols down the path in response to more students taking night classes.

She glanced up one more time at her apartment. Aidan's lights were still on. On a different night, she would have insisted he be ready for bed. But fifteen minutes late wouldn't hurt tonight. She'd rather he stayed awake while she was out of the apartment.

I'm an adult; I can do this!

But falling asleep had become a little harder to do this past month.

Adding to the waves of unexpected events was the abrupt exchange between her and Mano at the department meeting. With her new work schedule, she had barely seen him on campus. Twice, and from a distance. She hadn't spoken to him once. A part of her was grateful their paths hadn't crossed. The other part hadn't forgotten the feel of his back when she'd touched him.

Solid.

But his words had hurt. Not because they were untrue—she did tend to mother everyone who came into the Athletics Department—but because he didn't want her "mothering." Word through the grapevine (aka, Jackson) was that he was settling in with the rugby staff, and the student-athletes enjoyed his presence both on and off the field. She did notice on the admin's log that Brett McKenzie had seen Alistair twice already this past month.

Eden dug her fist deeper into the pockets of her jacket and increased her pace. It wasn't any of her business. She didn't give up fifteen hours of precious work hours and money to dwell on goings-on that Sarah was now in charge of. However, her ambition to not think more about Mano Palua wasn't aided by her son.

Mano was the one topic Aidan was willing to talk about. He and Matthew had begun throwing—or was it tossing? —the ball around with Mano for a couple of weeks now, and Aidan had nothing but praise for the coach.

"Hey!" The warning from the unexpected body came too late. She wiped her mouth then spat. Cold grass tasted…cold.

"Eden?"

"Mano?"

His hand stretched in front of her, reminding her of the indignity of her present situation. She ignored his offer of assistance. She rolled over before pushing herself off the ground, brushing away any grass or dirt. *At least the sprinklers don't come on until the morning.* The last thing she wanted was to walk in front of Mano Palua with wet spots on her butt and chest.

"Are you all right?" He was still partially hidden in the shadows. "I didn't see you. What are you doing wandering out here on your own at night?"

She returned her now trembling hands to the confines of her pockets. "What are *you* doing out here by yourself at night?"

He paused as if surprised by her question. "Running."

"Well, good to see you again."

She'd taken a few steps when he called out, "Neither of us saw each other on the trail, and I'm a friend. What if you bump into someone not so friendly?"

"We're not friends," she said hurriedly, continuing her walk. A few seconds later, he spoke again.

"I'm sorry."

His voice was loud and clear; she couldn't pretend she didn't hear him. She wanted to keep walking, to pretend their late-night encounter didn't just happen. *But he is helping Aidan.* She could ignore him professionally but not personally.

He was suddenly behind her. "I'm sorry. I was rude the other day." He sighed loudly. "Eden? Will you turn around?"

That meant she'd see him again. The last time she'd met his eyes, they were full of derision.

"Please?"

She inhaled, tempted to punish him now that he'd apologized. She hung her head, took another deep breath, and turned around. "It's fine, really."

"I also didn't thank you for…uh…looking out for me at the general meeting. Your intervention helped me calm down quicker. How did you know?"

She looked up. No derision but there wasn't much she could read in those dark eyes either. "I didn't. You just didn't look comfortable."

"Let me walk with you."

"No."

He then made a slow study of their surroundings before returning his gaze on her. "There isn't anyone around, Eden."

"I've done this walk many times by myself. It's safe."

"Is Aidan alone?"

"Our neighbor is home, if there's an emergency. He knows to get hold of her." She shuffled her feet. "Look, there's no need to be a hero here. I'm just going for a short walk. Needed to get some fresh air. Campus Safety is around. Thanks for the offer, anyway."

He studied her, his eyes never leaving her face. Even in the coolness of the night, she felt a warmth radiate under his intense scrutiny. "How about a compromise?" he said cautiously. "I'll stay here until you get back. In twenty minutes? Just so I know you're okay."

"People don't say 'no' much to you, do they?"

One corner of his lip lifted, and for a split second, Eden forgot she was still annoyed at him.

"Let's just say only a handful of people do."

She snorted at the hubris behind that statement, but she didn't doubt it was true. She looked around her. It was quiet and getting darker by the minute. "Listen. It's a free country. Stay here and wait; walk with me. I don't care."

He nodded then gestured for her to lead the way. He seemed

lost in thought, content at the space of silence that stretched between them. She kept her pace, which was usually too fast for most people, but Mano didn't seem hampered by it; his long strides kept up with hers so casually. His bulk belied a gracefulness she hadn't noticed before. Jackson had said he was working out with the team in the gym and outdoing most of them. Her gaze lingered on his biceps, the lack of light not hiding their size.

"So…you run much?" she asked. Inside, she cringed at the question and decided to keep her attention on the spotlight her flashlight provided as they walked.

"Old habits die hard. Helps clear my mind."

She told herself not to say anything more, but she was never very good at listening to that particular voice. "Um…how are you settling in at work?"

"You don't have to be polite to me, Eden."

But the dam had cracked. "No, I am interested. Because Jackson can't stop talking about you. Aidan can't stop talking about you. Patty can't stop talking about you. And Mrs. Henderson even emailed me saying she got you to agree to go to book club next month and that I should go, too."

"I'm not going to book club." His voice was calm, not irritated. "I thought you just wanted to get some fresh air, and I didn't think you wanted to have a conversation."

"But Mrs. Henderson said—"

"Eden, you seem nervous about something."

You. She laughed too loudly. "No! Of course not."

"The meet in San Luis Obispo?"

She stopped in her tracks. "How do you know about the meet?"

"Aidan wants to see you swim, but he tells me he's supposed to spend that weekend at his father's."

"He told you that?"

"Yeah. He's torn between having time with his dad and wanting to see you qualify for Nationals."

"Is he? He hasn't said anything to me."

They had reached the quadrangle in front of the chapel. Draped with light, it was a literal shining point for the campus. Soft laughter drew her attention to the shadows. A couple in a tight embrace only cemented the romance of the location. Mano followed her stare.

"Tom Harris said this was one of the original buildings on campus," he said quietly.

Eden nodded. "The story is that the nuns ran into this chapel as the fires came. There was only one road leading out of here at that time, and it was blocked off already. The miracle was the fire burned around them, leaving the chapel and its occupants safe."

Mano whistled softly. "That's a special story."

"There're miracles everywhere if we look for them." Eden blew out of her mouth and decided to go for it. It wasn't like she could be embarrassed any further. "If you don't know this already, I just want to thank you for working out with Aidan. I know I irritate you—"

"You don't irritate me."

She frowned and shuffled her feet. "But we've not spoken in a month. I must irritate you."

He took a step closer. "I don't do well with surprises, especially in front of people. When I realized Alistair was going to introduce me in front of everyone, I didn't handle it well, and you were the one I took it out on."

"But—"

"Yeah, I know. I've played in front of thousands of people for years. But I'm part of a team when I play; I'm doing a job."

"You've done hundreds of interviews. And you look good at them!"

He tilted his head slightly. "You've seen my interviews, have you?"

Heat flushed her face. "Aidan wanted to see them."

Amusement flashed in usually unreadable eyes. "What did *Aidan* think?"

"He didn't understand any of it. Said the accent was too strong." She stared. That was almost a smile.

"He's a good kid, Eden. And he's got a bit of natural talent."

"Seriously?"

"It's not often my opinion about rugby is questioned."

She laughed. And for a second, there it was. A real smile. With teeth.

"If it's any consolation," he continued, "Liana Murphy gave me an earful for how I behaved to you."

"She did?"

"Yeah. Along the lines of not showing my face in New Zealand unless I make it up."

A shiver ran through her body. Not from the chilled air. Not from fear. From him. His stare caught her in a net of awareness she wasn't sure she wanted to escape.

The rustle of the trees; the quiet laugh of two lovers in the distance; the low hum of nocturnal animals waking from their slumber—these were sounds she'd dismiss on any other night. But tonight, they only raised her consciousness about the man in front of her.

What would it be like to be touched by granite?

"We better get you back, eh?" he asked softly. "Getting late."

"What? Oh, right. Yes. Back. Better get back. Can't leave Aidan alone too long."

The walk back to the apartment was again without conversation, but it was no longer fraught with nervous silence. They exchanged a nod by the security gate; he waited until she waved from the balcony. She stayed there until he disappeared into the dark.

* * *

She dreamt about him. In her dream, she had reached to run her fingers through his hair, surprised by softness. He'd smiled then.

Not the brief flash she had seen under the shadows of a church but a wide, long-lasting one that was just for her.

"Eden? Got a minute?"

Eden started at the short, bald man now in front of her. She glanced at her phone then looked for Jordan. He drove them to practice this week. She caught his attention then nodded in Tommy's direction. Jordan understood immediately and gave her a thumbs-up.

"Of course," she said, pulling the sweatshirt over her body.

Tommy stared at a sticky note at the corner of his famous notebook. "I was just looking over your workout for the main set. Who designed it?"

"Linda Wellens. She's—"

"I know Linda. Okay, she's known you long enough, and you got here following her advice. But after the next meet, I'm thinking of changing it a little. How do you feel about that?"

Eden nodded. "I'm open to that."

"And you're starting to taper next week?"

"Yes. I began to drop some significant times when I switched from ten days to a full two weeks, moving down to fifty percent of my yardage in the second week."

"Sleep?"

"Nine hours." *As long as I don't dream of men from New Zealand, I'm sure I'll sleep nine hours.*

Tommy grunted then pulled a pen from the top of his ear, scribbling quickly. Eden made a conscious effort not to lean forward and try to sneak a look at Tommy's notes. She wondered if he still had his notebook from when he had coached Brandon.

"We'll stick to that." Tommy shut his notebook loudly. "Why mess with what's working, right?"

Minutes later, she joined Jordan in his car. He had his laptop opened, as usual, adding notes to a training spreadsheet that he would later share with the whole team. He looked up, a small smile resting on his face, as she slid into the passenger seat. He lifted a traveler cup toward her. "Hot chocolate."

"When did you get this?" She took the cup immediately.

"Ashley swung by the coffee place around the corner. She had sent a group message asking for everyone's orders." Jordan started the car. "She must have forgotten to add your number, so I asked her to grab an extra hot chocolate. I hope that was okay."

"I'll never say 'no' to a hot chocolate after a morning work-out. Thanks!" Eden brought the cup to her lips as Jordan drove the now-familiar route to Seven Hills. It'd been several weeks since she began swimming with the Berkeley club, and Ashley Jones was making her feelings clear.

Eden was competition both in and out of the pool.

They were both swimming in the same events, and until her arrival, Ashley was the only female swimmer in the morning swim sessions. She was good. A real contender for the national team headed for Worlds. But Eden suspected Ashley's angst against her wasn't strictly about swimming. There were some visual daggers thrown her way whenever she and Jordan arrived together.

If Ashley had been kinder, Eden would have cleared the air between them about her relationship with Jordan, which was nothing more than carpool buddies. But Eden decided not to be the better person in this fight. *Let her stew a little.* Mind-games were part of competition.

Thanks to the reverse commute and Jordan's driving, her quick chat with Tommy didn't put them too far behind schedule. She'd be back in the apartment in time to get breakfast ready for Aidan.

"See you later at the gym?" Jordan asked as he pulled up in front of her building.

"Of course. Can't wait. Two hours of torture? Sure." She took the steps two at a time, mentally preparing herself to switch from swimmer-mode to mom-mode. It was late-start Wednesday which gave her a few minutes with Aidan in the mornings. Except he hadn't taken well to the start of a new school year, or rather the idea of waking up before ten. He'd already earned one tardy, and it'd only been two weeks since the academic year started.

Eden threw her keys on the console then stopped in her tracks. "You're up?"

Aidan had a sandwich in one hand and a bag in the other. He rolled his eyes. "No, Mom. I'm just a figment of your imagination. Yes, I'm up. I've had my breakfast already and just made lunch."

She walked to him and put her hand on his forehead. "No fever."

He pushed at her hand. "I've got to get to Matt's. Mano said he'd do a session with us this morning since I'm staying at Dad's until Monday night."

"What? Now?"

Aidan pulled his water bottle from the fridge. "In ten minutes. And, no, I won't be late for school. Mano said being late was a sign of disrespect, and he won't work with athletes who can't respect time."

"Aidan! Wait for me. Let me walk with you."

"Seriously? Mom—"

"No, listen. I just want to make sure that Mr. Palua—and you should call him that, by the way—isn't doing more than he should."

"You know him. Do you think he's the type of guy who'll do something he doesn't want?"

Eden didn't have a response for that but followed her son out the door nevertheless. Aidan pulled up his hoodie, walking a few steps in front of her. When they reached the cul-de-sac, Matthew was already in front of his house, talking to Mano.

She stood at the corner as Aidan ran up to Mano. He nodded at Aidan then looked past her son to her. Dark, serious eyes met hers. Even from yards away, she felt the weight of his gaze, penetrating and invasive. She nodded in greeting, then sat down on the curb.

They began with a warm-up, then Mano demonstrated what

he wanted the boys to do. Aidan was always athletic, but she had never seen him look so invested in a drill before. Whether it was basketball, baseball, or even swimming, he practiced cautiously, as if unwilling to push himself beyond what was necessary. But not now.

She wasn't the only observer: Mrs. Henderson, in her pink robe, could be seen through the large bay window at the front of her house with a mug in hand and seated comfortably in a large wingback chair. Carolyn Henderson sat next to her grandmother, also with a mug in one hand and a book in the other. The Yuans' open door revealed shadowy movements that suggested someone was looking out every few minutes.

All the while, Mano stayed focused on the two boys. He didn't yell, but his voice carried through the cul-de-sac.

"Head up. Hands up. Be ready for the ball. That's it. Good. We're going for clean catches. Keep your feet moving," Mano instructed.

They stood in a loose triangle; Mano threw the oval ball with practiced ease. Even with her amateur understanding of the sport, Eden recognized how he'd adjust each throw. Testing each boy with a little more rotation, a little more speed, stretching them but never more than what he thought them capable. Then the words of instructions ceased. It was a fluid movement between three rugby players, tossing the ball back and forth as if they'd been doing it for years. Then they started to run up and down the cul-de-sac in a straight line, with the player at the end sprinting past the other two before passing the ball.

She should have kept her attention on her son, but it was hard to ignore Mano in motion. Muscled thighs flexed with every step. Biceps, no longer hidden by a polo shirt or a sweatshirt, gleamed.

He stopped the practice right on the hour. "Good work."

Fogged glasses couldn't hide Matthew's proud face. "Thanks, Mano. That was fun. Next week?"

Aidan shook his head before Mano could respond. "I can't

next week. Staying an extra day with my dad. We have family visiting from out of town." He drank from his water bottle. "But go ahead, Matt. No point for both of us to miss practice."

She felt Mano's eyes on her as she got closer to the trio, glad her jacket would cover up telltale signs of how his stare affected her.

"You look like you've just had a dunk in the sea," Mano said, the slight tease a welcome relief from the intensity of his scrutiny.

She rushed her fingers through her hair, conscious that her jacket wouldn't mask the flush of red that was probably spreading across her face. *Traitorous body.*

"She started swimming at five again," Aidan said.

Matthew's eyes grew wide. "In the morning? Like every day?"

Aidan nodded. "That's what world-class athletes do. My dad said, when he was preparing for the Summer Games, he'd be in the pool for at least six hours a day and another couple of hours in the gym. How about you, Mano? How much time did you practice?"

"About the same. Lots of gym work. Keeping strong helps prevent injury." Mano tossed the ball to Matthew, nodding at the Yuans' front door. "Hey, I think your mum wants you back in."

"Come on, Aidan. You know she made enough protein shake for the two of us," Matthew said, pulling on Aidan's shirt.

Eden waved at Patty who was sporting an extra-wide grin as she ushered the two boys into the house.

"Aidan seems to be really enjoying this," Eden said, now standing next to Mano. "I've never seen him this motivated about a sport before."

"Like I said last night, he has a bit of a natural talent."

"How about Matthew?"

Mano paused. "He tries very hard. He'll have a place on any team with a heart like that."

Eden smiled. "You'll win lots of invites to the Yuans' place if you keep Matthew interested in rugby. Patty's been trying for years to get him involved in a team sport."

"Why?"

"Why?" Eden repeated.

"Yeah, why? There's no rule that all kids need to be in a team sport. As long as they're active, it's all good. Matt says he likes to go for walks."

"Going for walks doesn't look as good on a college application as varsity volleyball or club soccer." She raised her hands in mock surrender at Mano's frown. "This is Seven Hills. People here want their kids to play sports. It's a sports town. St. Anne's is a sports college."

"What do the kids want?" He sighed suddenly and shook his head. "Sorry. None of my business. Just met too many parents who put all their ambitions on their kids. And when it doesn't work out, well, sometimes there isn't much of a relationship after."

Mano held up the oval white ball in front of Eden, turning away as soon as she took it from him. "Have a good day, Eden Pak." He walked determinedly to his house and raised a hand— but didn't look up—at Mrs. Henderson.

"Wait!"

Was that her voice? She didn't do confrontations. Not usually. Never with big guys whose faces she saw in her dreams. But her feet were moving to the hulking body that had obeyed her command. She moved in front of him. "You confuse the hell out of me, Mano Palua. I thought we were friendly again. Okay, some parents here are overambitious. But for the most part, this is a tight-knit community. We look out for one another. We only want the best. I'll admit it. I'm a helicopter mom. To everyone. But that's just me. Okay? That's how *I* roll."

"I wasn't criticizing—"

"Maybe not intentionally. You've been here a month. How many other parents with kids have you talked to? None? Yeah, I thought so. You've based your entire commentary on two sets of families, one of which is a single mom who probably doesn't spend enough time with her only son."

"Eden—"

"Furthermore...." But she stumbled on her rant when she realized they were no longer alone. Three figures had emerged from the Yuans' house with varying degrees of amusement, amazement, and embarrassment on their faces. Mrs. Henderson, still seated in her chair, edged closer to the window, her mug cradled in both hands.

"Furthermore?" Mano repeated, eyes hooded and his mouth set in a straight line.

But she wasn't going to be intimidated. She placed both her hands on her hips and raised her chin. "*Furthermore*, I've been nice to you. I could be a good friend, you know. I thought we started on a good note with me practically saving your life!"

"Saving my life? You took my temperature and gave me painkillers. A bit rich to think—"

"Okay, so I'm not your first choice for a friend. But I know for a fact that Tom Morris and Jackson have invited you over to their houses, but you turned them down. You didn't even have dinner with Alistair. No one has ever turned down dinner with Alistair. Don't you want to get to know any of us?"

"Look, I'm working out with your son. Isn't that being nice? Being neighborly?"

"No, *you* look. I said I was grateful. But—" She poked her finger repeatedly into his chest before he covered it with his hand. Her hands weren't small, but his were larger and heavier. And now one was keeping her hand hostage to the warmth of his body.

She told herself not to look away, not to back down.

Except every decision has a consequence, and she suddenly realized that, even if she wanted to, she couldn't look away. His eyes drew her in.

"Eden, I don't need friends." He stared at her lips, his eyes darkening when she licked them nervously.

Every competitor develops a knack for sensing a moment of weakness in the competition. Yes, she swam against the clock and trained to focus only on her own race. "Don't worry about the others!" was the common mantra from all her coaches, drilled into her subconscious since she was seven years old. But it was there, deep within each athlete, a sixth sense as to when to attack, when to summon the extra strength, when to push a nanometer ahead. For the win.

Mano wasn't her competition, but her instincts were screaming that something had changed with her touch. There was a small crack in the wall he had put up. It was a wall that was bigger and thicker than anything she'd ever encountered before. Was it there for him to hide behind or to protect against? Didn't matter. Even granite had its weakness.

She angled her head slightly, inching her face closer until she felt the soft caress of his breath on her skin. He stayed still, waiting. Ready to receive her lips.

When he did, a storm of emotions rushed through her body, shutting out the loud "Eewww" in the background. *Aidan?* She certainly didn't fully register the high-pitched squeal. *Patty?* Instead, she heard the softest of groans from him; felt his increased heart rate beneath her palm; sensed the warmth radiating from the gentlest of kisses that unleashed feelings long buried.

CHAPTER SEVEN

MANO BROUGHT THE CUP TO HIS LIPS, SIPPING HIS HOT TEA carefully. From the dining table, he watched the tall, broad-shouldered man emerge elegantly out of his dark blue car and move toward Patty's door. His hair was perfectly coiffed, even so late in the day. As soon as the stranger—who looked like he belonged in a TV commercial—turned toward his house, Mano knew he was to get his fourth visitor of the afternoon.

This was supposed to be an afternoon spent alone. But his two young protégées had appeared at his doorstep ten minutes after his return from St. Anne's as if they'd been lying in wait. Looking doleful and lugging a wagon of odd bits and pieces, they asked if they could use his backyard to work on a science project. He didn't know why, but he let them in.

Then Mrs. Henderson knocked on his door with more banana bread and a book. Somehow, the seventy-year-old grandmother got into his kitchen, brewed tea, and stayed in the backyard, supervising Aidan and Matthew on whatever the hell they were doing. And now, one more visitor. One more person he didn't need to meet would be invading his space.

Mano turned toward the open door at the back of the kitchen.

"Aidan! I think your dad has arrived."

Mano watched Brandon O'Callaghan laugh at whatever it was Patty said to him. He gave her a quick wave before walking toward the end of the cul-de-sac.

"Dad's here?" Aidan asked as he entered the house from the backyard. Matthew was close behind him. He reached Mano's side, and a large smile lit up his face. "Sweet! And he's driving the new car like he promised! Come on, Matt! Let's see if he'll take us around before we have to leave."

Aidan grabbed his backpack from the sofa and was at the door before slapping his hand on his forehead and rushed back to the dining table. "Thanks, Mano! We only have one more afternoon to finish the project. Is Tuesday okay?"

"Tuesday?"

"Yeah? Around five? You'll be home by then, right? That's not too late, is it?"

Mano grunted.

"Great! Thanks, sir!" Matthew raised his hand for a fist pump before running out onto the sidewalk, intercepting Aidan's dad, who had just reached the path to Mano's front door. Aidan, however, had stopped just at the front step, a look of indecision on his face.

"Uh, Mano?"

"Yes?"

"If you want to go out with my mom, I'm okay with that." He looked down at his feet. "She didn't say anything after you guys...you know...kissed. But I think she likes you. I just want to let you know you can ask her out if you want."

"Aidan, I don't...."

But Aidan had left before Mano could finish his sentence, though he wasn't sure if he knew what he'd meant to say. Eden's kiss was a surprise. The bigger surprise was his response to it.

He had wanted her.

He had wanted her to want him back.

Mano shook his head. He was overreacting to his physical response to Eden's touch. Mercifully, she had pulled back before he allowed himself to drown in a taste that was only hers. It'd been too long since his lips touched those of someone who cared for him. That was all. Nothing more.

Except two days later, the memory of the whisper of a kiss—more chaste than anything little Fred Dane had ever received from Jayne Molloy—followed him every waking moment.

Standing at the door, he watched Aidan run toward his father, embraced warmly by the tall man. Brandon O'Callaghan obviously knew Matthew as well, reaching out to offer a handshake. He nodded at the boys before turning slightly to unlock the car with his remote. Aidan and Matt didn't waste a second; they were in the sports car before Mano could blink again.

Brandon walked toward Mano's house with the confidence of someone used to success. When he was close, Mano didn't miss how those eyes assessed him from head to toe.

"Hi, you must be Mano. I've heard a lot about you from my son. I'm Aidan's dad, Brandon."

Mano shook the offered hand and met the intelligent blue eyes which continued to study him openly.

"Patty says the boys have been here all afternoon," Brandon said.

"They've been working on a project for their science fair in the backyard."

"What's wrong with their backyard?"

"Lydia."

Brandon nodded knowingly, a slight smile on his face. "Yes, she's a handful. A complete opposite of Matthew. I'm afraid my twins are like that. Drive my wife nuts." Brandon looked past Mano to the still-open back door. "You're not supervising?"

"I reckon if they need supervision, they shouldn't be doing it." A loud hiss and pop followed by an "It's under control! I'll put out the fire!" came from the back.

Brandon raised an eyebrow knowingly. "Ah, Irene Henderson is there. This should be interesting. She used to work for NASA. Rumor around here was that she was building her own spaceship in her backyard. The FBI visited once, I think."

"FBI?"

"Yeah. Don't let the pink bathrobe and banana bread fool you," Brandon said with a smile. "Well, thank you for letting them come over."

"No worries."

Brandon started to walk down the steps then turned around slowly as if changing his mind at the last minute. "Aidan also tells me you've been helping him out with the rugby. I must say I was a little surprised he wanted to try out for the team. His mom and I were both swimmers—"

"Eden is still a swimmer."

"What?"

"Eden still competes."

Brandon crossed his arms. "I stand corrected…she *is* a swimmer. Anyway, neither of us knows anything about rugby."

"It's something the boy and his grandfather have in common."

"Rugby's pretty dangerous. Especially without helmets and stuff."

"We're just throwing the ball around. It's only touch rugby at his school. There'll be no need for helmets…and stuff. But we don't use those things in our sport anyway."

"Right. Well, I understand you know a lot about rugby, so… thanks again."

Mano nodded, his legs apart, and his arms still crossed. Brandon walked back to the car without turning back. He glanced briefly at the Yuans' house before smiling at the boys still inside the car. A few minutes later, Matthew was on the sidewalk by himself, waving at Aidan as the car left the cul-de-sac.

Mano leaned against his doorframe as the sports car drove away.

"Brandon's a good dad," Mrs. Henderson's unexpected voice surprised him. He'd forgotten she was still in his backyard.

"I'm sure he is," he said.

"Always on time when it's his weekend. He may live in the city, but he's made an effort to get to know everyone who has contact with his son. Behind that TV-smile, he's protective of Aidan. I'd better be going. Trying a new banana bread recipe. With oats. I'll leave you a loaf tomorrow."

"You don't have too...."

She dismissed his protest with a flick of a hand as she walked toward her home. *TV-Smile? Dead on the money, Mrs. Henderson. Maybe you are some sort of spy.*

Despite the friendly demeanor, Mano sensed Brandon didn't trust him. Not that he could blame the man. It was the right thing to do. After all, he was still practically a stranger. He shut the door and increased the volume of the music from the turntable before moving to the kitchen. His landlord left a healthy collection of vinyl for him to explore, and he was currently getting to know Ella Fitzgerald. Her sultry voice filled the house without interruption. He turned on the electric kettle and reached inside the refrigerator for a box of cold cuts, tomatoes, and lettuce.

He wondered at Brandon's surprise when he referred to Eden as a competitive swimmer. Maybe Brandon wasn't privy to Eden's goal of qualifying for Nationals. As a medalist from the Summer Games, Brandon could help his son's mother. He was obviously doing well professionally and financially; he would understand the commitment it'd take to swim at the top level.

Assuming Eden said something.

Bet she didn't.

Mano reached for a knife and cutting board then began slicing the tomatoes as he stifled a yawn.

Last night he had been troubled with memories he was supposed to bury. He ended his misery by leaving bed and going for a run. Early light, crisp air, and running at a pace he hadn't pushed himself to since Ahipara, he had begun to clear his mind when he saw Eden emerge from the car driven by that slick-looking fella, Jordan Kennedy.

Jackson didn't like him.

Neither did Tom Morris.

Mano frowned as he layered the sliced bread with the turkey and cheese.

She had walked away after their kiss. Didn't give him a second look. Just left him to the stares and smiles of Patty, Matthew, and Mrs. Henderson, who gave him not one but *two* thumbs-up when he walked past her house.

One kiss didn't give him the right to feel *anything* at the sight of Jordan Kennedy checking out Eden Pak. But he did.

"Bet he's just a little bastard. No one is that perfect," Mano muttered.

A buzzing interrupted his thoughts. He automatically felt for his phone in the pocket of his sweatshirt. Still there. He followed the continuous sound to the sofa, feeling behind the cushions. Nothing. On his knees, he leaned his torso toward the ground. Partially hidden by the leg of the sofa lay a black phone. He reached for it.

Mom: Call me when you reach your dad's. Don't forget to thank Mrs. Yuan. Love you.

Aiden must have dropped it when he rushed out.

Mano tapped to reply, but the screen now requested a passcode.

He could leave it for Eden at the office on Monday, but a counter from an unwelcome voice said she'd be worried if she didn't see a message from Aidan when she next checked her phone.

Stay away.

You want to see her.

Make one friend.

She'd be at the gym. Every Friday afternoon, from four to six o'clock. He had seen her once when he was still familiarizing himself with the campus. She didn't see him though, so focused she was on her own sets, lost in whatever it was she heard through her earbuds.

Make one friend.

Mano nodded at Mrs. Henderson, seated, as usual at this hour, in her armchair facing the window. Carolyn sat next to her, a book on her lap, probably reading aloud. They did that every afternoon until Carolyn's parents came. Mrs. Henderson swore it was the only way for her to keep up with book club with her eyesight failing; Patty said it was one way to help Carolyn practice her reading without eroding the teenager's confidence.

The trail to St. Anne's was busy for a Friday night. Soccer season began tonight. Both the men's and women's teams were ranked in the top ten nationally. He learned quickly how much the local community embraced the college and its sports. He'd snuck into a preseason basketball game one night—a game that technically meant nothing other than bragging rights against a local rival—and was surprised at the number of families with young children in the stands, filling almost a third of the arena. Tonight, a steady stream of people walked to and from the stadium.

Twenty minutes later, he looked through the glass doors of the college gym. He scanned the front half of the area but couldn't see Eden among the exercise machines. He pressed his faculty card against the sensor then walked in. He nodded at Professor Fisher, red-faced on the treadmill. After passing a wall of bands and ropes, he found Eden in the weight room, 15-pound dumbbells in each hand. She studied her reflection in the floor-to-ceiling mirror as she performed another set of curls. The delicate sheen on her well-toned back suggested she had been here longer than he thought.

Her eyes widened when she saw him in the mirror. She turned swiftly, pulling the earbuds out. "Is Aidan okay?"

He nodded and held out the black phone. "He forgot it."

Her body relaxed as she smiled. She reached for the phone, an eyebrow arching. "I bet he hasn't realized it's missing yet. If there's anything that'll make Aidan forget about his phone, it's whatever new gadget Brandon bought this week."

"Brandon came in a new car."

Eden laughed softly. "I'll bet you ten bucks they're both sitting in the garage just pressing buttons as we speak."

What made him push back loose hair and tuck it behind the ear she favored to touch whenever she was nervous or in deep thought, he'd never know. But she stopped laughing immediately; her lips parted at the unexpected gesture. She met his gaze briefly but turned too quickly for him to guess what she thought of his spontaneous act.

"Sorry," he said. Though he wasn't.

"No, it's fine." She rushed her hand through the top of her hair. "I've never been able to tame my hair. This is the one haircut that keeps it reasonably neat."

"It suits you."

"Thanks." She threw a towel over her shoulder. The erratic pulse visible on her neck was intriguing. "Were you coming to work out?"

He dragged his attention back to Eden's flushed face. "No. The team has an early start at Cal tomorrow. I need to spend the night going over the playbook."

"Oh! You should have called about the phone. I would have swung by to pick it up. Thanks!"

"Nice night out. Didn't mind the walk."

"I'm done here. If you'd like some company, let me walk with you."

He'd averted his eyes as she bent over, so he missed seeing how she ended up on the floor. Only heard the loud yell followed by a string of expletives he hadn't expected to come out of Eden Pak.

Instincts kicked in. "Help over here!"

He knelt next to Eden, now hunched over and grabbing her ankle.

She groaned. "It seems you and I are doomed, Mano. Do you realize one of us falls flat on our face whenever we meet?"

"We didn't last time," he said, reaching around her waist. She instinctively wrapped her arm around his shoulder, leaning on him as she tried to get up. She was still damp from her workout, hair plastered from sweat, but he caught a whiff of gardenias.

"No, we didn't," she whispered.

He felt her tremble slightly, a soft pink spreading up her neck. Her lips parted, and the memory of what they tasted like teased him.

"Hey, Mano. Eden. What's going on?"

Eden's face went red at the intrusion. Mano bit back what he really wanted to say. He inhaled deeply, reminding himself that Eden was hurt. "Taylor, good to see you, mate. She fell. It's the ankle, I think."

"Let me take a look. Eden, can you get to the bench? Mano, would you mind getting some ice?"

When he returned, Eden was seated on the floor, one leg resting on Taylor's knee. Mano handed the bag of ice to Taylor immediately.

"I don't think it's a break, Eden, but it could be a pretty bad sprain," Taylor said apologetically. "Ice it for ten minutes. I'll come back to wrap it. You'll have a better idea of how bad it is tomorrow. But you know the drill: rest, ice, elevate, and keep it wrapped up. Are you still living at the Atria? I'll give Campus Safety a call. I'm sure we have a golf cart that can get you back home."

"It's okay," Eden emphasized. "I'll walk. Campus Safety will have their hands full with the games on tonight."

"I wouldn't recommend—"

Eden raised her chin. "I'll walk. It'll be fine."

Taylor raised his eyebrows, a soft smile softening the weight of his words. "The faculty newsletter said you're trying to qualify for Nationals at the next meet. Isn't that in a month? You might want to reconsider that decision."

"I never pegged you for being an asshole, Taylor," she said sarcastically.

"Sometimes the job calls for it," Taylor replied, grinning as he stood up. "Don't you live on the fourth floor?"

Her face turned white. "I'll manage."

Taylor sighed. "You can barely put weight on it."

"I'll help her," Mano said.

Eden shook her head. "I can take care of myself."

"You falling on your face on my watch obligates me morally to make sure you're okay."

Eden's eyes narrowed. "That's from *my* book of morals, remember. Not yours."

"When you visit a country, you follow their rules."

She lost the battle to suppress a smile, her eyes mirroring her amusement. The world suddenly disappeared from around them. She didn't hide that she liked him, and he wasn't sure what to do with that knowledge, with that gift of trust.

Taylor cleared his throat; his grin suggested he knew something was going on between them. "Looks like you're in good hands, Eden. Ice it when you get home, okay? I'll check in with you tomorrow."

Mano extended his hand to Eden, a repeat offer from a few nights ago. This time, she took it, wincing as she tried to stand evenly on both feet. "Humor me. Let's take the lift from Campus Safety."

"This isn't happening," she mumbled.

She didn't argue when he joined her in the golf cart. She remained quiet during the short ride to the Atria, her foot elevated in the back while he sat in the front. Ten minutes later, they stood side by side, eyeing the stairwell that would take her home.

"Okay, let's do this," she said, ignoring the offer of his arm as support.

He followed her, staying a step behind. Determination etched on her face as she began the slow ascent. She didn't complain, and he bit back the warning to take it slow. She had been the face of welcome, the smile of assurance, the voice of comfort and care. But right now, there were no smiles. Just a grim determination he was used to seeing in competition.

She worked in silence, one step at a time, an uneven pace, a slight pause before she pressed on the bare toes of the swollen foot. He understood this absence of noise, borne out of focus, and maintained for persistence. He didn't offer any help until he saw trembling hands when she took a break on the third floor. He decided he'd take the risk of her wrath.

The tearstained face that greeted him was like a kick in the gut. She looked resigned.

"I can carry you the rest of the way," he offered.

She wiped her eyes, lifted her chin, and—to his relief—nodded. He reached under her easily, her body filling his arms.

An hour later, he stared at her sleeping figure on the sofa. He had ducked into the kitchen, finding a packet of ramen in the small cupboard above the refrigerator. It was supposed to be a quick fix.

It wasn't quick enough.

He put the still-steaming bowl of noodles on the small dining set, glancing around the tiny but meticulous living area. He eventually found a throw in what he assumed was Eden's bedroom, elevating her leg further on a pillow when he covered the rest of her. His hand hovered over her cheek, slightly dampened from silent tears that had continued long after they had entered her apartment. But he pulled back before he could wipe them away. It wasn't his place.

Instinctively, he knew she hadn't cried because of the physical pain. That kind of pain was just part of the lifestyle of any topflight athlete. No, the tears flowed for something else.

* * *

She grimaced at the unknown restriction to movement then opened her eyes to the dark gray cushions of her sofa. Leaning on her side, Eden's eyes widened at the view of the large body lying on the floor. She recognized the light blue pillowcase from her bedroom, the one nod to comfort. Face up, hands crossed over his stomach, Mano's stillness mirrored the effigies placed on tombs of knights and kings.

Why didn't he go home?

Eden eyed the silhouette of her foot, still wrapped up. Flexing her toes, she began to rotate her ankle slowly. It was tight but not the searing pain of just a few hours ago. The weight of fear lifted slightly. The true test would be when she tried to walk on it.

The sofa creaked as she sat up, but Mano barely moved. She reached for her phone on the nearby coffee table.

Just past midnight.

Two missed calls followed by a text message from Brandon, sent at nine.

Brandon: Aidan couldn't find his phone. Tried calling. Will call tomorrow AM. He says good night.

She almost dropped her phone when Mano sat up suddenly, his gasp sharp and loud in the quiet of the dark. His hands went sharply to his head, scratching wildly into his hair, as if frustrated. He scrambled onto his knees, moving in a stealth-like, determined manner to the balcony door. She heard, rather than saw, the desperation in which he pulled at the blinds and wrestled with the lock.

She hobbled cautiously, her thoughts no longer on her injury but on the figure now hunched over her balcony.

"Mano?"

His head hid in his hands. "Sorry," he mumbled. "Didn't mean to wake you."

"You didn't. I was up."

He had stayed when he could have left.

So, she stayed. Next to him, close but not touching. They may have shared a kiss, but a barrier remained, one that prevented her from doing more than just being there. Would it be enough?

Voices carried in the trail below, students still meandering to and from the college campus on a Friday evening, but his ragged breathing silenced the questions of concern that were at the tip of her tongue. The irregular sounds slowly gave way to a calmer rhythm.

"How's your ankle?" he asked, his voice still distant.

"Not as bad as earlier." She paused. "How are you?"

"Better than a few minutes ago."

"These nightmares? They happen often, don't they?"

He hesitated to respond; his face still hidden. "I don't sleep well on most days."

She couldn't help it. He probably thought she was "mothering" again, but she had to offer some type of comfort. She never had the right words.

Just light rubs up and down a hard back. He stiffened initially but didn't move away.

"Why did you kiss me?" he asked.

She smiled. "No real reason other than I wanted to."

"You don't want to get close to me, Eden. I'm not good that way."

"I think you're a good man."

He bent his head as if in resignation before facing her. "You're the type of woman who deserves better."

Eden laughed softly. "Mano, it was a little kiss. I'm not asking for forever."

"You should, but not from me." He paused then spoke hesitantly. "I promised that once to someone else."

"Is she still in the picture?"

"No," he said immediately.

"But she's still in your heart." She moved her hand from his back, down his arm, and into a rough hand, squeezing it. "I've been in love before and had my heart broken. I can take the fact that you still love someone else without bursting into tears." He smiled at that, and she grew braver. "Let's be friends. Real friends. Talk to me. If it's a bad night, I'm here."

He stared. "But we kissed."

"Aren't you friends with the people you've kissed?"

He gave a little laugh. "I have to admit I haven't kissed many of my friends."

She raised her head, her voice teasing. "Then, I'm honored to be your first."

He left an hour later, refusing her offer for him to use Aidan's bed. She assured him she was fine. Her father would be there in the morning and would check the sprain.

When she reached for a hug, he returned it. He pushed her hair back behind her ear, an instant warmth flooding her face at his slight touch.

"I don't know how good a friend I'll be to you, Eden Pak," he said. "But I'll give it a go if you will."

CHAPTER EIGHT

"Move it, Holmes! Watch your man! Watch him!"

Eden rolled her eyes while Robert Pak yelled more instructions—punctuated with language she was still not allowed to use in front of them—to the St. Anne's players on the TV set.

Donald Harrison-Pak looked up from his crossword puzzle. His brown eyes peered over reading glasses. "Sorry."

Eden laughed. "Hey, it's less embarrassing than if we had gone with him to the game."

"I'm right here, loved ones, right here," Robert said, sitting down on the sofa again. "How's the ankle?"

"Good." Eden reached for the ice pack and wiggled her toes. "I'm not feeling anything while it's resting."

"That's a good sign. I'd take a week off from swimming if I were you."

"I can't. I still want to make that meet in San Luis Obispo. What do you think, Pop?"

Donald turned the page of his book but didn't look up. "The same rules apply for you in your thirties as they did in your teens. Dad handles all the sports questions. I keep you in shape with schoolwork."

"But I'm not in school anymore."

"My job is done," he said calmly.

"However —" interrupted Robert.

Eden braced herself for her dad's next words.

"—we're still very interested in anyone you may or may not have kissed recently."

Donald put his book down and removed his glasses. Eden didn't need a mirror to know her face was now a full shade of pink.

"You've kissed someone recently?" Donald asked.

Eden looked at Robert. "Let me guess. Aidan said something?"

Robert pulled out his phone and scrolled through a few messages. "Where is it? Ah, yes. 'Pop! Mom kissed Mano! In front of me! What if he doesn't want to be my coach because of that?'"

"This Mano? Is he Aidan's coach? The rugby coach he keeps going on about?" Donald asked.

"Yes and no," Eden said. "Mano's just helping Matthew Yuan and Aidan out a little. On a Monday afternoon. No formal contract or anything. In the cul-de-sac."

"And you kissed him?" Donald asked.

"Pop, I'm a grown woman," Eden protested. "I don't have to let you in on my love life."

Donald picked up his book again. "No, you're right. But it's good to know you have a love life again."

"Amen," Robert said, then he stood up abruptly again. "Holmes! Oh my god! Another try for Cal! I hope your man Mano has a plan for this team. The talent is there but the discipline? Stressing me out. Do you have any beer? Oh, wait—speak of the devil! Mano's on! Turn it up, Eden."

Reporter: You've been here for a couple of months now. What do you think about the game here at the college level?

Mano: I'm impressed. There's some good rugby going on, but it's a different style to what I'm used to. I'm looking forward to learning and contributing to the team at St. Anne's.

Reporter: What do you mean by 'style'?

Mano: Each country has a unique culture to its game. Understand the culture, understand the sport. I come with a lot of experiences that started when I was a toddler. Many of the kids here only begin playing rugby after trying out other sports. That changes the way you play. It's a good thing. Rugby's still so young in America. It's exciting for all of us who love the game.

* * *

Donald glanced at Eden, his pen now still. "So that's Mano Palua. Good-looking guy. Aidan likes him?"

Eden scrutinized her short nails. "Yes."

"Do you like him?"

Eden sighed. Out of her two dads, Donald had the knack to ask the right questions even if she didn't want to answer them. He also had the patience of a saint; he could wait until the sun went down, and on occasion, when she was testing the boundaries her parents had set for her, he did. He'd never push, but he expected an answer.

"I guess," she said. "We've agreed to be friends."

"But you've kissed him," Robert interrupted, throwing a knowing look at Donald.

"He wants to be friends, and I can respect that. He's still getting over a relationship, I think," Eden said.

Donald nodded, returning to his puzzle. "Good thinking, Eden. He'll be the type of person who can appreciate your determination to make Nationals. Not many men will, especially if it means coming in second for your time. Or, in this case, since you're a mom, third."

"Fifth," Robert said. "After us and her job."

"I'm suddenly not feeling very hopeful about ever being in a relationship again. Thanks, dads."

"As your father, I'm good with that," Donald said.

They left after lunch, promising to send a photo of them with Aidan and the twins later that day. It was something they had worked out with Brandon and Lisa a year ago, soon after the twins had turned two. A quick trip to the corner ice-cream shop gave Brandon and Lisa a break for an hour, and it gave Aidan some precious times with his grandparents.

Her dads had stocked up the fridge for the next couple of days, so there was no reason for her to leave the apartment. She glanced at the paperwork on the dining table and scrunched her nose at it. Nothing urgent there. She didn't even have laundry to do to avoid work-work, with Pop tackling it while Dad cooked.

She actually had free time. On her own. By herself. When was the last time that happened?

Eden moved gingerly to the balcony, ice pack in one hand, phone in the other. Bright blue skies beckoned her to relax. The trail below was busy, and she smiled at the sight of a young family dealing with the tantrum of a toddler while appeasing the cries of their older child screaming for them to "Hurry up!"

Putting on her earbuds, the voices of Aretha, Marvin, and Smokey took her back to her childhood. Pop always had them — and nearly everyone from Motown— playing when he cooked. Their music greeted her when she got home from school, when Pop checked homework, then in the car when he drove her to the pool or the gym.

Robert Pak would pick her up after training, take care of dinner, finish the last of the schoolwork, then bed. Regimented for months, for years. That's how they did it. The three of them. Juggling schedules to make things work. Her swimming scholarship to Cal was a family triumph.

Her unexpected pregnancy wasn't.

She had been scared—so scared—to tell them. Their disappointment at losing her scholarship was never voiced. They stayed by her side. They were there at every prenatal visit and at the hospital. Even in the delivery room. They, once again, adjusted their lives so Aidan was never with a stranger. They covered her expenses when she couldn't land a job. They never judged. They just loved her. Brandon had once asked her if she missed having a mother.

"I don't know what it means to have one," she had said. "I have two dads. They gave me everything."

It wasn't until she was in high school did she learn how much Pop hated the overnight shifts. But it made sense as a family for him to do it whenever he could. Nor did she know until she was an adult how hard her dads had to fight in court to have them both listed as her legal guardians. When she and Brandon became parents and discussed their insurance plans, only then did she understand the relief in Robert Pak's voice the day she had turned eighteen.

She was always their priority.

They sacrificed more things than she'd ever know to keep their family life intact.

If only she were as selfless as they were.

She pushed that errant thought to the back of her mind, annoyed that she had it. But it was there: the doubt that she deserved the opportunity to train again. It always surfaced when she hit a bump in the road.

She turned up the volume of the music, flexing and unflexing her ankle. No real pain but a little stiff. She closed her eyes and visualized the meet that she was training for. She'd swum at the Aquatic Center before. She knew what the lanes looked like and how the block would feel when she pushed against it at the sound of the starter's buzzer.

Clean strokes. Body long and flat. All within reach. She can cut those seconds off.

Her phone buzzed.

Mano: Look down.

She pulled her earbuds off and waved. "Hi! Did you just get back from Berkeley?"

He nodded, then typed into his phone.

Mano: Yes. Want some company?

She smiled.

Eden: Come on up! I'll buzz you in.

She greeted him at the door a few minutes later, his eyes automatically fixed to her foot.

"How is it?" he asked.

"Not bad," she said, closing the door behind him. "Tough game."

"You watched it?"

She nodded. "Dad made sure it was on the whole time he was here. Brett seemed particularly…uh…energetic?"

"It wasn't a party bus coming back, that's for sure." He shook his head at her offer of water. "Do you need help with dinner tonight?"

"My parents dropped off some groceries and some pasta. They're good in a crisis, and I've given them enough practice, they didn't even blink at this one." She put her hands on her hips and grinned. "This is the longest conversation we've had without someone being in pain."

Mano nodded solemnly. "This friend thing could work out, eh?"

"There is hope."

He stayed for dinner, telling her to rest her ankle while he brought out the pasta and salad. She peppered him with questions about New Zealand; he asked about her swimming meet and who would be attending.

"Just me."

"Your parents won't be there?"

"They're both working. My teammates from the clubs will be there, both old and new. It's been a long time since I needed anyone in the stands." She shrugged and reached for a snickerdoodle her dad always included. "Did you like having family watch you play?"

He nodded. "Didn't realize how much until I was in France."

"You played worse?"

He scowled. "I'm a professional. Who's in the stands doesn't affect me. But I like having my family watch. Not strangers. They cared about the team, the results. Me, personally? Not so much. You quickly learn who you can count on when things get rough in your sport."

"Yeah, I get that. After I became pregnant, it felt lonelier. But that wasn't really a surprise. Competing takes us away from the rest of the world. If you're not on the train, you get left behind."

She recognized the empathy in his eyes.

Mano leaned back in the chair and folded his arms. "How about Aidan? He said he wants to watch you swim. That he hasn't seen you compete all year."

"I know." She reached for her earlobe. "He used to watch me swim years ago, but I can't focus if I'm worried about where he is, what he's doing, if he's in trouble, who the strangers are around him."

"I can take him if you like."

"Thanks, but you're playing away that weekend," she said, her mind seeing the large calendar of matches and games on Alistair's wall. They—Alistair, Sarah, and her—stared at it often enough as they planned the logistics of home and away matches across all of St. Anne's sports teams.

"Brett doesn't want me to go."

Her mouth gaped. "What? What does Alistair say?"

He smiled. "Brett told Alistair I'm needed with the women's team that weekend. They're playing at home. A fair point, and I'm glad to help. They're a good team."

She frowned. "They are. But—"

Mano looked up. "They're playing Saturday morning, so I can take Aidan down with me in the afternoon. Will we be too late to see you swim?"

"My first event is scheduled for the evening. The next is on Sunday. But I can't impose on your time."

"It's not an imposition. Isn't this what friends do, eh? Or at least what my friends would do."

She mirrored his action and crossed her arms. "Why do I feel like I'm being bamboozled into a corner here. Is this you or Aidan?"

Mano allowed himself a slight smile. "He has brought it up a few times, wanting to see you swim, I mean. Until a couple of hours ago, I didn't know how I could help him."

Eden sighed. "I wish he would talk to me."

Mano reached for Eden's now empty plate, placed it on top of his, then stood up. "My mother was a netball champion in high school. She played at a time before digital cameras. I wish I saw what she was like as a player. Her friends said I had the same expression on my face whenever I competed. Let him watch you."

He spoke with such a matter-of-fact tone that she didn't expect the lump that formed in her throat or the sudden appearance of tears.

"Eden? What's wrong?"

She cleared her voice. "The only video I have of my mother is when she competed at Nationals at eighteen. I still watch it sometimes, you know."

Later that night, alone, she pulled out her laptop. After the fire that had destroyed a collection of memories, her maternal grandfather had dedicated himself to collecting photos and recordings from friends and relatives. Fortunately, her mother had a large family, and after a year, they were able to replace most of the photographs.

But the videos were harder to come by. Eden's mother was the youngest of six. She followed in the footsteps of her older siblings, all successful in their chosen sport. By the time it was her turn in the spotlight, there were fewer photos and videos.

They had this one though. One of her uncles had uploaded it to the website so that it would always be there.

She entered the memorized keywords to find the video.

Taken from a distance, eighteen-year-old Emily Collins walked to the seat behind the sixth block of a long course pool. She pushed a loose hair up into her swimming cap then reached for her earlobe. Eden smiled when her grandfather's voice came on. "There she goes! Come on, Em!"

Her mother finished fourth but took a second off her personal best. Her raised fist was in celebration as were the recorded cheers of her parents. No one would have thought then that in four years, Eden's grandfather would refuse to have any further contact with his youngest child because she had eloped with a young Korean-American who didn't go to church.

Mano was right. She had learned to keep her swimming life away from everyone. Initially, out of necessity. Busy parents whose schedules weren't flexible enough to allow them to be there conditioned her not to look for them in a sea of faces. Then the return to the pool was an escape. She didn't want to let anyone in.

But Aidan wanted in.

She stared at the frozen image of her mother's smile, a woman she only knew through the memories of others. She'd talk to Brandon tomorrow.

* * *

She returned to the pool on Monday. Tommy barely gave her ankle brace a second glance when she approached the pool. They quickly went over her goals for the morning set. She had arrived alone after waking up to a message from Jordan saying that he'd see her at the pool. The reason for his absence became apparent when he arrived hand in hand with Ashley, her satisfied smile suggesting that she had gained the prize she had sought since joining the club.

Eden's work week was going to be busier and longer than usual with Sarah out sick. She stepped in to chase paperwork, follow up with student-athletes on academic probation, and start planning recruitment trips for a handful of coaches. Then there was the email from Aidan's geography teacher. Two zeros already, which pushed his grade down to a D.

Time. She needed more time.

By the end of the week, she gave up on her high protein diet and indulged in a pizza and soda from the cafeteria. She had just sat down under her favorite tree when she spotted Mano's distinctive body walking out of the building. Carter Holmes—the source of much of Robert Pak's ire last Saturday—was listening intently to whatever it was. Hand gesticulations suggested Carter had a lot on his mind. Mano rested a hand on Carter's shoulder, and whatever he said next seemed to relax the youth visibly. He gave Carter a pat on the back then watched the athlete walk away.

He turned suddenly, and their eyes met.

She silently cursed her light skin, knowing her cheeks were probably a deep crimson in response to his attention. But she wasn't going to pretend she didn't see him. Before she could talk herself out of it, she waved him over. He looked surprised but moved toward her nonetheless.

"Her tree" was part of a grove of beech trees planted on gentle mounds. They formed a guard for a path that led to a small meditation garden that seemed never to have anyone in it. The grove provided enough shade to protect her from hot afternoons while none of the nearby buildings cast long enough shadows to make Fall afternoons too cool to sit outside.

"Hey! How are you?" she asked, scooting over even though there was no one else near them and plenty of space on the grassy area.

Mano sat close. His clean, fresh scent surprised her. "Could be better."

"Holmes?"

He gave her a side-glance as he opened a brown paper bag. "Yes, very perceptive. Brett gave him a bit of a dressing-down after last Saturday's performance. Came to me asking for advice."

"Sounds like you'd be the right guy for him to ask."

"I'm not sure. This position was supposed to be a simple consulting job. Just share my observations about possible areas to improve." He paused, and she guessed at the reason behind the hesitancy.

"I'm not on the clock right now," she said. "Sealed lips. Promise. Between friends. Alistair will never know you said anything."

Her heart skipped a beat at the smile he gave her, a genuine smile. With teeth. "I appreciate the reassurance. But there's nothing I'm going to tell you that Alistair doesn't know. Brett doesn't trust me. It's as simple as that."

"Sounds to me like you don't trust him either?"

Mano pulled out an apple and leaned on his side, his shirt tightening across his chest as he brought the fruit to his mouth. She turned away and bit into her sandwich.

"Eden, you've turned red."

"Shut up."

From the corner of her eye, she saw surprise then understanding cross his usually passive face. "Uh...am I making you uncomfortable?" he asked cautiously.

She sighed. "No. I can't help that I find you attractive. I've been cursed with a face that shows the world how I feel. But we're friends. But maybe I'll not look at your mouth so much."

His laughter was loud enough that others in the grove turned to look their way. "You are probably the most honest person I've ever met, Eden Pak."

"I'm just not smart enough to remember things if they're not true." She grinned. "Anyway, Brandon said he's fine with Aidan coming with me. There is a problem though. I'd emailed the team, and we don't have any extra room in the house we're renting. Most of the hotels there are booked out unless you're willing to pay an insane amount. I don't want you to incur any expenses for this, Mano."

"The whole team stays together?"

"It's cheaper that way, especially for what's considered a local meet. Aidan can sleep with me, though I don't think he'll be excited about sharing the bed."

Mano pulled out his phone and began typing into it. "Would you feel comfortable staying with me? There are a few weekend rentals still available in the area. My shout."

"You what?"

"Shout." Mano tilted his head. "As in, I'll pay for it. You and Aidan can be my guests."

Eden narrowed her eyes. "How much is it?"

"My shout," he repeated.

She tried to grab his phone, but his reflexes were faster than she expected. Off-balance, she fell on him. Her hands splayed out on his chest, and her eyes returned to his lips. Their breathing mirrored each other, shallow and rapid.

"Did you just fall again, Eden Pak?" His voice was deep and low. He lifted her body slightly; the adjustment brought their bodies into full contact.

Granite.

"Why mess with tradition?" She couldn't stop her hand from cupping his cheek, her thumb caressing the strong jawline. She hadn't realized how long his lashes were until now. A faded scar crossed his temple into hair she was sorely tempted to touch. Instead, she took a deep breath and pushed herself off him, her body already scolding her for the separation. She grabbed her water bottle and swallowed the water hurriedly.

"Let me think about the rental, okay?" she said.

"I'll book it. The boy wants to see his mother swim. He can stay with you or me. I'll send you the link. It's a nice place."

CHAPTER NINE

MANO KNEW HE WAS BEING A LITTLE UNDERHANDED WHEN HE SENT the link to the rental to both Aidan and Eden. She was right in that most accommodations were booked for the weekend. Only a smattering of high-end apartments was available at the last minute.

He didn't think twice about securing the rental as soon as he got home. It was a nice place: a two-bedroom townhouse with two bathrooms with a view of the San Luis Mountains. The Aquatic Center was only a ten-minute drive, and from the reviews, it looked like they were within walking distances to popular local restaurants.

It was a no-brainer for him, but Eden was proving to be a tougher sell.

Eden: You play dirty

He couldn't resist.

Mano: You can check. I've committed the least number of fouls on the NZ National Team.

Ten minutes later, his phone buzzed.

Eden: You still play dirty.

Another fifteen minutes later, she messaged him again.

Eden: Okay, you win. But I'll "shout" for groceries and stuff. Okay?

Before he could reply, another message appeared.

Aidan: Thanks! (And yes, my mom is making me type this.)

He welcomed the distraction from what felt like an unproductive month at the college. While Harry Winters welcomed his insights with the women's team, Brett had dismissed much of everything he had suggested from the start. He knew Jackson and the other trainers quietly absorbed his feedback, but anything he suggested directly to the head coach himself was thrown into the recycling bin.

Literally.

He had seen his handwritten notes there in the second week.

He got up from the dining table and watched the lights from the other houses in the cul-de-sac slowly brighten up the street.

He wasn't used to his opinion being disregarded.

More surprising, he wasn't fighting to be heard. He had good reason to bring up Brett's resistance to Alistair, but instincts said not to rock the boat. This was a short-term contract. Just do what he could. The nagging question was whether he was doing all he could.

If he could no longer contribute on the field, and his voice off the field wasn't appreciated, what was next? Unlike Mitch and Connor, he hadn't planned on staying associated to the sport he loved. He had planned on a regular job, coming home to Margot, and—when their kids were old enough—maybe tossing the ball around...like he was doing with Aidan and Matthew.

When Margot left, he let go of that dream. He was now back in his old world, but it didn't seem like that world wanted him back either.

The next time he looked up, he was completely shrouded in darkness. Startled, he checked his phone for the time. He had sat at the table, lost in thought, for two hours. He had missed dinner. He was sure he had half a sandwich in the fridge. And there was always banana bread.

He didn't bother with the lights. The darkness suited him fine.

* * *

Standing on the sidelines with Harry Winters was a far different experience from his time with Brett. Harry had included him in practices and in meetings with his assistants and trainers in the week leading up to their match. He even redirected a few players to work with Mano exclusively on the pitch, and the players were soaking it up. Videos of practices and matches flooded his email box. Mrs. Winters sent him lunch.

They lost by three points, but Mano appreciated Harry's post-match speech on what had improved and what else could be improved. He scanned the locker room as Harry spoke; the team was listening, taking notes. There was a thirst to get better.

He hurried back to find Aidan and Brandon sitting on his front porch. Matthew Yuan was there as well, pulling at his laces.

"Are you sure I can't go?" Matthew asked.

"Has your mother changed her mind?"

"Stupid family dinner," Matthew muttered. "It's always the same thing. We go to the restaurant and just sit there for hours. We eat the same thing every time: fried rice, fried noodles, fried prawns, sweet and sour chicken, tofu in black bean sauce..."

"Sounds like a good time, Matt," Brandon said.

"I'd rather watch people swim."

Aidan put his arm around his friend's shoulder. "I'll be back tomorrow night. Probably early. My mom said her last swim should be done by five."

"And we'll walk to school Monday morning, right?"

Aidan nodded solemnly. "I'll meet you by the bridge like we always do."

"Aidan...."

Aidan leaned his head closer to Matthew. "Like. We. Always. Do."

Mano held his fist up for a fist bump. "We'll go to the next rugby match together, eh? Your dad said he'll come as well."

Matthew nodded and returned Mano's fist bump half-heartedly. He walked dejectedly toward home, his hands in his pockets.

Brandon watched Matthew walk to his house before turning to Aidan. "Is there more going on, son?"

"No," Aidan replied quickly. "You know Matt. He just doesn't want to spend a whole weekend with Lydia."

Mano grabbed his bag from his bedroom and met Brandon and Aidan in his garage.

"Okay, be good," Brandon said, hugging his son. "Wish your mom good luck for me. And don't forget to let me know her times."

"I won't. Bye, Dad."

Brandon shook Mano's hand. "Thanks for taking him. Until Eden mentioned it, I didn't think he was interested in watching her swim."

"She didn't know either."

"That's what she said, too." Brandon paused then took a deep breath. "I appreciate that he had you to talk to. It's nice to see him excited about something again. He didn't want to do much of anything last year."

It was a three-and-a-half-hour drive to San Luis Obispo. Eden had left last night, and they agreed to meet her after her first race, which was going to be later tonight.

Aidan remained largely silent on the drive. Mano didn't try to encourage a discussion. If the boy wanted to talk, he would. That's how it had been this past month.

When they reached the rental, they were greeted by the smell of tomatoes and oregano.

Aidan rolled his eyes. "One more night of pasta. Can you die of pasta? It's all we've had at home this last week. Pasta, pasta, pasta. Glad I'm not Italian."

Mano picked up the note on the kitchen counter and noticed the lanyards under it. "She said to eat before we go to the Aquatic Center." He looked at Aidan. "She also said there's a hot dog in the fridge for you if you were sick of pasta."

Mano had never been to a swim meet before. It was busier than he had expected. He was unfamiliar with the vocabulary around him. Conversations about tapers, the difficulty of getting into swim-suits, and even shaving incidents were taking place around him.

He spotted Jordan Kennedy, surrounded by a group of people. Most seemed to want a picture with him. A couple had notebooks with them and were throwing questions at him simul-taneously.

"Where's your mom?"

"Probably in the warm-up pool," Aidan said. "She'll find us after her race. Oh—hey! It's Mrs. Wellens! Mrs. Wellens!"

Wearing a dark navy long jacket, a deeply tanned woman with the now familiar imprint of goggles on her face smiled widely as she opened her arms for Aidan.

"Look at you! How much have you grown over the summer?" Linda Wellens looked up. "You must be Mano. Eden said you were taking care of our guy here for the weekend."

"Good to meet you," Mano said.

Linda looked at Aidan again. "How long has it been since you last saw your mom swim Aidan?"

Aidan shrugged. "In a meet. Never."

"Well, I'm very glad you made it this time. Is your dad coming up tomorrow?"

"No."

She nodded. "Next time. Maybe he can get back in the pool again. Tell him the Beavers want him before all those folks in the city."

They made their way up to the stands, among excited family and friends. They didn't have long to wait for Eden's race—the 100 Meters Freestyle.

Mano almost didn't recognize her when she came into sight. She looked like most of the other swimmers he had seen so far. Their body types were similar: long-limbed, narrow waists, strong arms, thick muscular shoulders. She moved intentionally as she went through her pre-race routine. Every shoulder roll, arm swing, and tight slap on muscles had a purpose. He knew she was fit, but in this setting, among her peers, she looked menacing.

Introductions were made. Eden raised her arm when it was her turn, but she didn't look up even with Aidan loudly screaming her name. Her gaze stayed trained on her lane.

"Swimmers, take your marks!"

The deep-toned beep of the starting signal uniformly released the swimmers from their stationary positions.

"Go, Mom!" Aidan was up on his feet, yelling. "Come on! You got this!"

Mano leaned forward, aware that his heart had begun to race. Excitement coursed through his body, and he cracked his knuckles as he rested his forearms onto his knees.

She took a slight lead by the midway point. He could see—rather than hear—Jordan and Linda shouting from the sidelines.

There was an aggression in the pool he hadn't expected to see in a race. The show of power with each stroke or kick was also a surprise.

"Here she goes," Aidan cried. He began jumping up and down. "Go, Mom, go!"

Eden exploded off the last turn, surging forward. He didn't catch a change in rhythm or technique. It looked the same. But her kicks seemed to become stronger, creating small waves. Her arms reached deeper and pulled further.

She was the clear winner.

But he saw the disappointment in her shoulders before he heard Aidan's groan.

"She missed the mark by point four," Aidan said as he pulled out his phone. "A new PB but not good enough. I'm going to let Dad know."

Eden reached over the lines to shake hands with the swimmers closest to her. He watched her leave the pool and exchange words with a short man with a notebook.

"Is she done?" Mano asked Aidan.

"Yeah."

"Seems like a really long day for a couple of minutes."

Aidan laughed. "Welcome to the swim world, Mano. We wait a lot. That's why I gave it up. Dad didn't get that I hated the waiting. That's what I love about rugby. No timeouts. No waiting. We keep going and going."

Thirty minutes later, a deep sense of satisfaction filled Mano as he watched Aidan give Eden a hug. They shared a smile, the similarities between mother and son finally obvious to him. That was worth the long drive.

* * *

Eden stared blankly at the ceiling then closed her eyes, willing her mind to go silent. But it was alert. She had replayed her swim over and over again. She knew better. She needed her rest. Swim, race, let go. It was over. *Focus on the next one! Go to sleep!*

But she couldn't.

She sat up, deciding that a cup of herbal tea might help calm her down. She reached for the sweatshirt she had thrown casually on the foot of bed then stopped at the landing.

Mano's door was open.

She looked back into her bedroom. Aidan hadn't moved, his mouth was slightly opened while his eyes were shut.

She moved closer to Mano's bedroom and peered in cautiously. He could still be there, but she knew he had shut the door after they exchanged good nights a few hours ago. It seemed empty. Walking barefoot down the stairs, she looked furtively around when she reached the living area. "Mano?"

The curtain by the sliding door swayed gently as a light breeze entered the townhouse. She walked toward it and looked through the open door. Mano stood on the deck, his back to her, facing what should have been an unhindered view of San Luis Mountains.

"You should be sleeping, Eden," he said without turning. "You need your rest."

"Can't sleep. You?"

"The same."

She slipped her hand into his and squeezed it. A few seconds later, he squeezed back, their fingers intertwined.

"Did you ever get nervous before a big match?" she asked.

"All the time. They were always big matches to me. Even in France. For club or country, they all mattered."

"Weren't you expecting your matches in France to matter?"

"No, I signed on for the money. I thought if that was the reason for me to go, it wouldn't matter as much. I was wrong. I got to know the other fellas; they were all good people, good players. You don't want to let your teammates down."

She soaked in his answer. "Did you ever play for yourself?"

He glanced at her, surprise visible even in the shadows. "That's a strange question."

She shrugged. "I swim for myself. Selfish, I know."

"You've been called to answer a challenge. Different sport, but it makes sense."

"Is that what you do? Answer a challenge?"

He grunted. "Trust me. If I wanted to mess up my body, I could have found other ways to do it. But rugby called me. It made sense. Some things in life, you just do. Because you're meant to." He squeezed her hand again. "I'm glad I saw you swim today. You looked great in the water."

"I don't know about that. I didn't get the time I needed."

"You still have one more chance tomorrow, right? To qualify."

She nodded, now holding his hand in both of hers, seeking the comfort of his strength, hoping it would soften the anxiety she had forgotten she could nurse when something meant too much. "Yes. One more chance."

She left early for the Aquatic Center. She went through all her pre-race motions. Checked with Tommy one more time. Warm-up swims. Played her favorite pre-race music. Body felt loose; ankle felt strong.

But the water didn't welcome her. Her start was too slow. Her strokes far from precise. She won the race but—like yesterday—missed the qualifying point.

By one second. Point seven seconds to be exact.

A blink away from fulfilling a lifelong dream.

This time, there was no reason for her failure other than she wasn't fast enough.

CHAPTER TEN

From what Mano gathered, she spoke to no one about it.

He found a print copy of the faculty newsletter, which celebrated Jordan's and her appearances at the meet torn, in the recycling bin. Sarah could only shrug when he pulled it out and showed it to her.

Aidan said she continued to keep to her swim schedule, leaving the house at 4:30 a.m. and home by 7:30 a.m. Mano saw her at the gym on Friday, per the schedule before San Luis Obispo, except Jordan was working out with her now.

When Mano asked Aidan if she was going to swim at another meet, Aidan said Eden didn't want to talk about it.

"Granddad says she's acting like a teenager," Aidan said.

He stopped asking. He understood she had to reassess how much she wanted her goal. All athletes reached that point at least once in their careers.

Wasn't his dream.

They now met for lunch daily in tree grove, often eating in comfortable silence. Sometimes she'd ask about his past but always on neutral subjects: what do people eat in New Zealand? What exactly was a haka? Who was his favorite player growing up? When she laughed, he would sometimes join her. Then there were the occasional touches, the pat on his back, the squeeze on his arm, the friendly punch.

He didn't share with anyone that every time they touched his body would ignite with bursts of desire. The knowledge that she found him attractive was more of an albatross around his neck than an incentive to encourage it.

She wasn't the type of woman a man held only for one night.

He slept better after those lunch dates, then the guilt of finding joy in Eden's company would keep him up over the next few days. He had promised himself to love only one. He always kept his promises. Always.

A week after their return from the swim meet, he found a flier with a schedule to get ready for Halloween.

He stared at it suspiciously. Patty warned him not to disregard it.

"Are we all really supposed to get our decorations up two weeks before Halloween? A full two weeks?"

"You better believe it," she said, pulling out her phone. "Let me show you how we did it last year."

Longest fifteen minutes of his life.

But Aidan and Matthew didn't forget their side of the bargain. Without prompting, on the Friday the street was supposed to start decorating, Mano opened his door to the sight of the two boys lugging a large storyboard detailing their decorating plans for the house. His job was to string up the lights on the roofline, mainly because Mrs. Yuan wouldn't allow Matthew up a ladder.

Matthew handed Mano a piece of paper. "My mom emailed your landlord. These are instructions to where you can find all of her decorations in the garage attic. Can you bring it down by tomorrow?"

"I work tomorrow, Matthew," Mano growled, scanning the sheet.

"It's okay if you bring it down tonight," Matthew replied, pushing his glasses back on his nose.

Fortunately, the team's next match was in nearby Sacramento. He returned to find Eden on his front porch, sitting cross-legged, surrounded by boxes he had finally located at about ten o'clock the night before.

"I hope you like puzzles," she said, raising a wad of wires and light bulbs.

He didn't.

Three hours later, he returned to the porch, biting back the words he really wanted to use. Besides the lights, they pulled cotton to look like spiderwebs, hammered anchors so the giant blowups were secured, and hung ghosts from the trees. Aidan and Matthew were out front, working on the graveyard scene.

Eden burst out laughing. "I'm an adult. You can curse in front of me."

"I know that. But Mum made me promise on her deathbed to watch my language."

She stared at him in surprise. He wondered absentmindedly how many men would fall at her feet if she looked at them with those eyes. *"That's* what she made you promise?" she asked, incredulity lacing her voice.

"I had started to play top-level high school rugby, and... well...there's a lot of opportunity to expand one's vocabulary when it's just you and the brothers."

She grinned, and he suddenly felt the need to test whether her neck would fit his palm. He bet it would. When did he become obsessed with necks? Margot always wore her long hair down. He loved running his hand through it, as soft as silk were the strands. When she started losing all her hair, he tucked those desires away.

"Mom! Mano! Come out front! We're done."

"Thank goodness!" Mano threw another wad of lights into the closest plastic tub. "I'm just going to buy some new ones. How much could lights cost?"

"That's not the point."

"Saving time is the point."

"Is this why Halloween never took off in New Zealand?"

"What insane person lets their children take candy from a stranger? Isn't that what we tell them not to do the rest of the year?"

"Spoilsport."

"Common sense."

They turned the corner of the house. Eden let out an audible gasp. Aidan and Matthew stood at the entrance to the sideyard with wide grins, obviously pleased with the afternoon's efforts. The Styrofoam headpieces, although unimpressive singularly, looked remarkably authentic when displayed in a group of almost two dozen. The boys had strategically placed cutouts of scrawny hands, suggesting the dead were trying to emerge from their final resting places. The path that led to the backyard was lined with skulls on stakes, their eyes beginning to glow in the twilight.

"Can we see the full effect with the fog machine? Please? It's set up, just in case...."

"Just in case, eh?" Mano hoped he wasn't smiling, but the enthusiasm in Aidan's face was getting to him. He cleared his throat. "All right, let's give it a go."

He returned to the garage to turn on the fog machine then grabbed Eden's hand instinctively. It felt like the most natural thing to do as they watched the boys laugh and holler as the fog rolled from the corner of the house, a low moan occasionally coming from the same machine.

Mano smiled. "Well done, boys. I've never seen anything like this before."

"This is incredible," Eden agreed. She slipped her hand out of Mano's to start clapping, and he immediately felt the loss.

He tried to minimize his excitement about Halloween as the week leading up to the day started. His cul-de-sac had transformed into something he didn't quite understand and never thought he'd participate in.

His enthusiasm dampened significantly when Mrs. Henderson came by with his costume.

"We always do a theme on our street," she explained. He continued to stare at the costume she held out. "It's superheroes this year. The Yuans are going to be that family from that movie…what's it called? You know, where the mom can stretch all her limbs and the boy can run on water? No? It'll come to me eventually. I'm going to be a female Joker."

"There's a female Joker?"

"Suspend your sense of reality, son. It's *Halloween*! My grand-daughter wants to be Batgirl, so we'll match."

"Mrs. Henderson, thank you but…."

"No 'buts.' It's paid for. All the moms want to see you in it."

"Pardon?"

"Consider it our welcome-to-the-neighborhood present. You're causing quite a stir around here, especially when you're cutting the grass."

"Mrs. Henderson…."

"It's fine by me. Carolyn has brought more friends this semester. Nothing like a den full of teenagers to make a woman feel young again."

The gold, green, and brown costume hung between them. She looked at him expectantly. He took it and tried to smile. He suspected he failed, but Mrs. Henderson looked satisfied when she left his doorstep. "I'm sure I can find a trident before Halloween. Don't give up on me yet!"

When he Skyped with Mitch and Connor, they physically disappeared from the screen, their laughter loud and clear. It added salt to the wounds when their usually more sympathetic wives reacted the same way, leaving him staring at a blank wall for a good five minutes.

"What happened to 'thicker than blood'," Mano muttered.

"Mate, you got to send us pictures," Connor said, wiping tears when his image popped back on the computer.

"Not a chance."

"Come on. Fred will love it."

"No."

"Maybe you could convince them that you could dress up as Thor."

"Mrs. Henderson said they paid for the costume already."

"Who's 'they'?" Cat Dane had squeezed herself onto the screen, her arm around her husband's shoulder.

He hesitated then braced himself for the response to his answer. "Apparently, the moms in the neighborhood."

He switched off the connection when a second round of laughter echoed through his room.

Eden was more discreet when she surveyed the costume. In fact, she didn't say anything. She just stared between him and the offending garment.

"Well," she said, fingering the silver sequins. "It's…uh…eye-catching."

"It's tight."

"I think it's supposed to be skintight."

"I might need a drink on Halloween."

"Trust me, you won't be the only adult living it up."

"Suspend all reality," Mano muttered.

"What was that?"

"What Mrs. Henderson said. 'Suspend all reality.' Because it's Halloween." Mano looked at his costume again. "What are you wearing?"

"Me? Good lord, nope. I'm not a costume person. Besides, no one goes to the apartments, and the boys will be trick-or-treating with friends. They will finish at the Yuans' house to count their stash of candy. Patty has pizzas for them before and after the event. It tends to go late, so Aidan will sleep over tonight."

"If I'm wearing a costume, you should too."

"No way!"

"Why do I have to wear a costume?"

"I don't live on this street, remember? Mrs. Henderson will never forgive you if you don't wear *something*. She's already mad at you that you've not shown up for book club."

"This is ridiculous."

"Think how happy you'll make all the kids when they see you in your costume."

"This is not a good idea."

* * *

Eden knew she was staring.

As was Aidan.

"Where are you going, Matthew?" she whispered.

"Mom will want to see this," he said, running out of the front door.

She was more familiar with Mano's body now, but the tight-fitting gold spandex-like material brought out elements of his body she hadn't realized existed. She had suspected a six-pack under his shirt, but even the top swimmers she worked out with didn't quite have *that kind* of six-pack. Then there were the green tights that shaped a pair of buns no baker on Earth could form so perfectly.

"You look like a god," Aidan said, his eyes wide.

"That's it, I'm taking it off!" Mano said.

"No!" mother and son said simultaneously.

"Think of the children!" But Eden couldn't say it with a straight face, and it didn't help that Aidan doubled over the nearby sofa.

There was a pained look of restraint on his face when Patty and Mrs. Henderson came by—with the trident—and for a split second, Eden was sympathetic to his plight. Then he bent over to tie his shoes, and that moment was lost.

The man deserved to be seen tonight.

Matthew and Aidan had dinner at the Yuans before Charles took them and Lydia trick-or-treating for the first hour. The teens would then meet with some other classmates to canvas the rest of the neighborhood. They lived in a generous area, and last year's haul was so heavy Aidan's pillowcase tore at the seams. He was better prepared this year: he double-bagged his pillowcases.

After the boys left the street, Eden watched Mano offering a bowl of candy to the first set of trick-or-treaters. She had to choke back a laugh when she noticed the protective glance the young father gave his wife as she moved up the steps to get closer to Mano.

Then her humor was replaced with a soft, warm feeling. The King of Atlantis was on one knee, helping an indecisive little fairy choose between candy or chocolate. A cowboy and a turtle were behind her, but Mano didn't succumb to the panic of inefficiency. He let the fairy take her time.

Patty, dressed in a red bodysuit, came up next to her, a bottle of wine and two glasses in her hands. "You should go over there."

"This was supposed to be our night," Eden protested. "Remember? The plan was to sit on the porch together, complain a little, gossip a little, and give out candy."

Patty continued to hold out her offering. "I think he needs your help tonight. Besides, he may need a little protection from some of our single parents—moms and dads—wearing a costume like that. I'm buying Mrs. Henderson lunch for thinking of it."

"Oh, Patty!" Eden laughed.

The line toward Mano's place had grown in the last couple of minutes, and she gently maneuvered her way past princesses, knights, ninjas, frogs, a couple of sheep, and miniature basketball players.

"I'm glad you're here," Mano said through the side of his mouth when she reached his side. "This is a nightmare."

"The night is still young, your majesty." She grinned, reaching for the second bowl of candy.

Side by side, they distributed several hundred pieces of candy and chocolates. One little girl—judging from her age—was probably walking up to the door for the first time by herself. When Mano suggested she take more than one treat, her eyes grew large. "Really? Yay!"

Mano surprised her with the ease with which he greeted the youngest ones of the night. It was a nice change from the scowl he had recently thrown at a twenty-one-year-old, two-hundred-pound rugby player at practice.

When given, Mano's smiles came from a genuine place, but they remained rare. They were still so fleeting that their appearances caught her attention immediately. But she was learning the different nuances in his expressions. She'd take his half-smiles over someone else's fake full ones. He saved them for moments that meant something to him.

It was easy to associate his lack of expressions with lack of emotions. The opposite was true; he had them all. He had simply learned never to show them.

By nine o'clock, they were back inside the house and the doorbell finally stopped ringing. Eden ran to Patty's to check on Aidan but was promptly shooed back to Mano's with a pizza and brownies. "Don't come back. Aidan's fine. We'll make sure he'll be at school on time," Patty said.

When Eden returned, she was sorry to see Mano back in his regular shirt and shorts, relief etched on his face. He was leaning against the kitchen counter, a glass of iced water against his forehead.

"That was one of the hardest nights of my life." He looked up. "Patty sent food?"

"You know it! Aidan and Matthew are negotiating candy, and I was told not to come back again!" Eden pulled up the barstool next to him. "Dig in, I'm starving."

She closed her eyes, taking in the flavors of melted cheese

and tomatoes on a warm crust. Such simplicity became grand under the encouragement of hunger. But when she opened her eyes again, it was a different type of hunger that met hers.

He was going to hide it. It was what he always did whenever they touched. He did it well. But she was no longer a stranger. She was starting to understand this man in front of her.

He moved back slightly, as if in defense.

Was it the half bottle of wine she had consumed that encouraged her bravado? Or was it the hours of interaction with happy people that made her braver, bolder?

She reached for his face, gently cupping his cheek. He stayed motionless, as if paralyzed by her touch. She slid her hand up toward his hair, pulling on it lightly as she followed the curve of his head toward his neck.

"Eden, I don't think—"

"Shh," she whispered before claiming lips she wanted to taste again.

He was ready for her this time.

This wasn't the tentative brush of lips from weeks ago.

He responded immediately to her invitation, with a desire that ignited hers instantly. Strong, muscular arms wrapped around her body, pulling her firmly against him.

She fitted into his body, her long, lean length complementing his thicker frame. His hand followed the curve of her back, inch by inch, a slow, upward caress that was both tortuous and inflammatory.

She gasped in protest when he moved away. He leaned his head against hers, their joined irregular breathing loud in the quiet of the house.

He gently pushed her head into the crook of his neck, speaking into her hair. "I think you can feel how much I'm attracted to you, but this isn't good for either of us."

His words seared through her heart. She had expected them but didn't want them. "Was there a line I shouldn't have crossed? But I'd be lying if I said I'm sorry I did." She turned her head slightly. "I've told you before, one kiss doesn't mean I expect a tomorrow from you."

"The right man can promise you that. I can't."

"Can't or won't?" she challenged.

"Both."

"Scared?"

"Yes. I've been told to accept my limitations."

She turned her head, breathing in his scent in the crook of his neck. "I thought world champions didn't see limits."

"Eden," he growled.

Her fingers followed the lines of his neck down his torso then back up his neck. "No limits, tonight, Mano. Suspend reality with me."

"Eden—"

"Please."

CHAPTER ELEVEN

It began the same way most nights since Margot left.

He'd awake on an unknown beach, crashing waves so loud, it eradicated all other sound. He'd push himself up onto on his knees before sitting back on his hunches. Raising his arm to protect his vision from the sharp rays of the afternoon sun, a vast blue sky taunted him with its emptiness: cloudless with not a bird in sight. He'd scan the ocean but knew who he'd be looking for would not be there.

He waited for the cry from an unknown woman absent from his view.

He'd be faster this time. He'd get to her, to save her.

But there was no voice in the wind.

He frowned. She would always cry out. For him.

He started to run, feet sinking slightly in soft sand. He'd find her this time. He'd be quicker. He had always tried before, but whenever he thought he was close, the winds would die down suddenly. The waves ceased to exist; their erratic rhythm stopped abruptly.

A different kind of panic grew from within. He must save her.

But she didn't call for him.

* * *

"Mano? Mano? Hey? I'm right here."

It was barely a whisper but Eden's voice pierced through the seconds of confusion that came between dreams and reality. Now sitting up, he swallowed, aware of his racing heart. He struggled to breathe and ran a shaking hand through his hair.

Arms circled his torso from behind; her face pressed to his back. "It's okay," she said. "I got you."

But the walls had started to close in again.

"I need to get out…need to get to the backyard," he said. Without a word, she released him immediately.

He stumbled onto clothes strewn on the floor but didn't bother to pick any up. He should have turned back, but getting through this wave of anxiety was his only goal in that moment. He walked towards the backdoor automatically, urgency his guide.

Outside there were no walls. He held on the railings and raised his face to the dark sky. *Deep breaths. Keep breathing. Keep breathing.* Gradually, the pounding in his head subsided.

A blanket was placed over his shoulders then strong arms came around him. This time, he was ready for her offer of comfort and reached across her shoulders to draw her close.

"Sorry," he mumbled, kissing the top of her head.

"Don't be."

"I woke you up."

"I need to be going anyway. I have to get to the pool soon."

He nodded. "Is Jordan picking you up?"

She laughed softly. "No. He's been staying over at Ashley Jones'. She lives five minutes away from the pool, so I think that's an added incentive to stay there beyond just her companionship."

He blew out of his mouth then squeezed her shoulder. He had to be honest; he owed her that at least. "Eden —"

She placed fingers on his lips, speaking before he could

continue. "I haven't forgotten what you said before." Then she grinned. "But how about Sunday? Come over for lunch? Aidan's home for the weekend."

He should say 'no'. The team would be flying back straight after the match, arriving just before midnight on Saturday. He had planned to use Sunday to work and write down his observations and suggestions from the weekend match. The blinds were going to stay down, and he was going to try another vinyl from the eclectic collection in his living room. The plan was to be alone. Work. Hide the memories. But her hopeful eyes and friendly smile were hard to resist. "Yeah, all right. Sounds good."

"Great! Just show up! Our 'shout.'"

Mano smiled. "Your new favorite word?"

She kissed his cheek. "Yes! It is. It's catchy. What's another New Zealand phrase I should learn?"

He pushed back the front of her hair. Her smile deepened. "Well," he said. "We greet each other with Kia Ora."

"Kia Ora?" Eden repeated. "Kia Ora. That sounds so beautiful."

"You're beautiful." An immediate shade of red flushed her face, prompting him to reach for the neck that had beguiled him for weeks. He marveled at the babysoft hair under his fingers, a contrast to the strength he had seen in her shoulders when she swam.

"It fits" he murmured. She kissed him without reservation: gentle; warm; undemanding; giving.

Fifteen minutes later, he walked Eden to her car, the soft lights of the neighborhood provided direction but not attention.

She touched his face one more time. "Thank you for an incredible night, Mano."

He stayed rooted long after the Forester turned the corner. He saw what was in her eyes. He had seen those feelings before. Where once he had been proud to be the recipient of such emotions, now he questioned if he deserved them.

He wouldn't go back to sleep now. Her scent still lingered on him: a beguiling combination of gardenias and mystery. He would have kept her in his bed all night if it weren't for the nightmares he couldn't get rid of.

Just one night with her and already, without her presence, the house seemed emptier, colder. His hand hovered over the light switch. Dawn wasn't that far away. The dark was what he was used to anyway.

He returned to the bedroom and flipped opened the laptop that had stayed under his bed. Before he could think twice, Connor answered the call through Skype.

"Hiya! That was lucky! Just came into the kitchen to pick up a drink!" Connor's face grew serious when he glanced at the clock. "It's just about five in the morning where you are, isn't it? What's wrong?"

He wasn't used to sharing his feelings. He swallowed. "I slept with someone."

Connor stared blankly at Mano's confession. Then he blinked. "Hang on."

The screen went blank, then he heard the door shutting. Connor reappeared on the screen again. "First, are you all right?"

"Yeah."

Connor's shoulders relaxed. "Good—"

"I shouldn't have! I'm not good for her, Con. She's amazing. Beautiful, smart, kind. And she has a son who…. When she smiles, I almost forget," Mano exhaled. "I want to tell you it was mistake."

Connor's eyes widened slightly. "But you'd be lying to me – and yourself – if you said it."

Mano turned away from the screen, his gaze finding the petticoats of the can-can dancer on the wall. But it was the dark silhouettes of the men behind her he now studied: their anonymity more reflective of where he wanted to be.

"Mano, it's all right, mate," Connor said, his voice pulling Mano back to the present.

"I'm not sure if it is."

Connor hesitated then spoke again. "You know, Liana still checks in with Spurgeon once a year."

"I know. I spoke to him a couple of days ago. I'll talk to him again, but I don't feel…this can't be right, can it? Wanting to be with someone when your head is full of someone else?"

"Is this Eden Pak we're talking about?" Connor asked gently.

Mano nodded. "That obvious?"

Connor smiled. "Well, it's the only name you've mentioned other than Mrs. Henderson, and we didn't think she was your type."

Mano smiled. Just hearing Connor's voice helped lift a little of the heaviness inside him.

"Mano, you deserve 'amazing,'" Connor said.

"Wish I could believe that."

"I'm here for you, mate. Even across the ocean. Please…just remember that Spurgeon is also a phone call away."

"I will. Thanks, mate."

"And we'll be in Los Angeles for Steve's birthday in November. We'd love to see you."

"I'll think about it."

"We're thinking of bringing Fred with us. Make a longer holiday out of it. He's been wanting to go to Disneyland. And you know if he goes, Jayne will go."

"That sounds like…fun."

"It's going to be a disaster. It'll take at least three rugby players to keep them in control. We could use you, mate."

Mano smiled half-heartedly then took a deep breath. "I'm sure you'll have everything under control. You always do. How's Levi doing? Has he started teething?"

Connor nodded slowly before replacing his worried countenance with the smile that continued to be used in various ad campaigns around the world. Launching into a series of humorous anecdotes that suggested a life full of simple pleasures, Connor kept Mano company until the first light of day filtered through the trees in the backyard and the alarm sounded.

Mano stretched. "Time for me to start my day. I better go."

"Yeah, me too."

"Con? Thanks."

"No worries. Anytime."

* * *

During her morning swim, images of her night with Mano filled her mind. She had never been loved so tenderly nor with such attentiveness.

Turn; push; kick; breathe.

He had whispered her name often. Perhaps to appease any concern that it was she who was in his mind, that she wasn't a substitute for his former lover? This anonymous lost love may still hold Mano's heart, but Eden had no doubt she was who Mano had made love to last night.

He saw her.

He heard her.

It was her hand he had reached for before sleep claimed them both.

Turn; push; kick; breathe.

She was also certain of the anguish in his voice when he sat up suddenly. Whatever happened in his life before California didn't remain in his past. It followed him here. When she had joined him on the deck, she'd wanted to ask him what was haunting him. But it wasn't the right time. At that moment, he didn't need a lover to replace a former one.

He needed a friend.

Turn; push; kick; breathe.

After finishing her morning set, Jordan caught up with her in the parking lot, his practiced smile lighting up his face. "Hey, I'm sorry I haven't been living up to my end of the bargain," he began.

She reached her car and opened the door. "It's all good. At this hour, it's never bad. The carpool worked out great for a month, but it was never something I was going to depend on."

"Thanks for understanding. I hadn't planned on Ashley and I…well…but if it ever ends, I'll be back to carpooling again!"

Eden grinned. "Don't let her hear you say that, Jordan. It's not good for the ego to know a guy you're interested in already has a backup plan."

"That's true. "Anyway, I understand that Tommy's brought up making some changes in your sets. To get ready for Mesa. There's plenty of time to shave those seconds off."

She leaned against the car. "About that, I'm not sure if I'll sign up for that one."

Jordan's smile disappeared. "What do you mean? You would have qualified if you hadn't sprained your ankle."

"My ankle wasn't the problem."

"Is there a problem? What is it? Let me know. Let us know. We're here to help. We want you to get to Nationals. You're still coming to these practices. I think that says a lot," he said.

She tilted her head and frowned. "Why is my making Nationals so important to you? I mean, I appreciate the support and enthusiasm. But you've got a lot of people in the club that are going to get on the podium. I'm nobody."

Jordan looked away for a second. "Look, I really like you, Eden. You're the feel-good story of Bay Area sports this season. We just want you to succeed."

"But *why*?"

"My 'whys' aren't as important as your 'whys."

Eden rolled her eyes and shook her head. "Really? That's what you got? Who are you really, Jordan? Why is this club so important you? You spend half your free time recruiting; the other half swimming. Why?"

"I just want to help a fellow St. Anne's staff. That's all." He stared past her again. "We stick together, right?"

She nodded but had nothing more to say. She entered the car

quickly, suddenly eager to return home. She wanted to catch Aidan at the Yuans' before he left for school. She wasn't sure she understood her reaction to Jordan's questions. Part of her wanted to believe he was in her corner. After all, he was the team captain and the de facto face of the club. He qualified in his signature event—the Individual Medley—for Nationals and would, no doubt, be a contender again. His questions weren't in any way out of line.

But this was *her* dream; *her* ambition; *her* goal.

And it was hers to chase or give up.

Eden drummed her fingers on the steering wheel after merging onto the 24 freeway. It'd be eight minutes until her exit; then another seven minutes from there to the apartment complex. If she took the stairs two-at-a-time, she could be in her apartment in less than five minutes after parking her car. Plenty of time for a shower, finish the smoothie she had made before she left and start her walk to the Yuans' house.

Her bright face caused Aidan to frown when she walked into the Yuans' kitchen.

"What are you doing here?"

"Good morning to you, too!" Eden said, kissing Aidan's head. She extended her hand for a fist bump with Matthew before going round the breakfast counter to give Patty a hug.

"A good night and a good morning, I take it," Patty asked, arched eyebrows emphasized a knowing look. She pulled out a plate of scrambled eggs and sausages from the oven before adding sliced avocados. "Whole wheat or rye? Coffee's just been brewed." Patty glanced at the clock then walked to the nearby stairwell. "Charles! Lydia!"

"Thanks! I wasn't expecting breakfast," Eden said, pouring herself a cup before sitting next to Aidan.

"Ever since you told me how much you're supposed to eat in a day, I decided you shall eat everything I want to but can't." Her tone changed when she looked at Matthew's plate. "That's it?"

"Mom…."

"I wake up at six o'clock to make you pancakes, and you barely touch them!"

"Lydia will," Matthew murmured.

"It's not Lydia who has fallen off the height-weight chart. Matthew Yuan – finish that up!"

Matthew kept his head down but the stabbing action of his fork suggested his true feelings on the topic. Aidan gave Eden a 'don't-say-a-word' look before finishing the last of his pancakes. "Thank you, Mrs. Yuan."

"My pleasure. It's always nice to feed someone who appreciates a homemade meal."

Matthew stood up, stomped towards the sink and placed his half-eaten pancake in the sink noisily.

Eden brought her coffee cup to her lips and watched the two boys leave the kitchen quietly. Patty stood at the kitchen counter and massaged her temples with controlled motions. "That was uncalled for. I behaved like a twelve-year old."

"I say thirteen."

Patty smiled tiredly before reaching for her cup of coffee. She grimaced then put the cup in the microwave. "I thought it was supposed to be easier as they get older."

"Lots of good times but I don't remember it ever being easy. Even with help."

Patty nodded. "We waited so long to have children. Took us five years to finally get pregnant and have Matthew. I thought that was the hard part." Patty took out her now-steaming coffee. "Last night, the boys spent an hour going through the candy. Then another forty-five minutes negotiating exchanges. There was giggling. I should have put a stop to all of it earlier. But they were both happy." Patty smiled sadly. "I've forgotten what Matthew looks like when he's really laughing."

"He's a good kid," Eden said. "And you're a good mom."

"I want to think so. But he doesn't talk to either Charles or me anymore. And last week, I found porn on his phone."

Eden stilled her fork, the earlier sense of contentment pushed out by the immediate onslaught of fear. *"Porn?"*

"Oh yes. I freaked out and made Charles come home early to deal with it." Patty shook her head. "I wasn't as ready as I thought for whatever comes with teenagers these days. Anyway, that was a wake-up call."

"You don't think Aidan has it on his phone as well, do you? I mean…."

Patty met Eden's gaze squarely. "Well, even if he doesn't. It was on Matthew's. They spend all their free time together."

Eden pushed her plate away. "I guess I better go through his phone tonight."

"Better being the helicopter mom now than an unaware parent later."

A few minutes later, Eden accompanied Matthew and Aidan to school – or rather, until other kids from school began to appear on the trail. Aidan moved ahead before she could hug him. He didn't turn once to wave good-bye. The small act of indifference, on a different day, would become an amusing anecdote to share with her dads. Instead, it felt like a dose of rejection that cooled the day before it could begin.

She had an hour with him after school before she needed to leave for the gym. Maybe they could talk then.

But the earlier feeling of euphoria after a night with Mano was now burdened with the guilt of ignorance. She put on the backpack that had Aidan's clothes and Halloween candy as she watched the figures of her child and his best friend become smaller the further they went.

Others began appearing on the trail. Eden smiled at a slightly disheveled mom with a travel mug in one hand but in the other – her daughter's hand. The knot in her throat made it difficult to breathe. When was the last time Aidan let her hold his hand?

She started to run. Images of how many times she had said good-bye to Aidan this past month flooded her mind: at the

Yuans', before he left with Brandon, when her dads visited, with Mano.

Mano.

Even the newest person in her life had quality time with her son. Aidan talked to Mano; it was the rugby player who Aidan confided in, who her son shared his wish to watch her swim again. Aidan couldn't – wouldn't? – even bring it up with her. Her own son.

She rushed up the stairwell, frustration making the simple act of opening her door harder. When inside, she went straight to Aidan's room. She searched through his drawers; looked inside the closet; checked under the bed.

Nothing.

No drugs; no cigarettes; no alcohol.

She slumped against the foot of the bed and pulled her knees to her chest. The hollowness started in the pit of her stomach, and she rocked herself gently, tears quietly streaming down her face. She should be relieved. There was nothing here. But the relief didn't come. Not finding something was akin to battling the unknown.

Patty was always on top of things. She knew Matthew's schedule to the "T" and was on a first-name basis with all his teachers. She volunteered; she attended all the meetings. But if super-mom-Patricia-Yuan couldn't stop Matthew from being exposed to inappropriate and unsafe things, what were her chances?

Suddenly, all Eden heard was the uneven and shallow sound of her breathing. She took a deep breath to regain her bearings. Her son was safe. Nothing had happened...*yet.*

She doubled down, using techniques from the sports psychologist to focus on what she could control, to silence the doubt. She scanned the room and tried to remember the last time she actually spent time in here with Aidan. Lately, she would only enter to check if laundry was on the floor or if the trash can was emptied. This was now Aidan's world. He rarely invited her in.

Posters of basketball players used to don the walls. Now gone, they were replaced with a large white sheet with scribbles and a rough sketch of what had turned out to be Matthew and Aidan's science project. The only other thing up was a picture of the New Zealand rugby team…with Mano's fierce, unreadable face staring back.

He said he'd call her tonight.

Once she reached the office, she switched on "admin-mode." A large pile of paperwork kept her at her desk for most of the day, a much-needed retreat from her life as a parent and as a swimmer.

Jordan had sent her a message about joining the rest of the team for an informal social at Ashley's. "To build team spirit," he'd typed. She said she couldn't and was skipping the gym today. She wasn't sure if it was regret or relief that she didn't hear from him again that afternoon.

Aidan was surprised to see her at home when he returned from school. "Aren't you supposed to be at the gym?

"Not today," Eden began. "We need to talk."

Aidan narrowed his eyes suspiciously. "About what?"

"How about you get a snack first then get your bag ready for your dad's?"

The silence stretched between them. He'd glance at her occasionally as he put a sandwich together. She smiled whenever they made eye-contact, but he'd turn away in response. After finishing his sandwich, he disappeared into his bedroom, reappearing with a duffle bag ten minutes later.

"Are you ready, bud?" she asked.

He sat opposite her.

"I heard something this morning from Mrs. Yuan. And she reminded me that it's been awhile since I've checked your phone."

Aidan sighed, rolling his eyes. He reached inside the front of his jacket. "Is that it? I thought someone was dying. Here. There's nothing on there. Well, Mason Watson from my geography class does like using the f-bomb a lot when he texts me. But I don't use it."

She scrolled through his phone. "Have you deleted anything?"

"Oh, mom, come on." Arms crossed; Aidan's face screwed up in disgust. "It wasn't like I knew you were going to check it today."

She returned the phone, contemplating whether to bring up the topic Patty had raised with her that morning. But it was Aidan who decided where the conversation was going. "Matt's mom told you about the porn, didn't she?"

"What do you know about that?"

"He didn't download it. Some of the kids took his phone and did it. They know how to get past all sorts of firewalls. Matt's account is synched with his mom's. She knew right away. He didn't get a chance to delete it."

"Okay."

"You don't believe me, do you? I told dad about it. You can ask him."

"Dad knew? Why didn't you tell me?"

Aidan rolled his eyes. "He was the parent that was around that weekend, mom."

"You know you can talk to me about anything, right? Anything. I might get angry if I don't like what I'm hearing but it's because I care."

"Yeah, I know." Disinterest laced his voice. "Can I go now?"

Eden nodded. Emotional fatigue rather than physical lethargy kept her in the living room alone. A message popped up on her phone:

Jordan: Any more thoughts about Mesa?

She swiped at the screen to clear the message.

"No," she muttered angrily. "None."

She stared at her laptop on the coffee table, grabbed it then turned it on. Clicking on the icon for her weekly schedule, a bright, multi-colored spreadsheet appeared. Green for work; blue for pool time; yellow for gym time; pink for the non-physical part of her training like the sports psychologist, the masseuse....

But there was nothing on her spreadsheet that showed time set aside for Aidan.

CHAPTER TWELVE

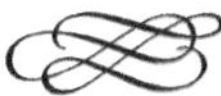

St Anne's Men's rugby team beat the higher-ranked Utah by one point.

Mano watched the matches from the stands; his absence from the sidelines made Brett more relaxed. A relaxed-Brett was better for the team.

Brett was a good coach. He knew his rugby; he liked the players; the players liked him. And even though Mano's notes still ended up in the recycling bin, most of his suggestions continued to find their way to the field. *Jackson probably memorized them.*

This first victory for St. Anne's must have been especially sweet. Mano learned—from Jackson, of course— that the head coach for Utah was Brett's nemesis from his college playing days. "Even made the Eagles before Brett," Jackson had said, grinning.

Winning must have also given Brett a reason to reassess his attitude toward Mano. On the bus to the airport, Brett found his way to the back and sat next to him.

"We needed this," Brett said. "They really took everything we talked about this week and applied it. It couldn't have happened without your input, especially the idea of having Holmes play as an openside flanker. That completely changed our attacking line. And he's only going to get better in the position."

"Just doing my job. This is a talented team."

"Yeah, and lucky. Not many people have insights from someone who played top level rugby."

"Not many will be able to say they're getting feedback from *two* people who played top level rugby."

Brett gave a little laugh. "That's a very generous statement."

"Test rugby is test rugby."

"It is," Brett said thoughtfully. "Listen, I know I haven't been…uh…friendly. But I don't trust people easily. Especially when they're forced on me. Alistair didn't ask. Just said you're going to be here. It's my bad. And I take full responsibility for any bad blood between us."

"You don't owe me an apology," Mano said. "This is your team. I'm just a visitor."

Brett held out his hand. "Well, I hope you visit often."

They were never going to be friends, but they were colleagues with the same goal. Seconds after Brett vacated his seat, Jackson took it. "I knew you two were meant to be BFFs!"

"If I see this is the newsletter, I know who to blame."

Jackson grinned and handed Mano a brown paper bag. "Thought you might like this. Just a bagel. They're not feeding us on the plane."

"Thanks. Have you eaten?"

"Yeah. But after we land, I know of an all-night diner in Oakland that is incredible. Do they have country biscuits in New Zealand? With real thick gravy?"

"I'm not sure."

"Then we're on! A little bagel isn't going to cut it for me…or do you have other late-night plans with a certain swimmer?"

"Jackson—"

"Aww. Don't go shy on me, Mano Palua! We all know the two of you have picnics under the trees on campus."

"Jackson—"

"Very romantic."

"Shut up."

"Holmes thinks we should have a team picnic one day. You've showed us how much bonding can happen when meals are shared under trees."

The snickering that came from across the aisle indicated this was far from a private conversation.

"I'll bond with you anytime, Jackson. Just say the word," Mano said.

Laughter erupted around them.

An hour later, they were on the plane headed back to the Bay Area. As soon as they reached cruising altitude, Jackson turned his head and closed his eyes.

If he were to follow his seatmate's lead, Mano wondered who would wander into his dreams.

It was the memory of Eden's touch that followed him all of Saturday. It was Eden's last smile before she drove away that occupied his mind. She had sent him a message to wish him "good luck" minutes before the match began. A simple message that he returned to whenever there was a moment that didn't need his attention.

Mano shut his eyes and tightened his hold on the armrests, preparing for the bolts of rage coupled with grief whenever he thought of Margot.

Instead, Eden's face appeared.

His body relaxed. She had welcomed his touch so eagerly and given so openly. When desire was replaced with soft laughter and gentle words, she watched him tenderly. Her touch then would warm rather than inflame. He would see her tomorrow. Lunch. With Aidan.

His eyes flew open and he swallowed hard. A shaking hand reached for the water bottle he had shoved in the seat pocket in front of him. He wasn't supposed to care for anyone again…not after loving someone else so fully.

Jackson continued to snore softly next to him. Around him,

heads were focused elsewhere. Nobody had noticed his sudden movement. There was a stillness on a night flight that contrasted with the power of a jet streaking through the dark. The ease in which tons of metal stayed up miles about the ground was no longer regarded as much of a miracle. People slept; movies were watched. The extraordinary was now ordinary.

Like his life.

He took one last look at a view of nothing before lowering the shades.

* * *

The plan was for him to wait until Eden sent him a message once they were home from Mass. He would then walk the ten minutes from his house to her apartment building. It was going to be a casual lunch. Nothing more.

Instead, he found himself standing outside the chapel about fifteen minutes before the service was over.

His heart quickened when he spotted her lone figure coming out of the chapel. Dressed in a pair of jeans and a soft white turtleneck, she suddenly stopped and raised her face to the sunshine that had broken through the morning fog. Inch by inch, she moved her face slowly, as if savoring, second-by-second, the feel of warmth.

Though she didn't see him, her being beckoned him, and he couldn't resist the lure of her peacefulness. When he was just steps away, she opened her eyes. Surprise followed by immediate joy spread through her face. "You're here!"

She didn't hesitate to go into his arms, her hands reaching to cradle his face. She must have liked what she saw as her smile widened. "You were supposed to wait for my call," she teased.

"I didn't want to wait."

"Oh."

"You're turning pink, Eden," he said softly. Her hands slipped towards his neck, pulling him down for soft lips to meet his. Any question of whether she wanted anyone to know of their relationship was quelled.

"Oh god. Mom!"

"Aidan O'Callaghan! You just had Communion."

Aidan looked over his shoulder. "Sorry, Father!"

Mano moved, relaxing his hold on Eden, who remained pleasantly pink. He schooled his face to prevent a smile. He placed a light kiss on Eden's forehead before turning to face the duo that was now within arm's reach.

Aidan glanced sheepishly at the priest before looking at Mano. "Just no tongue-kissing in front of me, please," Aidan said. "Are you done? Please be done."

"Yes, bud," Eden said grinning. "We're done."

"And we need to be introduced," said the priest, extending his hand out to Mano. "I'm Father Brian, but I know who you are. Aidan has mentioned your name several times." Father Brian looked Eden. "Eden, however, not so much."

"Isn't discretion considered a virtue, Father?" Eden asked.

"It is," Father Brian conceded. "But when you hear someone's name so often, discretion can be a hindrance. Anyway, it's good to put a face to a name. Are you a church-goer, Mano? No? Come in for the music then. The acoustics in the chapel are very good!"

"I may. Thank you for the invitation, Father," Mano said.

A small grimace crossed Father Brian's face before it was replaced by a wide smile. He waved at a fast-approaching couple. "I better get going. Eula is headed straight to me, which only means she didn't like my homily today. Have a blessed day, you three."

They began to leave the steps of the church when Aidan pulled on Eden's arm. "Did you tell him? About granddad and Pop coming over too?"

"No," she said as Mano draped his arm casually over Eden's shoulders.

"It's my fault," Aidan explained. "I told grandad you were

coming, and he wants to meet you. You don't have to stay when they get here, though mom did make curry. It's really good. Even Matthew likes this one."

"I thought you said it was just going to be hot dogs," Mano said.

"It was and still is. But my dad hates hotdogs, so you know… it's hot dogs and curry for lunch."

"Why not?" Mano said.

"Why not!" Her laugh prompted his own smile and he pulled her closer into his body. Kissing her on the temple, Mano inhaled deeply, contentment filling his body with the now familiar scent that was just hers.

There were no awkward introductions at lunch. Robert Pak basically launched himself into Mano's line of sight and cornered him. Donald barely got in a handshake before Robert pulled out his phone and played various videos of matches Mano hadn't seen in years.

"This one was incredible! How did you see the gap there? There were three Pumas in front of you!"

Mano glanced over Robert's shoulder into the small screen. "Well, that was ten years ago…"

Robert pulled his phone back to study the video. "Now, I know Argentina isn't New Zealand, but there were still three of them! Wait, I definitely want your opinion about this one! 2014 in Ellis Park."

Mano crossed his arms. "The one we lost?"

Robert Pak paused then met Mano's gaze through the top of his glasses. "Uh…nevermind."

Eden laughed. He glanced over his shoulder to see amusement dancing in her eyes; they exchanged smiles. A little corner of his heart mended.

Aidan and Robert controlled the conversation over lunch: school; rugby; holiday plans; rugby. Curry, hot dogs, potato salad, and rice crowded the table. These odd combinations were familiar. Such a mix of interests, cultures, and cuisines dictated the family gatherings he grew up with. Missing were the familiar faces of his childhood, but present were the family ties being strengthened between Eden, her fathers, and her son.

Soon enough, dishes were cleared so that the salt and pepper shakers, condiment bottles, and glasses could become substitutes for props, second-rows, flankers, fly-halves, locks, hookers….

Aidan stared at the bottle of relish. "And it's the same name for that position in the women's team, Mano?"

"Which one? Hooker? Yes."

Aidan pointed to Donald's wine glass. "And there's no other name for a 'Number 8'?"

"No," Mano said.

Donald looked at Eden. "I think Aidan's getting serious about this. I'm married to a rugby fan. I wish you well."

Eden tilted her head. "Ah, but it's different raising one, Pop. You can feed the passion without needing to share it. Considering you hate the water, you did a pretty good job raising a swimmer. Parental love is different."

"Not sure if I'd agree with that," Donald said. "Your losses were my losses."

She reached to cover his hand on the table. "I know."

Eden's phone buzzed. She frowned when she read the ID. "Excuse me, I have to take this. Won't be long." She walked toward her bedroom quickly.

The two dads exchange a look that Aidan picked up on. "It's probably Tommy."

Donald glanced at Robert before looking back at Aidan. "Her coach?"

Aidan nodded. "It's because she won't commit to Mesa."

Mano crossed his arms. "I'm missing something."

Donald looked at Mano. "Tommy doesn't call unless it's serious. He's the type of coach that prefers to tell you things in-person. A bit old fashion but it's respectful. I've always liked him. Hands-on."

"Mom's worried about the costs of going to Mesa," Aidan chimed in.

The three adults turned to the youngest member there.

"Aidan Pak O'Callaghan, this better be based on fact and not something you're making up," Donald said.

"Fact," Aidan said confidently. "She left her laptop open last week. I saw the spreadsheet she was working on. The Mesa trip's going to cost her a few thousand dollars. Tommy wants her to get there three days early, and to fly in the masseuse she's been using. That's almost a whole week of hotel costs for somebody extra. She'd have to take time off from work. And she's using up her savings because she's working part-time this semester. But she'll do it. I know she will. She's that close."

"Wait. When did she switch to part-time?" Donald asked.

Robert stared at Donald. "You've been a swim-dad for decades. Do you think she was going to make qualifying times for Nationals working forty hours a week?"

"Robert, we could lend her the money," Donald said. "She deserves one more shot."

Robert shook his head, shoving his hands into the front pockets of his jeans. "I've already suggested it. She knows what the costs for Grandma Mattie's caregiver are. She helped you find the lady."

"Am I right to assume Eden doesn't like to ask for help? That she just likes to give it" Mano asked slowly.

"Yup." "Yes." "Sounds right."

"Been like that since she was a teenager," Robert said. "When she became pregnant, Don and I had to call in the troops to make her realize she needed to move back in with us."

"The troops?" Mano asked.

"My mother and my sister," Donald replied. "They had her packing in ten minutes."

The bedroom door opened, and they all stared at her expectantly when she reappeared in front of them.

She scanned their faces one by one. "What?"

"What's going on Eden?" Donald's tone was clear he wasn't interested in half-a-story.

"Just letting him know I'm quitting the team," Eden said as she sat down at the table again. "No biggie. He just called to make sure I had thought it through. Very nice of him. Coffee, anyone?"

Aidan's reaction to Eden's news kept Mano's attention. A wave of indecision and vulnerability washed over a face he was used to seeing as proud, occasionally bordering on defiant. Aidan swallowed as a tide of red rose up the teenager's neck.

"What do you mean you're quitting the team, mom? How about Mesa?" Aidan asked, his voice cracking slightly, as if trying to gain control of his emotions. "You're still going, right? It's another chance to make Nationals. You don't have to train with the Berkeley club. You could still train with the Beavers."

Eden reached for Aidan's hand but he stood up abruptly, the dining chair almost toppling at his abrupt action. She covered her response to the rejection quickly, a hand reaching for an earlobe. "Going to Mesa wasn't part of my plan, Aidan. My goal was to qualify at San Luis Obispo."

"You need to go," Aidan insisted. "You need to keep trying. You hurt your foot. And it was a short course. Dad said your turns suck."

"Aidan, listen. I gave it a shot. I was close but not fast enough. I'm proud of my time, but I need to move on. I'll still keep swimming at the Masters level. Besides, I want to spend more time with you."

"No, you don't!"

"Aidan—"

"I won't be the reason why you didn't make your dreams come true. Not again! You need to do this!"

Stunned silence was broken by the sound of a slamming door.

Mano wanted to reach for her, to offer the comfort of his

arms, her pained face calling for him to protect her. But Robert was there for his daughter before Mano could act.

"Let me talk to him…." Robert began.

Eden shook her head. "No, this one is on me." She kissed Robert on the cheek. "If you and Pop need to go before I'm done talking with him, please go. I'll call you tonight."

"Eden, Aidan does raise some good points." Donald said. "Mesa is still within your reach. We're here for you in any way."

Eden squeezed Donald's hand. "As you've always been. I've got this, Pop. I do. I know what I'm doing."

Then she turned to Mano. The questions in her eyes glued him to the spot. He spoke quickly, wanting to extinguish any doubt she could have. "I'll stay until you come out. No worries."

* * *

Eden knocked gently on the door before turning the knob.

Aidan sat at his desk. He looked up briefly before returning to his drawing, his pencil moving aggressively on the paper. Eden sat on the floor behind him, leaning against his bed. She touched her earlobe before pushing her fingers through the carpet. She didn't want to be there; she didn't want to have this conversation with her son. When did it become so hard to share a dream with people?

"Aidan—"

"You're quitting."

"No —"

"Bullshit, mom."

"Hey! Watch your language, young man!"

"You're stopping because you didn't make your times. Sounds like quitting to me." His back was still to her. The scraping sound of pencil on paper filled time before she could answer as the adult she was supposed to be.

She took a deep breath. "Bud, you can't control the outcome of everything you do. I gave it as much as I could. It's okay. But I need to go back to work fulltime; I want to spend more time with you, with Granddad and Pop. And you know Grandma Mattie is getting older. She may be here with us for very long."

Aidan glanced over his shoulder. "So, in ten years, it'll be everyone else's fault you didn't make Nationals."

"No! Of course not. Just like you're not the reason why I didn't make it to Nationals thirteen years ago."

Aidan threw his pencil on his desk and rested both his hands on the back his head. "Dad said everything was perfect for him to make the Summer Games. He had the right conditions, the right coach, and the right swimmers to compete against. Don't you have that now? To make Nationals?"

"I don't need to swim Nationals to make my life perfect. Things are pretty good."

Aidan shrugged. "Whatever, mom. If your goal is to almost-make-it, I guess you achieved it. Is that it? Want to check my phone again?"

Eden closed her eyes and pursed her lips. At the door, she pushed back against the desire to grab her son and hold him tight. If he pulled away, she may not be able to keep a calm front. "Say goodnight to your grandparents and Mano, please," Eden whispered. "Manners, Aidan."

Neither of her fathers had left, bringing the level of cleanliness in the house up a notch while they waited for her. Lemon scent lingered; her pots shined. Even the toaster gleamed. Mano was on the balcony, a phone to his ear. She put her arm around Robert, his quick but reassuring touch said enough. Mano's low laugh caught her attention; its tone somehow an emotional anesthetic to the angst that simmered inside. Through the glass doors, their eyes met. A soft smile rested on his lips as he leaned against the metal railing.

He continued to watch her as she made her way to him.

"I know, mate," Mano said. "I miss you too. Maybe, mate. No, Los Angeles isn't that far away. Of course I want to see you. Yes, I want to see Jayne too. Fred—"

As if needing to concentrate, he turned around as a voice from far away kept his attention. "Yes, mate. Let me talk to your dad one more time. Will you get him? Bye, mate." Mano sighed. "I love you, too, Fred."

She smiled at the confession, no longer able to resist touching him again. Eden rested against his back, soaking up his strength then wrapped her arms around his waist. His free hand covered both her hands, his warmth a welcomed contrast to the cooling air.

"Con? That wasn't fair play, mate. No, Los Angeles isn't far...I'll think about it...No, there's no need for all of you to come up to visit me. Don't believe you, mate, I don't want to talk to Cat. No, don't have Liana call me...The contract is over in December."

She held him tighter at those words, an instant and instinctive response at the idea of him leaving her. It was inevitable, of course. They never talked about the future. He didn't want to, and she knew that when she first kissed him.

There was an end date to his time here. With her. She swallowed the hope that he'd want to stay. Others loved him in New Zealand. And he loved them, including an anonymous figure who still held a large part of his heart.

She knew she could love him. It'd be easy to fall in love with him.

But she wasn't there yet.

And he didn't love her.

Yet.

She shook her head, rubbing her face into his back, willing wishful thoughts to go away.

"We'll talk more later. I have to go," Mano spoke into the phone.

His large body heaved as he slid his phone into the front pocket of his hoodie. He turned and she met him halfway, her body molding into his as they embraced. "You all right?" he asked.

"Everything okay?" she asked back.

"Yes, but I want to know if you're okay."

She nodded. "Teenagers suck."

"He's a good kid."

"He's nice to you."

"He has to be."

She laughed softly and pulled him closer, his breath warming her neck. She would have stayed there longer if Aidan's words didn't continue to dance in her head.

"He thinks I'm a quitter," Eden said, pulling away slightly. She patted his chest with both her hands and searched his eyes for assurances. "Why can't he understand that some goals will never be reached?"

But he wasn't able mask his thoughts quickly enough. She stepped back suddenly, as if to avoid his touch. "You think I'm a quitter," she said loudly.

He pushed his hands into the pockets, his dark eyes meeting hers. "No."

She frowned. "You think Aidan's right, that I should try for Mesa."

He stood straighter, his eyes dark and unapologetic. "Yes."

She blinked and without another word, turned and reentered her apartment.

* * *

Eden walking way without looking back brought Mano to the minute – the second – he heard Margot's voice on the recording. He didn't have a say in his ex-fiancée's decision to end their relationship. His opinion wasn't sought. The anger that came after the despair wanted the conversation, wanted the argument, wanted the opportunity to fight for the life they had planned. He was mentally conditioned to battle, to overcome obstacles, to work through pain. He was trained never to give up until the final whistle blew.

Except, in love, there was no opponent to fight.

Love?

He shook his head, pushing the thought as far away as possible. Seconds that seemed like minutes passed. He fought for his breath, got it back, and the heavy pounding in his head eased. Three faces stared expectantly.

Donald nodded toward Eden's door.

But it was the front door that beckoned, teasing him with the safety of retreat, of returning to the sanctuary of being alone. Easier not to get involved. He wasn't good at the friendship-thing; he failed at the relationship-thing. It'd be smarter to walk through the door, down the stairs and head home. He could handle the silence waiting for him in the little house at the end of a cul-de-sac.

Yet, whatever awaited behind Eden's closed door, he knew he couldn't leave until they spoke. No apologies; just an explanation. She deserved that.

He prepared himself for a confrontation, for her anger. He knocked softly. "Eden?"

The door opened immediately. Flashing eyes, crossed arms, and a raised chin greeted him. "What?"

He blinked, suddenly muted at her beauty. She rolled her eyes and slammed the door.

"Eden! Please, open the door."

"No!"

"We need to talk."

"Talk."

"Through the door?"

"Yes. You laughing at me doesn't win any points, Mano."

"I didn't laugh."

"You smiled."

"I didn't."

She opened the door again. "You're still smiling!"

The apartment shuddered at the second slam. Throat clearing from down the hallway drew Mano's attention. Robert gestured for him to open the door. Mano shook his head. Donald appeared and pulled his husband away and gave Mano an apologetic glance.

Mano cracked his neck and loosened his shoulders before knocking on the door. "Eden? Please. I didn't realize I was smiling."

The door flung open again. "You're not good at this boyfriend thing, you know! One: if you're going to disagree with your girlfriend, do it nicely. Two: don't laugh at her when she's angry at you. Is that why you're here alone and not with what's-her-name?"

She rushed her hand to her mouth, horror immediately replacing anger. "Oh shit! I didn't say that, did I? Oh, god, Mano. That was terrible. That was totally uncalled for. I'm just mad at… I don't know…anyone! Everyone! And you're here, right now, getting the worst of me. I'm so, so sorry!"

Eden's words should have elicited a response reflective of his loss. It had before. He was ready to bear down on feelings before they overwhelmed his ability to think rationally.

But the expected anger didn't cut through him.

Instead, it was Eden's fear and sorrow he reacted to. Her eyes had begun to well up; her hands continued to cover her mouth as if no longer trusting herself to speak. "Walk with me," he said. "We should talk. In private."

She stared at his outstretched hand, confusion crossing her face. When she reached for it, he exhaled as relief flooded his senses.

"Let me grab a sweatshirt," she said, weakly, her face pink.

Intuitively, hand-in-hand, they walked towards the chapel. She may decide he wasn't worth the effort after hearing his story – who wants to stay with a broken man? – but she deserved to hear the whole truth about him. Otherwise his advice about something as basic as whether she should continue swimming or not didn't hold value. It had to be the truth about everything.

They stopped in front of a bench strategically placed between two river birches. A quick brush sent a scattering of golden tear-drop leaves to the ground, revealing a plaque dedicated to an "Alison Yasmin".

"I'm sorry," she said. "That was mean and stupid and spiteful and—"

"And true," Mano admitted.

Eden shook her head vigorously. "No. Definitely not true about you. You're one of the good guys, remember?"

Mano scrunched up his nose and stared ahead. "I'm not perfect."

"Who said you were perfect? I just said you're a good guy. No one's perfect."

"There was a time when I was pretty famous in New Zealand. I've been on a few of those stupid 'Eligible Bachelors' lists. A lot of people thought I was the 'perfect guy.' But I don't think I was a very good boyfriend. Always on the road. Not there for birthdays, for family. I couldn't have been a good fiancé, either." He turned to look at her. "Or she wouldn't have left, right?"

Eden winced. "I don't know why your fiancée left you, Mano. All I know is that you have a good heart."

He looked away. "I wish I could promise you something."

"Like what?"

"A future?"

This time, she turned away. Adjusting her body, she crossed her legs as she pulled on the collar of her sweatshirt. "I grew up knowing that the people who loved me most weren't there for me. I never knew my parents, Mano. But they loved me. I know they did. It wasn't their choice to die. They weren't even doing anything stupid. They were driving home from work. An accident happened. Guess what? I'm okay. I have a good life. I've been loved, and I can love." She gave him a sideways glance. "Don't get me wrong. I like you. A lot. If what we have ends tomorrow, I'll be sad. I may cry. And I would probably be upset at you for a little while. But I'll be okay."

He reached for her hand; a dry throat prevented an immediate response.

He wanted to say something, to thank her for her patience, for not wanting to know why he couldn't promise more than one day at a time. Instead, he stared at their clasped hands and marveled at the fairness of her skin to the darkness of his: different but complimentary.

"My friends will be in Los Angeles at the end of the month and want me to join them in L.A. for Thanksgiving." Mano paused and searched for the right words. She needed to know. "They're afraid for me."

"Afraid *for* you? What do you mean? Why?"

"I...struggle."

She didn't move. Fear enveloped him. He prepared himself for her retreat. Darkness threatened to appear, from within, from a place void of light. He blew out of his mouth repeatedly. Then she squeezed his hand.

"Go on," she whispered.

She was still there. Next to him. Encouraging.

"I talk to a doctor once a month," he began. "Dr. Spurgeon. He's in New Zealand. Good bloke. Works with a lot of athletes. You know, teaching us how to deal with the stresses of success and failure. I started private sessions with him after Margot – the woman I wanted to marry – left. She was my whole world. Thought I was going to lose her to cancer but she survived that hell. What I wasn't ready for was her not wanting me in her future."

"She said that?"

Mano shrugged. "She didn't say much. She just left. Basically told me to move on."

His voice sounded hollow even to his own ears. *But not angry.* No, not angry. That was a first. Her hand continued to hold his.

"And that's why you're here? In California? To move on?" she asked.

A short laugh escaped him. "Sort of." He looked towards the curved dome of the chapel; stained glass glowed, seemingly, from a single light source inside. "The idea was just to get away. And here, no one would be interested in who I was or who I am. To start fresh, Spurgeon said, I needed to reclaim my privacy. Too many eyes on me back home. That was the price of success."

"You seem to be doing okay. I mean, aren't you?"

He shifted slightly. "Yes."

"The nightmares?"

"Spurgeon says there's no schedule to heal from loss. Day to day."

She squeezed his hand again. "No, there's none. Grief comes in stages. To this day, sometimes out of the blue, my dad calls me to talk about my biological father, his brother. They were really close." Eden turned to Mano, a large smile on her face. "Thanksgiving in Los Angeles? Why is that such a bad idea?"

"It'd be good to see them. Connor's my best friend; Mitch would do – and has done – anything for me. They're my rugby brothers, brothers by choice. But I don't want them to be worried about me anymore."

"I don't think you can stop the people who care about you from doing that."

Mano pursed his lips. "I know, but I don't like it." He paused. "They want to meet you. They think you're good for me."

"You told them about me?"

He elbowed her gently. "Yes. And Aidan. And Mrs. Henderson. She's who they really want to meet!"

Her laugh surprised him as was her pulling him into her arms. He reached around her waist automatically, and when Eden's lips touched his, he responded immediately. The warmth she emanated brought him further away from the edge of sadness he almost fell in. He inhaled her scent and savored the taste of her lips. Mano started to believe that maybe—just maybe —he was entitled to a moment of perfection.

CHAPTER THIRTEEN

Eden had told herself she would sleep in. There was no longer a reason to keep to the crazy schedule of an early morning workout. She'd still swim, she argued to herself. Just at a more acceptable time. Like normal people. Except her body was still in the habit of waking up before her alarm went off.

She turned in her bed and reached for the extra pillow next to her, scrunching her nose slightly at the cool sheets. She would have preferred a warm body next to her last night. A specific body, but Mano declined her invitation to stay over. Ten years ago, she would have taken that as an ultimate rejection, that he was no longer interested. A warm bed with an eager partner? What healthy man would turn that down?

But Mano did, and rejection was the last thing she felt when he kissed her goodnight. Instead, his last words to her before leaving was an apology for hurting her with his answer. That wasn't his intention, he said. And with those simple words, she knew she was a little closer to falling in love with him.

Eden looked at the clock again and groaned.

The college pool would be open… *No! Sleep in! You're done!*

Fifteen minutes later, she flung the covers and changed.

Biting a banana quickly, she scribbled a quick note to Aidan. When she pushed through the doors to the swimming pool, she stopped and took in the scene. The two end lanes were already occupied, a lone swimmer in each of them. The sound of their clean strokes barely discernible over the continuous hum of the invisible air filter.

Any questions about whether she made the right decision to quit the Berkeley club disappeared. This was right. Swimming here, as a Beaver, was right. She wasn't from the world of "all-or-nothing anymore. Her life was bigger than that.

With no swim plan to follow, she luxuriated in the first streamline off the wall, consciously breaking away from the now automatic movements of the past months' schedules. She took a deeper breath than necessary as she broke through the water, then reached further and kicked harder than she was supposed to.

No rhythm; no plan. *Just follow the black line.*

She expected to see the face waiting for her in the next lane when she took a break.

"Welcome back," Linda Wellens said.

"Good to be back." Eden raised her chin. "You know already? It just happened last night. Who told you? Tommy or Jordan?"

"Tommy. Want to talk about it?"

"No."

Linda nodded then—more out of habit than functionality—pushed hair strands up her swim cap before disappearing under water.

An hour later, Eden returned home to see the scribbling next to her earlier note to Aidan:

Matt and I are having extra practice with Mano. Aidan

She smiled then frowned. When it was time for Mano to leave, it wouldn't be only her heart that would be broken.

Eden sighed.

If only the heart would listen to the brain more often. But all the best things in her life had come from listening to her feelings, and she wasn't going to change that philosophy just because loving Mano could be hard.

Nope.

Loving him, she decided, was going to be the easiest part of this whole relationship.

She reached for her phone and messaged Aidan:

Mom: Let me know when you're at school. Have a good day, bud. Love you.

* * *

Mano looked at his watch again, uneasiness pooling at the pit of the stomach. Nine minutes and twenty seconds.

Even if they had taken a break, they should have been back from the sprint. He silently cursed himself for not running with the boys. But it was supposed to be an exercise in explosive speed, just between the two of them. To the aged bench before the trail curve.

Mano walked back to his porch. Patty usually glanced out of the window every five minutes while they practiced. Used to annoy him, but now that he'd had spent more time with his neighbors, he knew her presence was more to watch Matthew than him.

He glanced at his watch again then looked around. Eerily quiet. Even the squirrels were absent from the trees. Instincts propelled his walk toward the trail. Then something in his gut made in run.

They should have been back by now.

He turned the corner and slowed his pace. He heard yells in the creek that paralleled the trail part of the ways and moved toward the embankment. He spotted backpacks thrown at the start of a track that would lead down to the creek. A couple of bikes laid flat.

He peered down; his heart stopped.

Matthew laid face down on large flat section of rock, a large boy on top of him. Matthew's face grimaced in pain as his captor twisted Matthew's arm into his back.

"You think playing rugby's going to stop us? You little yellow-skinned…You people come here and take our jobs! Get back on the boat you came from!"

"I was born here! I'm an American, just like you!" Matthew cried out.

"Let him go!" Aidan screamed; his arms held behind him by two other boys. Veins strained in his neck, in his face. He pulled and pushed, desperate to break free. "Matt!"

Anger flashed through Mano's body. He ran down the steep hill; his only goal was to get to Matthew and Aidan.

He must have yelled, as the boy holding down Matthew looked up in his direction, fear erasing the anger from his face. "Let's get out of here! Run! Run! Go!"

Now released, Aidan rushed to Mathew's side, pulling his friend close to him. By the time Mano reached them, the three attackers had nimbly climbed up the other side of the embankment. They obviously knew the terrain, and their voices were less desperate when they recognized they weren't being followed.

Mano knelt next to Aidan. "Aidan? It's me. Let me help."

But Aidan was focused only on the sobbing boy in his arm. Tears rolled down Aidan's flushed face as he rocked his friend. Mano gritted his teeth when he saw the scratches on Aidan's neck and face. There were going to be bruises.

Whatever pain Aidan felt didn't seem to register. Instead, his focus was only on Matthew. Aidan rocked this friend back and forth, Matthew's face hidden in Aidan's chest. "I'm sorry, Matt. I'm sorry, Matt. I'm sorry. I should have done more…it's my fault. I promised you I'd protect you. I'm sorry…I'm sorry."

Matthew's quiet cries could barely be heard above the moving water. Looking up, it'd be easy not to be spotted. They were less than a few meters from a busy footpath, but in the age of earbuds and headphones, would anyone have looked over the bushes?

Mano stayed by Aidan's side. "Matthew? Mate? It's Mano. I want to check if you're okay. Could you look at me, please?"

Matthew's arm grew tighter around Aidan.

"Mate, I have to call your mom—"

"No!" Matthew pushed away from Aidan, scrambling backward before being stopped by the side of another large boulder. "No! She'll be so angry! Don't! I don't want her to know!"

Mano held up his hand. "Okay…okay. No worries. But can I just please check you? I'll touch you gently. Just to see if you're hurt."

Matthew looked at Aidan who nodded. "We trust him, remember?" Aidan held out his hand. "I trust him."

Mano stepped forward while holding his hands up. Matthew met Mano's eyes briefly then nodded. Mano released his breath. "Matthew, mate? I'm going to first check your face and neck. If you don't like what I'm doing, or if it hurts, let me know. I'll stop. I *will* listen to you. You're in charge here, yeah?"

Careful to let Matthew know when he was touching him at every point, Mano gently patted along Matthew's face, watching to see if the latter reacted to his touch. Then he'd gingerly squeeze Matthew's arms and legs. But Matthew didn't react or say anything. He just sat there, his eyes now flat and distant. *He's going into shock.*

"Aidan, we have to take him home," Mano said. "Then we'll call mum, yeah?"

Aidan bit on his lower lip and nodded. Mano squeezed Aidan's shoulder, wishing he could erase the pain in eyes that trusted him. He inhaled deeply, forcing himself to focus on what he could do then turned to Matthew. "Mate? I'm going to carry you. You all right with that? On a count of three."

Relief spread through Mano at Matthew's slight nod but the latter's body remained limp in his arms. He made quick work of climbing up the steep hill. He glanced over to make sure Aidan was close, extending his arm to pull the latter up the final stretch as the ground gave way slightly to Mano's weight. Then he ran, one arm holding Matthew close, the other urging Aidan along as fear rather than conscious effort propelled him toward Patty's.

Patty opened the door before they actually reached it, as if she had been expecting their arrival. The horror in her face stunned Mano momentarily. She swallowed the cry that was half voiced but her training as a physician kicked in. She assessed the situation quickly and directed Mano to the living room sofa to lay Matthew down. Seconds later, she appeared next to him with an icepack and a first aid kit. "What happened?"

No emotion passed her face as she heard Mano's brief account of what he had witnessed, her hands moving deftly as she checked her son. Questions posed to Matthew were unanswered. But if she were alarmed, Mano didn't see it. She was a doctor—not the mother—at this moment. At one point, Matthew turned his head away, hiding deeper into the sofa. Silent tears ran down his cheeks. Aidan pushed past Mano and Patty and reached for his friend's hand.

"I'm sorry, Matthew. I'm sorry. I wish I had been stronger."

Patty gently covered the boys' hands with her own, and kissed Aidan on his head. "I know Matthew's very, very lucky you're his friend, Aidan. That won't change after today." She looked at Aidan. "I want to check you over. Will you be okay with that? I'm sure it's something your mom would want me to do."

As Patty examined Aidan, Mano stepped into the hallway

and reached for his phone. His hand paused briefly over Eden's name, regretting that it fell on him to tell her that her son had been in danger. He inhaled deeply then pressed the "CALL" button.

* * *

He's fine; he's fine. Mano said he's fine.

She should have driven over but her instincts were to run the short distance from home to Patty's. She'd be faster this way. No red lights. No one to stop her movement. She was fast. She could be faster. Her son was hurt…

He's fine; he's fine.

Mano waited at Patty's front door. His figure was unfamiliar in the environment she knew so well. He reached out for her hand and repeated the words she had been saying.

"He's doing all right, Eden. Patty's checked him. Just a couple of scratches."

She bit on her lips as she moved determinedly to the living room. She needed to see Aidan, to hold him. When he was finally in her arms, fear of what could have been overwhelmed her. Trembling, she rubbed Aidan's back, needing the reassurance that he was really there, that he was standing in front of her, that he was in one piece. No relief came until then.

In the back of her mind, she recognized that Aidan allowed her that moment. There was no struggle to break free, just a silent, tight, strong embrace that said more than words ever could.

When her shaking became manageable, she looked over to her friend. Patty hadn't moved since her arrival, her figure seemed smaller as she stayed still and focused on Matthew. Aidan's wide eyes met hers. "He hasn't said a word, mom," Aidan whispered. "He won't even look at Mrs. Yuan. The police are coming. I'm going to have to talk to them, won't I?"

"Let's take a minute here, bud. Are you okay?"

Her insides tightened as Aidan's eyes welled up. He nodded. "I'm fine."

"You sure? Want to tell me what happened?"

Feigned detachment kept the cries of horror from leaving her lips. How could kids do that to other kids? They were all babies. She wanted to ask why this was the first time she was learning about the bullying, but she didn't know if her voice would remain calm when everything inside was burning and sharp. Anger, fear, disappointment, resentment...the emotions were tightly interwoven. She wasn't sure why they were there. She knew she had to be grateful. Her son escaped being hurt. But rage simmered inside. "I'm going to call your dad now, okay?"

"No, it's okay. I don't want you to bother him. He's at the studios right now. I'm fine."

"Aidan, you're not, nor have ever been, a bother. You are important. He needs to be here. He will *want* to be here."

But it was Charles Yuan who arrived next. Usually the quieter parent who would defer to Patty's "rulings" in the house, Eden finally understood why he was considered one of the most respected prosecutors in the County. He took control of the situation, monitoring the strangers that were suddenly coming and going. Standing guard over his wife and son, Charles' quiet presence was unexpectedly calming.

When Brandon arrived, he pushed through a police officer whose arms only fell back at Charles' nod. Wild and angry eyes caused Eden to rear back instinctively. Relief flooded his face only when Aidan was in his arms. A woman appeared out of nowhere, flashed her ID at Charles who pointed to Mano. Mano squeezed Eden's elbow before leaving her side. Wrapping her arms around herself, she moved to the corner of the room.

The detective that Mano had been talking to introduced herself to Brandon and asked if Aidan was able to speak to her. After glancing at his father, Aidan nodded. They began to move away before Brandon stopped and surveyed the room, his gaze resting on her face. "Eden, come on. You should be here."

"Aidan, do you want me there?" Eden asked.

Aidan shook his head. "If dad's going to be there, I'm going to be fine."

Eden swallowed hard, reminding herself that her heart wasn't going to break into pieces. Charles smiled kindly at her before directing the detective, Aidan and Brandon to his study. The sound of the door shutting seemed to silence everything around her.

Anger threatened to crack her shield of numbness. She had to do something; her next words were aimed at no one in particular. "I'll boil some water and get the coffee maker going."

A weak excuse but it allowed her escape. None of this was normal; Patty was usually in charge; the boys were never quiet; police shouldn't be in her friend's living room.

Trembling hands managed to get the electric kettle going and avoid making a mess as she ground fresh beans, then added them to the coffee maker. She knew Mano was in the kitchen before his strong arms wrapped around her waist, pulling her close. She leaned against his body easily, wanting to disappear into his strength.

"He's fine, Eden." His voice soft against her ear.

"Yes. For now. Those kids still go to school with them!"

"Patty and Charles will be on top of this. You and Brandon will also make sure Aidan's all right. Look, you can't fight enemies you didn't know existed. Until an hour ago, none of us knew about these boys, these bullies. Now we do."

She walked out of Mano's hold, braced herself against the countertop and hung her head. "But why? Why didn't we know earlier? I was worried about drugs, about porn..." She turned around and pointed in the direction of the living room. "...of him being the one getting in trouble. I never once thought he could be a victim."

"You heard him. They targeted Matthew. Aidan was trying to protect his friend. That's why they wanted to play rugby."

Eden blinked. "What?"

Mano crossed his arms. "It was Matthew's idea that if they both got on the rugby team, they'd be safe. Because rugby players stick together."

Eden raised her fingers to her lips, the tears no longer containable. "I thought I had a good relationship with my son. I don't understand why Aidan anything. I just don't get it. Why didn't he talk to me?"

Mano pulled Eden into his arms again, gently molding her head into the crook of his neck. He didn't give an answer; he wouldn't give her false pretenses. Whether she liked it or not, she had to accept that her child didn't want her to know parts of his life. He kept this a secret by choice.

When they returned to the living room, Brandon and Charles were in quiet conversation with the detective. Matthew was nowhere to be found. Patty was by the window. She took Eden's offer of the mug of tea, her blank stare unchanged as she sipped the hot liquid.

Neither woman turned when the police announced they were leaving. Eden watched Charles and Brandon as they followed the detective to her squad car. The two fathers continued to talk on the street after the cars left. Brandon's wild gesticulations only ceased when Charles placed his hands on Brandon's shoulders.

"You know," Patty began, her face still toward the street. "This is my fault. I wanted the suburban life. If we had stayed in the city, like Charles wanted, Matthew would have been surrounded by a lot more Asian kids. But I wanted the good schools; I wanted trees and a garden and hills and…swim club and soccer…."

Eden blinked away tears when Patty's voice broke, unable to find words that could offer comfort. Maybe there weren't any. Seconds later, Patty left her side, and Eden remained frozen to her spot. Any desire to say something or to follow her friend evaporated at the final look Patty gave her. "Thanks for the tea,

Eden. I hope Aidan's okay. We will always welcome him here, but I'm keeping Matthew home for the time being."

Patty didn't wait for a response, and suddenly Eden found herself alone in a room that was void of the energy and warmth she had always associated with it.

Brandon drove them home. She sat in the back, half listening to Aidan arguing with his dad about whether he should skip school the next day.

"I've a test to make up, dad."

"Your safety is an issue, Aidan. You're not going."

"I want to go. I'm not scared of seeing those guys."

"Look, Mr. Yuan and I want to talk to the principal first."

"Isn't the deal that mom is in charge of the stuff that happens here? You're in charge of what goes on in the city."

Brandon met Eden's eyes in the mirror. She cleared her throat. "Stay home tomorrow. Your dad's right. Your principal needs to know what happened today first. Then we need to know if it's a safe place for you."

"It's just a couple of kids! I'm not afraid!"

"Aidan, you're not going to school tomorrow."

Aidan slumped deeper into the front seat. "And you wonder why I don't say anything to you both? No one listens to me," he muttered.

Food would be the last thing on anyone's minds, but as soon as they entered her apartment, Eden headed straight to the kitchen. She pulled out the bottle of juice and a jug of water, grimacing at the loud slam of Aidan's bedroom door. A few second later, Brandon joined her. He grabbed the sliced bread and reached for sandwich meats while she began slicing apples.

"Thanks," she said.

But no words of kindness or courtesy were returned. The absence of civility at a time when she had hoped for support ignited her temper.

Whispered words of anger flew between them. She took

Brandon's criticisms and flung a few of her own. Their voices grew loud until one of them would glance at Aidan's room, prompting their argument to resume with more controlled tones. Logic disappeared; emotions reigned.

* * *

The screen of Mano's phone remained blank.

Are you okay? Is Aidan okay?

But he didn't type the words into his phone. *She'll call if she needs you. She said she would.*

Even when it was crazy, if they were all together, he could understand what he could do. He could see they were fine. He could protect them.

His notebook remained blank. Unusual. He was usually meticulous at notetaking during these meetings. Xs and Os dotted the white board in front of him. On another board, columns of paper hung loosely, numbers telling a story of the last few weeks. Spoken words washed over him.

Brett knew what had happened this morning. Only the basic facts just in case…though now that Brandon was there, it wasn't really his place to be there for them.

He reached for his bottle of water. Hand held steady. *Good.* A question about the Men's next opponents was thrown at him. His answer seemed appropriate. Nods around the table. Then the screen on his phone lighted up, and his attempt at a normal day ended:

Aidan: I need to talk to you.

Mano held his phone up to Brett, who nodded briefly. Outside, he prepared himself to hear anything then pressed Aidan's number. "Hey, mate. You all right?"

"Yeah," Aidan whispered. "But Dad's still here. He's so

angry. They're fighting. I haven't heard them argue like this ever. It's my fault, Mano. Everything's my fault."

"Mate, calm down. It's not your fault. Your parents are adults. They're just scared, and sometimes it sounds like they're angry."

"Dad wants me to go home with him tonight."

"You all right with that?"

"Yeah, but I don't want mom alone. Could you—"

"I'll be there for her, if she needs me."

"Promise?"

"Yeah, mate. I promise."

"Thanks."

As soon as he ended the call, heaviness pressed into his chest. But the walls of the hallway started closing in; he fought for air; suppressed the need to yell out; rejected the desire to crumble. Shaking his head to clear his mind, he scrambled towards the light shining through the glass panels of the nearby doors. Once outside, he sank to the stairs, echoes of his own voice loud in his head, the memories came rushing back.

I'll be there for her…I promise.

The last time he had uttered those exact words were to Antoinette and Michael. He had fulfilled his promise to them. He knew there was nothing to feel guilty about. But the weight in his heart didn't lift with that knowledge.

The quadrangle in front of him began to fill as students transitioned between classes. Activity broke his reverie. He stood up. The meeting was still going on; he could still catch the tail end of it. Do his job. But his feet took him to the white domed building he had studiously avoided entering.

The heavy wooden door swung open with ease. He raised his eyes to the rose window, its colors muted now that the afternoon sun was shining through the stained-glass triptych behind him. Yellows, blues, oranges beckoned him to move forward, down the aisle. He resisted, his heart already in his throat.

The doors opened suddenly behind him, and he instinctively jumped to the side, pressing his body against the wall.

A young woman walked steadily towards the pulpit before genuflecting, sliding into the first row. He should leave. He didn't belong here. This wasn't his church. He turned to escape but heard voices in the narthex.

In the shadows, Mano followed the wall, his hand fingering the cool stone wall. His hand floated past the statute of St. Francis whose peaceful countenance was still brightly colored in the dimmed light of the enclave that housed him. A potted plant lay at the statue's feet while dollar notes were squeezed into its folded hands. The earlier voices were now gone, yet Mano stayed inside.

When the student left, he made his way down the side aisle to the front of the church. He paused at the front pew, indecision stopping his movement. Years of faithful worship still resided in his subconscious, and it reminded him of holiness of the location, even if his soul was not quite mended to trust in the message of religion.

He knelt, and a wave of humility swept through his being. He sat in the pew quickly, its hard surfaced welcomed. Time disappeared, but his past continued to burden him. Mano pressed his head to his hands.

"Mr. Palua?"

Mano blinked. Soft lights were now lit; the dancing colors that had welcomed him earlier had disappeared, replaced by elusive shadows.

"It's Father Brian. We met a few weeks back." The priest had slid into the row in front of Mano. "I hadn't realized anyone was in here. I've just locked the front doors."

"What time is it?"

"Just past six."

Two hours? But he just came in….

"Is there anything I can help you with?" Father Brian smiled gently.

Mano exhaled, clasped his hands tightly then lowered his head. "I've been asked to help someone, to be there for her. I'm not sure if it's the right thing to do."

"Why wouldn't it be the right thing to do?"

"Because being there for someone caused a lot of pain last time."

Father Brian frowned as he absorbed Mano's words. "Tell me something, Mr. Palua…Mano. Did you know it was going to end like that? With all that pain?"

Mano looked up. "No. No one did."

"Will supporting this person now also end in a lot of pain?"

"I don't know. Maybe. I hope not."

Father Brian looked toward the altar. "There's bravery that comes from facing one's fears. There's also bravery in going forward not knowing what's ahead. I don't know you well, Mano. But I saw the way you look at Eden. I also saw the way both Eden and Aidan look at you. There's a lot of love there. I'm guessing this has something to do with them. Trust yourself. Because they trust you."

He knew they did. A kind, compassionate woman and her brave son gave their friendship freely to him from the first moment they met.

Mano inhaled. The heaviness was still there but he knew how to push through pain. The question was whether he wanted to. A hand appeared in front of his face. Mano took it and met the priest's eyes. "Thank you."

"You're very welcome." Father Brian stretched as he stood. "These seats are so uncomfortable. Take your time. The doors will lock automatically when you leave. I trust you won't steal any of our candlesticks. I don't know why, but they're popular with the college crowd."

The light from St Anne's guided him back to the trail. He stopped in front of Eden's apartment building. Soft light flared through gaps in the balcony curtain.

He checked his phone. No messages.

He had made a promise to the boy. More importantly, he had made a promise to her.

Mano: Need a friend tonight?

He wasn't going to move until he heard from her. The curtain pulled back slightly; he could just make out a figure.

Eden: Yes.

CHAPTER FOURTEEN

EDEN WOULD COME TO THINK OF THE NEXT FEW DAYS AS SOME OF the most stress-filled in her life. She spent hours on the phone: talking to various representatives of the school district, the school, doctors, psychologists, therapists…everyone and anyone she thought could help Aidan.

She spent an afternoon helping Charles pack the children's clothes and collecting favorite toys and books. There was a degree of finality in the manner in which Charles slammed the trunk of the car, though he insisted this was just temporary. Mrs. Henderson appeared suddenly with a container and handed it to Charles.

"Banana bread. With chocolate chip streusel. Matt's favorite," she said. "Tell that boy he's made of sterner stuff. I'll keep a look out on things. You have my number, if you need anything."

"Thank you. I want to be back by Christmas," Charles said. He looked up and down the street. "This is our home. We'll be back. Patty just needs a break from being worried all the time." He turned to Eden. "We're staying at my brother's for the time being. It's not too far from Brandon's place. I think it'd be a good idea if the boys caught up whenever Aidan is in the city. What do you think?"

Eden nodded enthusiastically. "Aidan would love that."

Charles waved out of his car window as he drove away, first to her then to Mano who was just walking into the cul-de-sac.

Mano kissed Eden on the cheek when he reached her, then did the same to Mrs. Henderson.

"Oh my!" Mrs. Henderson grinned as she fanned herself dramatically. "Don't go anywhere. There's another loaf of bread with your name on it."

Mano held Eden's hand as he led them back to his house. "How did the meeting go this morning?"

Eden groaned. "Adulting sucks. Overall, as good as it could be. It was tense and awkward. I felt for one set of parents. Who wants to hear that their kid is a bully and is capable of such horrible, angry behavior? Said they're working on getting help for their son. Hope we'll allow him to apologize directly to Matthew and Aidan. But the other two? It was like they live in a bubble. Thank goodness Charles was there. He was doing his full lawyer thing."

"What happens next?"

"Those bullies are suspended for a week."

"Just a week? Not expelled?"

"No. And our boys are allowed to keep up their schoolwork through distance learning for as long as we feel it's in their best interest."

"Seems like the bullies got off easy."

"Honestly? And maybe I'm just being a wimp about it, but I don't care about them. I just need Aidan to be okay. Has he talked to you?"

"He sends me a message every day. He wants to come back to Seven Hills."

Aidan repeated the same desire when she met him, Brandon, and his family at the airport. They were leaving for Louisiana to spend Thanksgiving with Lisa's family. But she didn't have a definitive answer for Aidan. She couldn't leave her job; the rents in the city were higher than before she moved into the suburbs.

Brandon was there but… "Your dad and I have a lot to talk about, okay, bud?" she said as she hugged him.

A few days later, it was her time to board the plane to Los Angeles and meet the people who meant the world to Mano. She had initially been reluctant to join what should have been a private reunion. Then Liana Murphy called and sealed the deal with a name.

"I still cannot believe I'm going to meet Mark Johnson," Eden said. She would squeal but it was a full flight so she redirected her energy into giving Mano a side hug. "I'm going to meet the Sexiest Man Alive in less than a couple of hours."

"Maybe longer if L.A. traffic lives up to its reputation." Mano adjusted the air vents. "Mark's really more of Liana's friend. One of her best friends, actually. He was a bit annoying when we first met him, but he has grown on us. And for the record, he hasn't been the sexiest man in a few years."

"He's still hot! Silver Fox hot! And we're staying at Veronica Boyd's house? The *Impulse* albums were the only non-Motown ones Pop would let me play in the house, and he still has them!"

"Now, Veronica's nice. Very generous."

Eden studied Mano. "You really are famous, aren't you?"

"Not in this country."

"Mano, the rest of us aren't used to rubbing elbows with people who have their own entries in Wikipedia with multiple paragraphs."

"Brandon and Jordan both have fan clubs," Mano pointed out.

"Okay, that's true." Eden's smile softened as she placed her hand on top of Mano's, squeezing it slightly. "Thanks for inviting me. Getting away is probably what I need right now. With Dad and Pop working over Thanksgiving, I wasn't looking forward to being alone."

"I would have stayed."

Eden shook her head. "And miss seeing your godson? I wouldn't have let you."

Mano took her hand, still in his, and lifted it to his lips. "I know.

They continued to hold hands until the moment they drove through large metal gates and parked in front of a mansion the likes of which Eden only saw on TV or in high end real estate magazines.

"Come on! None of my friends live in places like this!" She eyed Mano suspiciously. "Do you live in something like this in New Zealand?"

Mano shook his head. "Far from it. My house is about the same size as the one I'm renting in Seven Hills. But no backyard. I do all right. Rugby players don't make the kind of money your professional athletes do."

She continued to stare at the front of the mansion when its large front doors opened and she felt the rush of blood to her face. "I think I'm going to die...."

Eden had followed Mark Johnson's career since he burst on the scene as the star of the "Skycatcher" action series. A couple of shirtless pictures of him was still on her phone somewhere, and here he was, walking toward her with a smile that left her immobilized.

"Breathe, Eden, breathe," Mano whispered into her ear.

"I'm dying...." she whispered back.

"Hi! You must be Eden," Mark said when he got close. Eden didn't know what possessed her but she started to cry.

* * *

He shouldn't have laughed but it was rare to see the actor known for being the epitome of suave and sophistication look completely confused.

Mano reached for his pocket and pulled out a packet of tissues. "Eden. Are you all right?"

Eden dabbed her eyes and inhaled deeply, her attention now on Mark. "I love your movies! Both my fathers love your movies, and they don't usually agree on many things! My son loves your movies! His father loves your movies! Now that I think about it, you're the common love in all our lives!"

Mark grinned. "You could very well be my new favorite person. I haven't been greeted by such enthusiasm in a long time."

After years of knowing Mark, Mano was no longer suspicious of the actor's smooth manners. He took the hand Mark now offered, genuinely pleased to see the actor again. "Good to see you, mate. I understand Natasha is here as well."

"Yes. It was a last-minute thing. She wasn't planning on coming but suddenly wanted to see everyone before the baby arrives," Mark said.

Mano nodded. The actor and his veterinarian-wife had been trying for over a year to get pregnant. "Then I'm especially glad I flew down."

Voices, screams, and a yell of "Don't drop the baby!" drew the collective attention of Mano, Eden, and Mark to the entrance of the house.

Before Mano could blink, a little body flew into him. Joy immediately flooded his being as tiny arms wrapped themselves tightly around his neck.

"Uncle Mano, you're here. You're really here!"

He blinked back unexpected tears. "Yeah, mate. Said I'd be here, didn't I? Have I ever broken my promise to you?"

He felt his godson's head shake before a pull on his shorts claimed his attention. He looked down to see dark blue eyes peering at him.

"My turn."

Jayne Molloy held her arms out, but Fred tightened his hold on Mano's neck. "He's *my* godfather, Jayne. You didn't let me hug Uncle Mark for ages."

"You're being mean, Frederick Dane. It's because I beat you at footy, isn't it? You're such a sore loser. You're not my best friend anymore!" Jayne stuck out her tongue and ran toward the house.

"I don't want to be your best friend! Who wants a girl for a best friend anyway?" Fred yelled before returning his face to Mano's neck.

"It's been like that all week," Connor said as one arm embraced both son and friend while the other carried Fred's younger brother, Levi. "Cat said I'd better get used to it. I told her we're moving to Auckland if this continues when they're both teenagers."

"You'd never leave the South Island."

"A man can pretend to have control." Connor studied Mano. "You all right?

Mano met Connor's eyes. "Yeah."

Connor glanced at Eden who was playing peekaboo with Connor's youngest son. "You brought her," Connor said, under his breath.

Mano nodded.

"I'm glad."

Despite her star-struck reaction to meeting Mark, Eden seemed comfortable and relaxed with people whose names were more common in popular media and the gossip news. As part of New Zealand's national rugby team and especially after he became captain, Mano had access to celebrities from most walks of life. The more they won, the more famous people they would – and could - meet. Success was always attractive.

Fortunately, his teammates kept it real. As did their wives, bringing them down to reality whenever their egos got too big.

"Mitch, help with the bags, will you? They just arrived." Liana ordered.

"Steve, you help, too," Veronica added. "Into the casita."

Mano held out his duffle bag for Mitch.

"Just today," Mitch muttered as he grabbed the bag roughly.

Liana's delight at seeing Eden was reciprocated. Whenever he looked over, she seemed engaged in conversation with an adult or child. Little Levi Dane seemed particularly enthralled by Eden, content to stay in her arms when she read to him later that night.

"She's amazing," Cat Dane said, as she pushed her arm through his. "He usually doesn't go with strangers."

"Yeah. She's good with people," Mano said. "Everyone she works with, including the uni kids, like her a lot."

Cat grinned. "Be careful, Mano. Your feelings are beginning to show."

"What do you see?"

Cat looked him over. "That you're in a good place."

"Told your husband that I was fine, that he shouldn't worry."

"Not a chance he wouldn't worry about you. You're family. Thank you for coming down. If you hadn't, we would have probably flown up."

"I know," Mano said. "Figured by meeting you lot here, it'll save me from cleaning up the mess you'd have left at my house."

Cat laughed then hugged Mano. "I like where you are now, Mano Palua. And I think Eden's lovely."

Later that night, as he watched Eden sleep, Mano agreed with Cat. Eden Pak was indeed lovely. She wasn't intimidated by Steve's interrogation of her swimming career, Cat's not so subtle questions about "the-two-of-you," nor any of the regular chaos in a house with seven children. She took everything in stride. It was as if she were always meant to be part of this family of friends.

But moments of perfection usually end before their significance can be truly appreciated.

With the weather warmer than usual, the decision was to move Thanksgiving lunch to the pool area. Veronica's chef prepared an eclectic spread that gave a nod to both the American holiday and Steve's birthday.

Afterward, Connor and Mano sat by the pool's edge watching children while Veronica held the women captive with the latest designs for her baby-clothes collection, to be named after Natasha and Mark's baby.

But so in tune they were to each other's moods that as soon as Mitch appeared, his large strides making quick work of the distance from the mezzanine to the pool, they all stopped talking. Liana stood up immediately, her eyes widening slightly when Mitch stopped in front of Mano.

"Corrine is on Neela's phone," Mitch said, holding his mobile. "She wants to talk to you. I thought it was your cousin when it rang. Sorry, mate. I can hang up, if you want. But wanted you to know just in case you wanted to speak to her."

It was as if the world stopped. All because of a phone call. Mano stared at Mitch then at the phone then at Connor. Even the children in the pool sensed a shift from the casual atmosphere of a few seconds ago.

Veronica frowned, cleared her throat and yelled at her son. "Max? Why don't you get all the kids up and head to the games room?" She pushed her husband forward, unspoken instructions in her stare. Sighing, Steve whispered loudly, "But I want to stay – shit! Stop pinching me, woman! It's my birthday! Okay, you win! Right, kids! Ice-cream, yeah? Last one out gets NO toppings!"

Liana exchanged a glance with Mitch then nodded. "How about the rest of us go inside as well? I'm ready for some of that lovely lemonade you made this morning, Veronica." She helped gather the baby clothes while Cat packed up Levi's gear.

"We'll be in the kitchen," Liana said as she touched Mitch's arm. She looked at Mano. "Whatever you need, you have."

Connor stood next to Mitch and looked at Mano. "Mate, if you want some privacy, we'll go too."

Mano shook his head as he took the phone from Mitch, his eyes catching Eden's. "Corrine was Margot's best friend. The last time we spoke, I was still trying to find out where Margot disappeared to."

Eden guessed Corrine must have played a bigger role in

Mano's life than she suspected. And in watching Mano's friends watch Mano, Eden realized he hadn't exaggerated their fears for him. It was there, obvious and unapologetic: Mitch and Connor stood like bodyguards. Their friendly faces now taut and grim. A vein ticked furiously on Mitch's temple, the only moving part on an impassive countenance.

Eden returned her gaze to study Mano; she didn't see what they saw.

She didn't see anything that scared her.

He looked serious; he paced; he clenched and unclenched his free hand, stopping whenever he spoke. She recognized the voice: moderated and clear. His coaching voice. No anger. "Look, Corrine, I wish I could help, but I don't know if Margot will listen to me…. That doesn't sound like a good idea. I'm not sure if I know her anymore... Yeah…no, stay in touch. You have my number now."

No, there was nothing in front of her that surprised or scared her.

He frowned again and nodded. "No, no…don't do that. Please don't cry. It's all right. Everything will be all right. I should talk to Antoinette first. It's been awhile."

He nodded then his eyes found hers again.

A second nod.

But it was for her this time. Just to let her know he was fine, that he was in control.

She moved towards him automatically, her hand slipping into his quickly.

He held it firmly as he continued to talk. She tuned out his conversation with the unknown Corrine on the other side of the world. They stood side by side: he faced his friends while she soaked in the view of Los Angeles, shiny and bright.

When he finished his conversation, he sighed.

"Corrine and Margot grew up together," he began. He, too, kept his gaze on the city view in front of them. "She's like a second daughter to Margot's parents. She wants me to help bring Margot home."

"Why?"

"Margot's father doesn't have much longer. He's been ill for a while."

"Does Corrine know where she is?"

"Yes." Mano inhaled deeply. "Already tried to see her. Margot doesn't want to go home."

Eden squeezed Mano's hand. "And Corrine called because she thinks you can help convince Margot to go home?"

"Yes, but I don't know if that's a good thing. Margot's the part of my life I'm trying to forget."

Eden turned and searched his face. "Who says you're supposed to forget her? She'll always be in your heart. Just because she's not here, standing where I am, doesn't mean you need to forget. She's a part of your history, of your life...in making you the man I'm falling in love with."

Mano's head jerked; his eyes wide at her words. She put her fingers on his lips, wanting to continue before she became aware of what her confession could do to their relationship. This wasn't the time to talk about it. He had his past to deal with. When she knew he wasn't going to interrupt, she traced the contours of his face to his chest, smiling as her palm caught the increased rhythm of his heartbeat. "I think you're ready to trust your heart again. Your brain is saying going back will hurt; your heart is saying it's the right thing to do."

"Do you mean that? That you're falling in love with me?"

She smiled. "Have you known me to say anything I don't mean? No filter, remember?"

She looked past him and smiled at Mitch and Connor. "You're a lucky man, Mano Palua. Your family stands behind you, ready to help at a moment's notice."

He looked over his shoulder. A few weeks ago, she wouldn't have seen it, the softening in Mano's face or the warmth that simmered in his eyes. She kissed him quickly on his cheek. "Talk to them. They know you best. But deep down, you know what you need to do. Whatever the decision—stay or go—it'll be the right one."

She began to move away, to make way for the two men who continued to give them space, but Mano pulled her back into his arms, his lips claiming hers.

Los Angeles disappeared; Mitch and Connor disappeared; the sun disappeared. But not the heat that automatically flared inside her at his touch, or the sense of completion at being in his arms. *Will it always be like this?*

"Yes."

Eden opened her eyes to see Mano grinning at her. "I asked that out loud, didn't I?"

"Yes," Mano repeated. His eyes emphasized what his words said. It was a promise.

She kept smiling as she made her way up to the main house, pausing when she realized she had entered an unfamiliar wing. Cautious curiosity led her forward. Wide tall windows suggested moving along the hallway would eventually lead her to where she was supposed to have entered.

She ran her fingers along the wooden paneling that encased the nearest window. On the opposite wall, art was meticulously hung in precise spacing. It was an eclectic mix of modernism, Romanticism, Dadaism, and other -isms she couldn't identify. She tried to tell herself that not everything could be original. Surely not the Chagall that was mere inches from her face. The last time she saw the same image was in a college textbook.

The final grouping was personal but no less impressive in composition or impact. There was a shot of Veronica facing a full stadium of people, no doubt in her days with *Impulse*; then there was a large black and white photograph of Steve with a medal around his neck, arms raised in triumph; then there was a familiar looking magazine cover of the three Boyd children modeling clothes from Veronica's new line. And, lastly... Eden eyes widened. *No way...at the royal wedding!*

Laughter guided her to the open kitchen where Cat, Natasha, Liana, and Veronica sat around a large island.

"Oh, there you are!" Cat pulled out a bar seat. "Got lost? Trust me, we all do at one time or another. Even Steve, and he lives here!"

"It's quite a house," Eden said.

"It's a bloody mansion," Veronica said, pouring a glass of lemonade in front of Eden. "I wanted something smaller, but my husband has a thing for grandeur, doesn't he, Liana?"

Liana nodded. "Always has. When they got married, it was his idea to light up all of Glasgow with fireworks."

"Most embarrassing day of my life," Veronica muttered. "Mum loved it though. You'd think a woman who spent her entire life in a small village that had more sheep than people would hate all the fuss. But she and Steve are like two peas in a pod. Big, big, big. Fancy, fancy, fancy. I'm just a simple girl at heart."

Eden didn't miss the amused look exchanged by Cat and Liana while Natasha burst out laughing. "Yes, that's you, Veronica. Simple!"

"I am!"

Eden drank her lemonade, recalling that the last time Veronica Boyd attended an awards show, the singer-now-designer made headlines by wearing an evening gown made mostly of crystals, pearls, and little else.

"We're glad you're here. I hope you've been comfortable," Cat said. "We can be a lot."

"Amen!" Veronica raised her glass. "Only the strong make it through a weekend with us! Way too many egos and competitive spirits in one house!"

Natasha rubbed her protruding belly. "Don't mind them, Eden. They're harmless underneath the glitz and glamor of it all. I'm the only one never to have made a cover of a magazine, and they still let me sit at the dining table once in a while."

Eden grinned. "Mano calls you his family."

"We are," Cat edged closer to Eden. "He's mentioned you as well. And Aidan, who we hope to meet one day. He never talks about anyone, especially the women in his life. We didn't even know Margot existed for months, did we? And he's brought you here with him? You must be special."

"He's pretty special to me and Aidan," Eden said honestly.

"He's proud of what you're trying to do with your swimming. Says you came out of retirement and now you're one of the top swimmers in the country?"

Eden shifted on her seat. "For now. Records don't last. But I've decided to stick to just swimming at Masters level from now on."

Liana frowned. "What do you mean? I thought you were headed to the National Championships. Alistair sends me the faculty newsletter."

"No. I'd set myself a deadline to qualify at my last meet, and that didn't happen. Also, my son needs me right now."

"Fair enough," Liana said.

"Yes," Cat said. "If you feel there's no more to be done, you should close that door. Move on."

"Oh, yes. If you are done, *definitely* close the door," Veronica said. "Forever. The End. Finito. Fini! Nothing worse than living with someone who keeps chasing a dream they just won't give up. Steve's always wanted to qualify for the World Cup with Scotland, but it didn't happen."

"He can always aim to manage a team to the —"

Veronica held her finger up at Liana. "Hush! No! Don't say it! Don't even suggest it!"

"But—"

"No! Retiring hasn't been easy for him!" Veronica looked around then lowered her voice. "He's a bit lost. His whole life was about perfecting his skills on the field, of being mentally strong...but no one talks about what happens next. When the contracts no longer come, when all they're offering is being on the telly to talk about the game, to talk about other athletes...."

That's not Steve. I worry he's going to spend too much time thinking about what he didn't do instead of enjoying everything he has accomplished."

"Has he given more thought about talking to Dr. Spurgeon?" Liana asked.

Veronica rolled her eyes. "Not really. If it were anyone else who'd suggested it, Liana, he would have chucked the card in the bin right away. All I can say is that he did put Spurgeon's number in his mobile."

"For Steve, that's a good first step," Liana said.

"Yeah, it is," Veronica said. "One day at a time, yeah?"

"Is that the same Spurgeon Mano talks to?" Eden asked.

Cat's eyebrows shot up. "He's told you about Spurgeon, has he?"

"He has. Is he a psychiatrist?"

Liana shook her head. "He's a psychologist. I've worked with him when I went through post-partum depression. He has worked with Mano and a lot of other athletes on how to deal with pressure and stress. He has a keen insight to who we are as professionals. Apparently, we're a case study in itself!"

Veronica nodded and held up her glass. "You can say that again!"

Cat tilted her head. "You're good for him, Eden. Six months ago, we had a hell of time worrying about whether he'll see Spurgeon."

Eden shrugged. "I haven't done anything."

"You've made him care again," Cat noted. "That's enough."

Liana nodded. "To be honest, I wasn't happy with Mitch for giving him Alistair's contact information. I wanted Mano to stay close, to be with us." Liana looked at Eden. "But Mitch was right. For Mano to get back to who he was, he needed to get away, to trust himself with people he didn't know."

Cat huffed. "If Margot didn't do what she did—"

"Cat—"

"No! I'm not letting her off the hook. Yes, she was sick, but disappearing like that? Not a word to anyone? That was just immature and selfish. Her poor mum! Having cancer doesn't give anyone leave to be mean!"

Liana sighed. "Oh Cat. Margot…well…Margot…it's not easy to live in the shadow of someone famous. When they got together, Mano had just earned the captaincy." Liana explained to Eden. "In New Zealand, the captain of the national rugby team is one of the biggest public figures. The captain's face is everywhere. His opinions matter; he is, in a way, public property. And she was…uh—"

"Young," Veronica interrupted. "She was young and unprepared for so many things thrown at her. Margot is beautiful and people loved the idea of her and Mano. There was a lot of attention. A lot of expectations of a happy-ever-after. It's hard to be in a fairy tale when you live in real life."

"You two are far more understanding than I am." Cat blinked repeatedly as she studied the random lines of the marbled countertop. "I've known Mano for as long as I've known Connor, and I'd never seen him so hurt as when she disappeared. He always knew what to do. And then he didn't."

"He seems to know *now*," Eden said. "He knows what he has to do; he'll help Corrine."

"You sure?" Liana asked.

Eden nodded. "That's what he does. He helps people."

Three sets of eyes stared at her. "What?" Eden asked. "Why are you looking at me that way? What did I say?"

Liana's dark eyes glistened. "The truth. And you reminded us something we'd forgotten. You're right. That's who he is: someone who helps people."

Mano stayed in Steve's study most of the evening, finalizing his plans to leave for Auckland the next day. Eden turned down the offer to stay the full weekend as planned, managing to secure a morning flight on Saturday. But she was unable convince Mitch that she was just fine taking the shuttle to the airport. His glare gave her insight into what he must have been like as a rugby captain. She made a mental note to quiz her dad about the man.

Sleep eluded her that night. Mano had stirred a few times, but her hand on his back seemed to settle him. She finally gave up, slipping out of the bed as quietly as possible and made her way to the small but comfortable living room. Pushing the curtain aside, she studied the bright stars then noted the stillness of the palm trees that stood over them. Her gaze settled on the pool where underwater lights kept it from being dark and mysterious.

It wouldn't be the first time in her life she'd brave the cold air of winter to get to the pool.

She relaxed as soon as her body touched water, diving deeper until her body skimmed the bottom of the pool. She pushed forward, adjusting her movements fractionally to go as far as possible. Then she turned, angling upwards, but this time on her back. Blurred ripples passed her goggles. Slowly, she floated to the surface again, turning instinctively as her body cut through the surface.

Muscles took over; her mind went blank.

She only slowed when well-formed calves appeared in the water, their owner still absent from view.

"Did I wake you?" she asked when she reached him.

"No," Mano said. "Watched you from inside. You're a fish." He held a steaming cup.

"You really know how to compliment a woman," Eden smiled as she took the mug but remained in the water. "Thanks. This is great. Aren't you cold?"

"This is nothing to the winters we have back home," Mano glanced around.

"Everything all set?"

"Yeah. Leave tomorrow night. Mitch's brother, Tim, will meet me at the airport. I'm sorry for leaving you like this."

Eden smiled. "I'm a big girl, Mano. I can handle a two-hour flight home alone. Besides, we have all day tomorrow with your friends. Feels like I've known them for ages."

"They like you, too."

"Will you call Aidan before you leave?"

"Of course."

"Do Brett and Alistair know?"

"Yeah. And Jackson. They'll send me videos, and I'll write things up."

"How long do you plan to be there?"

"Not sure. A few days? Maybe a couple of weeks."

"I can water your plants."

"I don't have plants."

"But you are coming back, right?" Did the world stop as she waited for his answer?

"I plan to."

"Good. I'll be here. Waiting."

He entered the water fully-clothed. Their shoulders touched. "There's a lot of darkness inside of me."

"And a lot of light. You're a good man, Mano. And I love you."

"Eden..."

"I choose you. I don't mind waiting. And when you're ready, we'll see where this journey goes, right?"

He took the cup from her hand and placed it on the deck. With one hand he gently cupped the back of her neck. His eyes darkened as his thumb traced her jaw before resting on her lips. "You're the first and last thing I think about every day."

She kissed him before he could say more. The chilled air, the cold water, the unknowns of tomorrow were no competition for what they felt whenever their bodies touched.

CHAPTER FIFTEEN

CHRISTCHURCH, NEW ZEALAND

THERE WAS SOMETHING COMFORTING WHEN HEARING FAMILIAR accents after a long time away. It became real then; he was home. He breezed through Immigration and found Tim where the latter said he'd be, in a discreet corner of the airport, far from the excited crowd armed with flowers, placards, and balloons.

Mano moved quickly, keeping his sunnies on and pulled his cap low. He only slowed his pace when he stood a few feet away from the tall figure engrossed with a phone. If he knew his former roommate, Tim Molloy would be checking any number of facts and statistics that nobody else would care about.

"Tim?"

"Oh shit! You scared me!" Tim gasped, one hand clutched over his heart.

"Aren't you supposed to be looking out for me?" Mano said, shaking his head as Tim reached for his bag. "Did you drive the ute?"

Tim dangled the keys in front of Mano's face. "I know this wasn't the practical car of your dreams so if you ever want to sell it…"

"Lucky for you that I don't. Besides, you're a uni student which means that you're poor."

Tim burst out laughing. He casually draped an arm around Mano's shoulders as they exited the airport terminal. "Not for long. Once dad retires and I inherit the farm, I'm sure I'll be able to pay you back."

"Your folks all right? Mitch said your dad was a bit under the weather."

"He's better now, but yeah, it took him longer than usual to get back to his old self."

"He'll be all right."

"Yeah. But for the first time, he actually looked his age. Won't slow down though."

"I don't think anyone in your family knows what that means," Mano said.

Tim grinned. "Yeah, you're right there."

Buildings and roads he once knew like the back of his hand seemed different for no reason. Store fronts, street signs, even the sound of the buses demanded his attention. Familiarity should bring comfort; instead it reminded him only of how long he had been away.

And yet his time in California wasn't the longest he had been out of his homeland.

Different this time, he realized, was wanting to know what was going on elsewhere while he was back in New Zealand. Normally, he was quick to forget about his experiences overseas. He was home and that was all that mattered before. He glanced at his watch.

Since Aidan was still with Brandon, what would Eden be doing now? A vision of her curled up on her sofa watching something on Netflix came. He smiled at the idea. He sent a message:

Mano: Just arrived.

Seconds later, his phone sounded:

Eden: Oh good! I'll be up for a couple more hours, if you
want to talk. Love you.

Tim's chatter on their drive back became background noise, an accompaniment to the passing scenery. He searched the blue skies, a gauze of white cloud breaking the perfection of the color.

"Corrine wants to see you today."

Mano's head turned sharply. "We didn't talk about that."

"No worries. Blake suggested giving you a day at home. She's been staying with him and Neela."

Mano returned his attention to the moving view outside. "I want to talk to Antoinette first. Whatever Corrine thinks, I want to hear it straight from Antoinette that she wants me to talk to Margot. I won't do it without her permission."

Tim nodded. "Neela's coming over after her morning training. Blake couldn't convince *her* to wait." Tim paused. His quick glance over was felt rather than observed. "She's been worried. About you. About how all this might—"

"It won't."

Mano pressed a button on the dashboard and music filled the ute. Tim understood that conversation would cease between them at this point.

When they pulled into the driveway of his townhouse, the front door opened quickly. The stocky figure of his former teammate and flatmate—now married to his cousin—stood at the doorway, his famous smile on display and an apron tied around his waist.

"Welcome home! Though I wish it were under better circumstances," Blake said. "I just got a batch of choc chip cookies out of the oven. Good timing!"

Blake wasn't one to hide his feelings, and Mano found himself enthusiastically enveloped by a tight embrace. "Miss you, bro."

"You taking care of my baby cousin?" Mano asked.

"More like she's taking care of him," Tim snickered as he walked past the two men. "Put him on a diet. Retirement has packed on the weight, hasn't it?"

Mano smiled at the banter between his two former flatmates. It used to drive him crazy, but it wouldn't feel like home if those two weren't arguing about something. They had been an odd threesome: two professional athletes and the younger brother of one. But it had worked.

They were a tight unit, one always there to support another. During the darkest days of Margot's treatment, when he would spend half of his time in his car driving to practice, to the hospital, to team meetings, back to Margot's house, to somewhere for something, either Blake or Tim—sometimes both— would be waiting whenever he got home with a pat on the back, a warm meal, and silent companionship.

"Ten minutes, Mano, yeah? For lunch?" Blake yelled.

He stopped at the doorway to his bedroom. It'd been months since he was last there. The room was virtually untouched but he guessed Tim must have checked in from time to time as there wasn't a speck of dust anywhere.

Shutting the door behind him, he sat on his bed then reached for his phone. His really wanted to hear Eden's voice. He wanted her to hear his.

"Hi!" she answered the call after only one ring. "Are you home?"

"Yes. Did you get home okay? How was the flight?"

"You have the best friends! Mitch and Mark drove me to the airport. I'm going to pretend it has nothing to do with the fact it was either taking me to the airport or decorating the house for Steve's birthday. I hope I didn't leave any drool over Mark when we hugged. He smells so good. But get this: he one-upped Mitch and got me on a private plane! Mitch is so cute when he's angry. Is this an ongoing thing between the two of them?"

Mano smiled. "Yes. Been like that for years."

"How fun!"

"How's Aidan?"

"He sounds good! Going to Louisiana was probably the best thing for him. Lisa's parents are amazing, and she has a lot of nieces and nephews. He's the oldest one there, and Brandon said he has all the little ones following his orders."

"He was born to be a protector."

"Yeah. Patty and Charles are sure they won't be sending Matthew back to school for the rest of the year. I haven't told Aidan that."

"I have a feeling he knows."

"Probably. The boys have talked, which is good." She paused. "Brandon suggested Aidan finish school in the city as well."

He heard her fighting through the hysteria at the suggestion. "What do you think?"

"It makes sense."

"What do you want?"

Seconds stretched before she answered more determinedly. "I think he should stay in Seven Hills until he finishes middle school. He likes it here."

Mano smiled. "You son's not a quitter. He's like his mum."

She cleared he throat. "Well…."

"You're not, Eden."

After their call, his gaze lingered on the lone object still on his side table, now lying on its front. It was a simple frame, bought on a whim to showcase photos that were also impulsively taken in a photobooth. On their first date, he recalled. Except there weren't any more photos, the glass had cracked at his hurried removal. Did he cut himself? He couldn't remember. Darkness had enveloped him then, so strong the rush of anger, sadness, despair – nothing good – that he could barely see in front of him. He had been alone when he first heard her message on his answering machine. They had already talked; she had written a note. There was no need to emphasize her decision to destroy him. But she left a message anyway.

Mano leaned to the side of the bed and pulled out a drawer from the side table. It was still there. He opened the small velvet box. The single emerald-cut diamond ring glistened inside.

Forget me.

It wasn't only what she had said, but how she had said it. He knew her. He heard the relief in her voice. And because he still loved her, he tried to honor her request. It began by taking the ring she had given back to him. Then the rage began to dictate his actions: ripping photos, throwing out her gifts to him. He tore through the house determined to eradicate all memories of their past.

Forget me.

The knock on his door brought him back from the past. "Mano?"

"Coming." He placed the ring back into the drawer.

"Not my idea, and I just found out," Blake said through the door. "But Neela's just parked the car. And Rieann and Joe have parked behind her."

Mano swung his legs off the bed. "What?

"Just giving you fair warning."

Sure enough, his cousins weren't apologetic in showing up unexpectedly. Rieann pulled Mano into her arms before he could say a word. "Why didn't you let us know you were back, eh? I had to find out on Blake's Twitter feed, of all places!

Blake held up his hands in surrender. "Hey, all I tweeted was about the choc chip cookies being a welcome home treat for my former flatmate. Honest!"

Joe pushed through, lifting Mano off the ground with a bear hug. "You don't think we'd let your first day back be without some good food, eh? Dad wants you to visit him soon. Said there's good fishing going on. You haven't met Sam's little one yet, either."

Joe patted Mano's cheek affectionately. "You look good. Told Rieann there was nothing to worry about."

"Real subtle, Joe." Rieann rolled her eyes as she began to pull food containers out of a plastic bag. She slapped at Tim's hand dismissively. "Back off! Mano gets first pick."

"I was just taking a look, Rieann!" Tim protested.

"Yeah, I remember you saying that before half the ham disappeared on New Year's Day."

Mano's grin disappeared when he spied the youngest of the Smyth siblings standing by the door. Hair pulled back, worried eyes met his. Neela was often quoted in articles that he was one of her inspirations when she decided to be a professional rugby player.

He knew better. Given how many records she was on track to break this year, Neela Smyth could very well be the most decorated rugby player in the family.

"Hiya," she said tentatively.

He did as he used to do and placed his hands gently on her shoulders. She responded to his gesture by leaning for the traditional hongi. It was a greeting they'd committed to sharing, just the two of them, when he found her crying in the backyard decades ago. She was tiny then, left behind while her brothers and sister accompanied their father on one of his boats. She became more like a sister to him that day than the little cousin who followed him everywhere.

"You look good," Neela whispered. "Tim said that Mitch said you were laughing in Los Angeles. That got me worried."

"Because I was laughing?"

"Yes. You don't like to laugh out loud."

"To be accurate, Mitch actually said he giggled," Tim interrupted.

Mano glared at Tim, "Mitch wouldn't say such a thing."

"Aha! You did giggle!"

Rieann rolled her eyes. "Food's getting cold. Tim, be useful and get us plates!"

It didn't feel like he had been away for months. Teasing and endless talk circled around him at the dining table. Joe was quick to bring up news from the family business; Rieann kept him up to speed with how their extended family was doing; Neela and Blake were his source for all things rugby.

Tim sat on a barstool busy eating what he could.

A strong sense of contentment washed over him as he watched Rieann laugh. She was a cancer survivor, too. Unlike Margot, Rieann didn't want walls around her to keep her safe.

* * *

It wasn't jetlag that kept him up that night. Thoughts and memories of the life he had here flooded his senses. He tried to focus on what he planned on saying to Antoinette. Instead, all he heard was Margot's last words to him before she disappeared.

When he heard Tim's heavy footsteps descend the stairwell, he glanced at the clock. Dawn was barely breaking but Tim was on yet another research expedition to the coast. Most people would balk at the odd hours, but Tim loved it. Still, Tim loved farming more and couldn't wait to return to his parents' farm to help run it full time. That had always been the plan: one more year with Tim as a roommate then Margot and he would have this place to themselves, a perfect time to start a family.

As soon as 9 o'clock came, he dialed Antoinette's phone number. She picked up immediately.

"Mano! Son! You are home!"

"Good to hear your voice, Antoinette." And he meant it. His nervousness ebbed. She sounded good. "How are you?"

"I'm better now that I've heard your voice. When did you get back?"

"Flew in yesterday."

"Will you have time for a visit? I know how busy —"

"Of course, Antoinette. In fact, that's the reason I phoned."

"Oh? Well I was wrong. I thought it'd be because you wanted to know if you should look for Margot."

He froze. He shouldn't have been surprised though. Antoinette always seemed to be a step ahead of everyone she knew.

She laughed quietly. "Mano? Son? Are you there?"

"Yes."

"Corrine's been here. I know what she feels you – and she – should do."

"What do *you* think I should do, Antoinette? Be honest."

She sighed. "I won't pretend I don't want to see Margot. But I also feel she should want to come home, that she would want to say good-bye to her father." She waited, as if thinking deeply, then asked the question no one had yet. "Would *you* like to see Margot again?"

No.

Yes.

Maybe.

"Mano?"

"I don't know."

He heard her smile. "Neela hinted that you may have moved on. I'm glad. You must tell me about this new love of yours, Mano. She must be special."

"She is," he said immediately.

"See me soon? I want a good look at you. It used to be so easy to keep up with your life, what with you being in the papers and in the internet all the time. But once you retired and left the country, it's like you disappeared as well!"

"I'm sorry. I should have —"

"Ah, none of that! No need to be sorry for living your life. How about lunch today? Michael's usually at his best at that time, but I can't guarantee he'll be able to recognize you. He doesn't always know me either."

His morning was spent counting down the minutes until it was time to leave. He thought he'd be nervous, to face the woman whose daughter he had promised to love forever.

Instead, he retreated into a neutrality of emotions whenever he was placed in moments of pressure.

He may have been gone for months, but the drive to the care facility remained familiar. He pulled the ute into the half-filled parking lot then walked up the path between manicured lawns, toward the ramp that led to a covered veranda. A figure dressed in yellow had come out; she raised her hand in greeting. Within five minutes of his arrival, he stood before the woman who was to have been his mother-in-law.

Barely a meter and half tall, the former dancer stood taller and had her arms wide open.

"You look well," Mano said as he bent to kiss her cheek.

"Thank you." Antoinette tilted her head as she studied him. A bright smile briefly distracted Mano from the dark circles under her eyes.

"Today's a good day," she began. "Michael had a wonderful morning. We had a good conversation. We laughed. And now you're here." She cupped his cheek. "Yes, today *is* a good day."

She hooked her arm into his and led the way to Michael's room. Antoinette was stopped by a nurse near the doorway of what looked to be a large social room. A sitting area was empty but behind it were several round tables, each with different activities keeping half a dozen people occupied. A lone figure stood by the window; another sat reading by the unlit fireplace.

They reached Michael's room at the end of the hallway, entering it after Antoinette gave a quick knock.

Michael frowned when they entered.

"It's me, darling," Antoinette said as she approached her husband. "Mano's visiting."

Michael stared at Antoinette before smiling. "You're very pretty, young lady."

Antoinette's musical laugh filled the room, and she raised her hand toward Mano. "Come closer, Mano. He won't bite!"

Eyes that didn't recognize him fell on Mano's face. "Mano? Do I know you, young man? I'm forgetful."

Antoinette brought out a photo album and sat in the armchair next to her husband. She urged Mano to come closer then began to show Michael photos of their past. If Michael were surprised to see himself in photos he didn't know, Mano couldn't hear or see it behind the occasional questions Michael would ask.

Michael seemed content to just listen to Antoinette speak.

Mano was in several of the pictures. Margot had introduced him to her parents early in their relationship, and his time with the family was well-documented. There were photos of him at a family dinner; when they attended one of his club games; playing cards; having a barbecue in the backyard; the day Margot and he became engaged.

Later, Antoinette and Mano sat quietly on the veranda of the care home, tea and a plate of untouched biscuits were on the small table between them. Music from inside kept them company.

"I will forever be grateful you helped us get him here, Mano," Antoinette said. "I intend to pay you back, you know."

"No, please, Antoinette," Mano said. "We're family not by blood but by choice. I first fell in love with your daughter, and then her parents. I'm glad I could help."

"But you didn't marry—"

"My feelings for you and Michael are unchanged."

"What about your feelings for Margot?"

She studied him intently; he remained silent.

"Corrine thinks you'll be able to bring her back," Antoinette continued. "Michael doesn't have long, Mano. And I think, deep down, even if he doesn't recognize her, he would want see his daughter one last time. I'd like for him to have that. But it still needs to be her choice, though. It's important that she has a say in things."

Mano heard the quiet plea behind the brave words and the cover of grace. Antoinette would never put herself first. Her needs had always been secondary to her family: moving to the

South Island when her life was in Auckland, stopping her painting to care for her daughter, then her husband. Always done with love, without judgement.

Just like mum. They would have been fast friends.

And that's probably why he had to try, because his mother would have. Mano sighed and covered Antoinette's hand with his. With a soft squeeze, he left her without another word.

There really wasn't a decision to be made. He wouldn't have left America without knowing he was going to see his ex-fiancée. Before, he had avoided looking for her in deference to her last words to him. It had driven him almost crazy with anger and grief…and perhaps fear. Her directive became an excuse to ignore his past without fully understanding it.

As he pulled out of the carpark, he could make out Antoinette's figure still standing on the veranda. If he were truly honest, finding Margot for someone else was easier than doing it for himself.

Mano drove straight to Neela's house afterward, his earlier numbness now mixed with a taste of adrenaline. It was the same type of feeling he had before a big match: so much on the line, but to make it to the end of eighty minutes meant focusing on one play at a time.

Results were never guaranteed.

Both Blake and Neela were sitting on the front steps of their house, bottles of water in their hands, and a rugby ball between them. Neela waved as he pulled up, her face glistening from sweat.

"You all right?" she asked through the lowered car window.

"Yeah. Corrine in?"

Neela nodded. "In the house. She's giving private lessons while staying with us."

"Private lessons?"

"Yeah. Piano and voice." Neela looked to the front door. "Little Billy is in there right now. He's a good kid, but not quite the talent. Why do you think Blake and I are working out here?"

He paused just outside the large rumpus room that Blake affectionately called "his library." Keys were struck on an unseen piano then a clear, melodic voice broke the chord into individual notes.

Corrine used to volunteer as a music teacher at the learning center he had helped start through their church. Then he cringed as the next set of notes – sung by a younger and, very enthusiastic voice – pierced through the air.

He poked his head through the opened doorway. Corrine saw him immediately but kept her focus on her student. Only a slight nod in his direction acknowledged his presence. She joined him in the kitchen fifteen minutes later, accepting a mug of tea after a brief hug.

"How was Michael?" she asked.

"Okay. I've nothing to compare it to. He looks good but he didn't recognize Antoinette or me."

"If he's up and talking, it's a good day. There have been days he just wants to stay in bed. And she sits with him. All day. Even if he never sees her."

"She had an album of photos. Looks like she takes it out often. They've had quite a life...quite a love story."

Corrine nodded but continued to stare into her mug. Instincts told him she had something to say, but he didn't expect the loud wail.

"I'm sorry, Mano! So, so sorry!"

Tears had appeared suddenly, and the anguish in her voice matched the sorrow etched in her face.

"I've felt so guilty this last year." Corrine pushed a strand of hair behind an ear and wiped her eyes with the back of her sleeve. "I lied to you. I knew from the beginning where she was. Have always known. I loaned her the money to leave Christchurch, to leave you."

She didn't wait for him to say anything. It was as if a dam had broken, and the words came flowing quickly. Her hands moved wildly; her voice was keen and urgent. But he didn't hear anything; he only saw her pain.

Corrine received the brunt of Margot shutting herself off from the world during treatment. He hadn't noticed how much so until Corrine had asked if he would say something to Margot. She missed her friend; wanted ten minutes to say "hello." But Margot guarded her time carefully. "I don't want to see anyone," Margot had said. "I don't need anyone to feel sorry for me. It's my fight. Corrine will wait. She'll understand. She always has before."

He blinked as the memories merged with the present.

Sad eyes met his. "When she phoned, I couldn't say 'no' to anything she asked of me. I was just so happy to have her back in my life again," Corrine said. "I missed her so much when she was sick. She only wanted you. And her mum and dad. No one else."

Leaning over, Mano reached for Corrine's hand. She grasped it firmly.

Neela appeared in the kitchen with a box of tissues. She pulled out the empty chair, sat next to Corrine, and covered her former roommate's shoulders with her arm. "Hey, I thought we agreed there won't be any more tears while you stay with us," Neela said softly. "At the rate you're going through all our boxes of Kleenex, I might have to start charging you for them!"

Corrine blew her nose into a tissue before looking at Mano again. "Well, I guess you coming home means you're going to get her?"

Mano crossed his arms. "I will try to *see* her. That's all. I'm still not sure why you think I could convince her if you couldn't. You're her best friend."

"I *was* her best friend. You took over that role when she fell in love with you."

"Well, I don't think either of us can claim that title anymore," he countered.

She smiled sadly. "No, I guess not."

He didn't miss the gentle squeeze his cousin gave Corrine. Impulsively, he asked, "Do you want to come with me?"

A shadow of surprise and something else crossed Corrine's face. Fear? Reluctance? Whatever it was, she replaced it quickly with firm shake of her head. "Thank you, but no. She's already seen me. Might be best for you to do this alone."

CHAPTER SIXTEEN

Her eyes opened before she heard the soft vibration of her phone, almost as if her subconscious knew he'd be calling. Eden reached for it, aware of the bubbles of joy that accompanied the anticipation of hearing Mano's voice.

Mano: Did I wake you?
Eden: No. Was hoping to hear from you. Want to talk?

The phone sounded, and she pressed the green icon quickly. "Good morning! Technically, that's true, isn't it?"

"Yes," Mano said. "Just about midnight here. Sorry I didn't call earlier. Spent some time with my cousin and Corrine." He paused. "Planning to see Margot tomorrow."

"How are you feeling?"

"Ready." He sounded determined. "Spent the last six months wanting to see her. Then not. It's time."

"I'll be here when you get back."

"I know."

"I love you. You got this, babe."

"Babe?"

"Too ordinary? How about 'Honey'? Hunk-of-mine', perhaps?" Eden grinned. Pulling her covers as she rolled over, she imagined Mano's face. *He's frowning.*

"What's wrong with my name?" Mano asked.

"Don't you want a nickname?"

"No."

Eden laughed. *He's smiling.* She remained awake fifteen minutes after he said goodbye. No embellishment; no nicknames. Just a "I miss you, too."

I'll take it.

Sighing, she stared at the blank ceiling and knew she wouldn't go back to sleep. She reached for her phone.

5:45 am.

Brandon, Lisa, and the children would have just reached the airport in New Orleans. Once they were checked in, she'd get a call from Aidan. Brandon would make sure of it. He always did.

Maybe it was time for Aidan to live with Brandon. It wasn't as if San Francisco was far away. It'd be half an hour on BART to the city center, then she would hail a taxi to Brandon's house in North Beach. It had always been a possibility. Even her fathers knew it would happen, hence their efforts to build an independent relationship with Brandon and Lisa.

Eden decided on a hot chocolate to keep her company on the balcony. Nobody was about so early. The trail leading to the St. Anne's was decidedly empty, a reminder of how vacant the campus could be over the holidays.

Alistair still snuck onto campus over Thanksgiving break which meant Eden spent much of her first day home going through a dozen of his emails. She was certain another dozen would be waiting today. College hoops was in full swing; commitment letters from next year's Freshman class continued to be processed; the fencing team needed a new trainer to travel with them.

She welcomed the emails and texts from Alistair; they were expected and strangely comforting. Normalcy in one part of her life was welcomed.

Surprising but equally comforting were the text messages from Liana, Cat, Veronica, and even Mark Johnson (she took a screenshot of that one with the intention of printing then framing it). Each had separately checked in with her through the day and sent photos. That little Levi had wormed his way into her heart already. It'd been awhile since she'd last held babies. She wasn't so old that another baby couldn't be in her future.

Eden grinned.

She'll keep that idea to herself for the time being. Even granite had its breaking point.

A few hours later, Aidan texted her as soon as the plane landed at SFO.

Aidan: Dad wants to know if it's okay if we stop at Pop and Granddad's to drop off presents. Lisa brought them beignets.
Mom: Granddad would never forgive me if I said 'no.'
Aidan: OK.
Mom: I'm going for a swim later in the afternoon, so don't worry if you don't hear from me.
Aidan: OK. Can we have Mexican tonight?
Mom: Of course! Tradition!

Only one lane was occupied when she entered the pool. After her first set, she found herself alone…except for a pair of expensive Italian shoes facing her when she reached the side.

Settling her goggles on her head, she swallowed the panic that immediately surfaced at the unexpected. "Where's Aidan? Is he okay?"

Brandon sat down and began to take his shoes and socks off. "Yes. He's at the apartment with your dad and Pop. We left a message on your phone that we're coming straight here. With Mexican. The twins were jumping on your bed when I left."

Eden grinned. "You abandoned Lisa to deal with that?"

"Her idea," Brandon said. "She thought our conversation should be just between us."

Eden eyed Brandon suspiciously. She pushed off the wall and watched him put the exposed half of his legs into the water. "What conversation?"

"Have I ever thanked you?"

"For what?"

"For taking care of our son? Especially while I was training for the Summer Games. I mean, you could have made it really difficult for me."

"Oh, come on, Bran…"

"No, I'm serious. I'm not sure if I ever did. Just for the record, I was grateful. Still am. Forever will be."

Eden swam back to the side of the pool. "You don't have to thank me for taking care of Aidan. He's my son too. That's what I'm supposed to do."

"But you didn't insist I stop training or stay back instead of going to the Games or—"

"Hey, I was from that world too. I knew I had to stop, but there was no reason why you had to. You gave me what you could as a boyfriend."

"Your dads didn't think so."

"No, neither of our parents were happy with how we handled things."

Brandon chuckled. "No. And when we said we weren't planning on getting married…"

"It was like World War Three happened," Eden laughed. "At least it wasn't my side that used the 'b' word!"

Brandon's face shaded a little. "I'll never forget that. I couldn't believe that came from my grandmother. You weren't worried about it though. That's what attracted me to you in the first place. You marched to your own beat, Eden. You always have. I hope Aidan gets that from you."

"This feels like a fairly surreal conversation. Are we sharing feelings, Brandon?"

Brandon smiled. "We've come a long way. But, look, Lisa and I have discussed this. I want to help."

"Help? What kind of help?"

"If you won't go back to Tommy, let me help coach you."

She knew her mouth was hanging. This was the last thing she ever expected Brandon to say. He was done with swimming. He wouldn't know a thing about coaching.

"I know enough."

Eden shut her mouth. "You have a job; you have a wife; you have twin daughters who are in the middle of potty training!"

"The Yuans are open to switching houses with us right now. They know us; we know them. They want to stay in the city for the time being. Moving to Seven Hills for a few months will give Lisa and me an idea of whether we want to raise the girls in the suburbs or in the city."

"Wait— when did this happen?"

"Called Charles while we were in Louisiana." Brandon looked around him. "Aidan and I had a good talk as well. He really wants to stay out here. Despite everything he's been through, he likes it here."

"And Lisa is okay with this?"

"It was Lisa who brought up the idea," Brandon said. "Eden, it's your turn to go for the dream. I remember how much it meant for you to qualify, to do what your mom did. You can do this."

She shouldn't be suspicious but... "And you moving here? This has nothing to do about whether I'm still capable of raising our son?"

Brandon studied the swirls his legs were creating in the water. "We had a bit of a scare. We've managed to make it work so far. It's a good thing. And Aidan's a really good kid. I'm so proud of him, of who he's becoming."

"Me too," Eden said softly.

"We were so young when he was born. Things could have gone really wrong. For whatever reason, even when neither of our parents thought we could do it, we did it. Aidan has always been a priority between us. Neither of us forgot that. And we've always agreed that Aidan lives with the person who can best help him at the moment." Brandon raised his head to look at Eden. "You're that person right now."

Her throat caught at the sincerity in Brandon's eyes. "Thank you. I hadn't realized how much I needed to hear you say that to me."

Brandon smiled. "I know you had to cut hours while you were training. Do you need any money to tide you over?"

"What? Oh my god, can this conversation get any weirder?"

"I mean—"

"No! I'm okay. Really."

"Is Mano lending you money?"

"Is that really any of your business?"

"Oh, so you are taking money from him."

"No! Oh geez."

Brandon laughed. "It's so easy to rile you up, Eden. I hope Aidan doesn't get *that* from you."

"Don't you have to get your nails done or something?"

"Grasping for straws, are we? You're blushing. You must really like him. You're usually more straight-forward if you don't like a guy. This is good. Time for you to get back in the game."

Eden pulled herself up from the pool and accepted the towel Brandon offered. "It's easier for you guys to get back in the game. Single moms aren't exactly at the top of most men's wish list."

"You're a catch for somebody, and by the way he looks at you, I think he likes you back."

"I know he does, but there's someone in his past he can't forget. He has *a lot* from his past he can't forget."

"Seriously? Is she still in the picture?"

Eden sighed. "Not actively. But she's the reason he went back."

"And?"

"And that's where he's different from anyone else. But I get it. I can understand why he's struggling to let go of the life they had."

"*I* don't get it. And you, of all people, shouldn't be on the sidelines waiting for some rugby player to get off his ass and start paying attention to you. You deserve better."

Eden shrugged. "Maybe. But can you imagine being the one who earns that kind of love, that kind of loyalty? That's pretty special, don't you think? Being loved no matter what."

"What kind of Kool-Aid are you drinking? If you love the guy, hold on to him and don't let him go."

Eden stood up and pulled the towel closer over her. "Logical, but this is emotional."

"If you say so. But back to the swimming: why was San Luis Obispo the deal breaker? You know you pretty much have right until Nationals to qualify. Tommy says you're very close."

"Very close," she repeated softly. "I'm a better swimmer now than I was fifteen years ago."

"There is Mesa. And others."

"Yes, but I need to go back to work at the start of the year. My savings will only last so long on a part-time basis."

"I'm willing to help out with money, Eden."

"It's not just the money. St. Anne's has bent over backwards to accommodate my training schedule. But I don't want to lose my benefits. San Luis Obispo was the deadline for me." Eden shrugged. "Logical. Not emotional."

Brandon stood up and surveyed the pool area. "It all smells the same, doesn't it?" A smile stayed on his face. "Mesa is still on the table, if you want it. It's a good meet for you: you do better in the long course anyway. Your turns were always your Achilles heel."

Eden elbowed Brandon. "That's a lie!"

Brandon smiled but his eyes grew serious. "I want to help. I owe you. Let me. Let us. You have your team: your dad, Pop, Aidan, me, Lisa. And now Mano. You can do this."

IT WAS GOING TO BE ABOUT A THREE-AND-A-HALF-HOUR DRIVE TO Tekapo from Christchurch. Mano declined offers from Blake and Neela to join him. Tim also offered to go.

"No thanks, mate," Mano said.

Tim frowned then smile. "Hang on, you have to drive through Geraldine. How about me joining you until there? And you can pick me up after you see Margot."

"No."

"There's a really good bakery there. Right on the High Street. Maybe you could—"

"No."

"They have the best scones."

Mano shook his head as he walked out of the townhouse and got into the ute; Tim stood at the front door, hands resting on his hips, his frown back.

Mano lowered the window. "Go to work! I'm sure there's an endangered species somewhere that needs your attention."

He checked his phone one last time. Still no message from Corrine. He had asked her to let Margot know he was coming. The last thing he wanted was a scene in a public place. After he entered the name of the motel she was now working at, he followed the traffic through the city center then out of it.

Tekapo wouldn't have been the first place he thought Margot would run to.

The last time he was there, he was about ten years old. Surrounded by wide open spaces, Tekapo's lake was famous for its unique turquoise color. It drew stargazers from around the world as part of UNESCO's Dark Sky Reserve.

His lips lifted slightly at the memory of his dad and Uncle Malcolm impulsively loading up him and his cousins into a big truck one late afternoon and starting to drive. The kids didn't bother asking where they were going. As long as they were together, it was going to be all right. Back then, he didn't remember the turns and twists or the teasing views of the mountains before they disappeared whenever the road changed direction.

Joe, Sam, and he were quite the trio back then. His cousins drew him out of his preferred place of few words, encouraging laughter with irreverent jokes made in hushed voices. When the truck finally stopped, golden rays reached toward them from afar, then almost suddenly, red washed the sky of the last of its blue. Did they have dinner that day? Was he cold? He remembered his father's arm draped across his shoulders in the dark as the stars exploded above them. Bright and large, he had tried reaching up for them even though he knew his fingers would never touch the magic.

He hadn't been back since.

And never with Margot.

Whenever they sought escape from his fame, they headed higher into the Southern Alps. In such grand surroundings, there was plenty of space – both physically and mentally – for quiet moments when everything seemed perfect.

Maybe that's why she chose Tekapo.

There would be no memories of them there.

Like for him in Ahipara.

Mano tightened his grip on the steering wheel. His feelings for her couldn't have been wrong. The whispers of love, the gentle caresses, the feeling of contentment in each other's arms... they were real. They must have been.

She loved me once. None of what we had was in my imagination.

He glanced at the sign that welcomed him to Geraldine. He drove past the bakery on the high street but didn't have second thoughts about stopping. Tim wasn't that big a fan of scones.

The phone sounded as he entered the carpark of a motel just off the highway

Corrine: Are you there?
Mano: Just pulled in.
Corrine: She says she'll come out.

The dark, looming mountains in front of him, still lightly dusted with snow, should have drawn his attention. Instead, he kept his eyes glued to the rearview mirror, now angled to the glass doors of a brick building.

When it slid open, Mano reared instinctively, a rush of adrenaline shot through his body at the sight of the petite woman walking out.

He got out of the car; his movements drew her attention. She stopped. Her body tensed up.

As she watched him, he watched her.

She had managed to gain back some of the weight she had lost during chemo; her hair was long again, now tied back into a ponytail. The nose piercing was new.

Margot raised her hand, hesitantly, in greeting.

He responded in kind then walked toward her. She stayed rooted to the spot. He half expected her to turn around, to return to the safety of the motel, but she continued to stand her ground.

"You look well," Margot said when they were face-to-face. She broke their eye contact, stared at her feet before rushing through her next words. "I know why you're here. I don't want to see him. I told Mum; said the same thing to Corrine. Not sure why they think you'd change my mind."

"How are you?" Mano asked.

She raised her head and met his eyes again. They were clear, proud, and unapologetic. "I'm happy. Everything's been real good."

"I'm glad."

"How about you? Corrine said you've been in America. You didn't fly back just for me, did you?"

"I'm good. And, yeah, I did." He paused. "Why won't you go see your father?"

She stared past him; he was sure she wasn't seeing the view either.

"Dad won't remember me. What's the point?"

"You don't know that."

Irritation laced her voice. "If I go back, Mum will make it hard to leave again. I can't stay in Christchurch. There's nothing for me there."

"Your mum, Corrine—"

"—belongs in my past, Mano. Don't you understand? I've been given a second chance to live, to do the things I've been afraid to do before."

"None of us would have stopped you from doing anything—"

"Not out loud! But I would have felt your disapproval!" She took a deep breath, as if to gain control of her emotions. "I just want to do things without feeling I owe anyone an explanation. Mum should understand. She gave up her whole life in Auckland for dad. Broke my grandfather's heart apparently." Margot laughed softly. "Full-circle, I guess."

"Margot—"

Her touch on his arm surprised him. "I *am* sorry I didn't talk to you before leaving. To tell you to your face why. You deserved that. I was—am—too much of a coward. It's just easier and less complicated for me to just go."

He nodded slowly then gently drew his arm away from her touch. "You disappearing hurt more than anything. I thought we could always count on each other for the truth."

"I didn't lie. I told you to forget me. I tried to do the same. But the past comes back when it wants, doesn't it?"

"Yes," he said, softly. "It does."

Margot looked over her shoulder. "Listen, I've got to go back to work. But tell Mum I *will* call her. I just don't want to go home right now." She turned before he could say anything. A part of him wanted more from her; he deserved answers to so many questions. But a stronger voice knew he had all he needed. She had said enough.

Margot stopped at entrance of the motel just as glass doors opened automatically. "Thanks for coming, Mano. Really. You didn't have to. You've always been more than I deserve."

And then, suddenly, he was alone again.

He walked back to the ute but wasn't ready to drive back. Instead, he headed to the shores of the lake. In the distance, kayaks speared through the still-calm water. A young couple was scrambling on the rocks. Their laughter and shouts reached him. Rain was forecast for later that day. He angled his face to feel the fullness of the sun. The clouds remained white and non-threatening.

For now.

He sent a group message to Corrine, Neela, and Tim:

Mano: She didn't change her mind. I'll tell Antoinette myself.

He switched off his phone immediately, shoved his hands into the pockets of his jeans and headed east for no reason.

Her voice surprised him. Different from the soft, musical tones that used to warm his heart whenever he heard it.

Today, he didn't recognize it at all.

It was the voice of a stranger.

Memories of their time after the diagnosis flashed through his mind: her anger, her fear, her fight, a surprising need to keep people out of her life. His cousin had fought her cancer quietly but not secretly. Rieann had warned him that this could change Margot, that it could change them. She told him to be prepared.

But Rieann and her husband's relationship didn't change; instead, it seemed stronger because of her illness. He followed Trey's example: he made sure he was there by Margot's side for all the treatments. If practice and work schedules allowed, he took Margot to her doctor's appointments. He asked Connor and Mitch to take over all his sponsorship duties. Fortunately, his friends had enough name recognition in rugby to appease the powers-that-be so there was little fuss about his absences.

He had promised Margot that he wouldn't leave her, that he would take care of everything, and all she had to do was fight the disease.

Which she did.

His pace quickened on the track. The wind had come up slightly; the rhythm of the waves lapping the shoreline had increased in tempo. Mano looked behind him; the couple was still scaling the rocks, camera in hand. No doubt still in search of the perfect selfie.

The sky remained blue; the sun continued to shine.

Uncle Malcolm's words came back: *small signs tell you when big changes are coming.*

He scoured the horizon. He could just pick out a large mass of dark clouds moving toward the lake.

Small signs.

He had missed them with Margot. So big was the battle, he didn't pay attention to her changing. He just wanted her alive for him, for her parents, for tomorrow. He never once asked her what *she* wanted. After all, they were the perfect couple. The

World Champion and his beautiful girlfriend. What could go wrong?

Nothing went wrong. She just changed.

He stopped walking.

I lost her before she left.

He heard his own breathing; the pounding in his head began.

He fought back.

Inhale. Exhale. Inhale. Exhale.

His body listened as he watched the rain approach him steadily. The pain in his head lessened.

Mano blinked and stared at his hand, fast becoming wet. He then transferred his attention to the mysterious blue lake where stronger waves grew in response to the changing weather. Raising his face to the dark clouds now overhead, Mano shut his eyes and savored nature's baptism.

He was tempted to stay until he was completely soaked, to rid himself of parts of the past he didn't want. But Eden was right. Like it or not, the sorrows were just as important as the joys.

He looked at his watch. Antoinette would be waiting for news. Time to go.

He retraced his steps back to the motel carpark and reached the ute as the rain began to fall harder. He checked the back and found his old gym bag. He grabbed it just as the rock-climbing couple rushed past him. The young man tried to shield his lady-companion with a thin coat, but it only sagged under the volume of water. Still, they laughed as they ran into the motel.

He changed his shirt and toweled off his hair, then waited out the rain before driving straight to Antoinette's house. He thought he had perfected the art of hiding his emotions as captain of the National Team, but Antoinette's smile faded as soon as she saw him.

She bit her bottom lip as a trembling hand held the door open.

"I'm sorry," Mano mumbled.

"You tried," Antoinette said. "Did you both have at least a chance to talk?"

"Not for long."

"It's still hard for her."

"She said she'll call you soon."

Antoinette slipped her hand into Mano's. "I'm sure she will. But stay for tea. I hate eating alone. You still need to let me know about your new love."

Over stewed beef, boiled potatoes and peas, Antoinette firmly opened a new chapter for them, one that had nothing to do with Margot.

She didn't produce an album full of memories. Instead, she asked to see pictures of his life in California. She smiled when she saw Eden's face, fawned over Aidan and didn't stop laughing at his Halloween costume.

When it was time to go home, Antoinette held him tight. "You will always be my son, Mano. We don't often choose who enters our lives, but we have a choice in who we keep."

* * *

Eden's phone call was right on schedule, letting him first have a conversation with Aidan, before shutting the door to her bedroom. "You know, there is technology these days that would allow us to talk and see each other," she said.

"Do you want to switch to Skype?"

She considered the choice. "No. I actually like hearing your voice in my ear. It's like our talks in the dark. Well? What happened?"

It wasn't hard to relate the facts. Harder was explaining how he felt.

"And she just walked away?"

"Well…"

"Didn't you want to stop her? Or spend more time talking? At the very least, I think she owes you an explanation."

"She gave me one."

"That she wanted to live her own life? Wow. Cat was right."

"Cat? What did Cat say about Margot?"

"Nothing," Eden said quickly. "And don't say that I mentioned Cat's name."

"Who would I say anything to?"

"Oh, I don't know. But don't say anything!"

"Have you made a decision about working with Brandon?"

"Oh, no you don't, Mano Palua. You're not switching the subject on me. I'm here to… you know… for you to unload your burden."

"Pardon?"

"You know, to be there for you."

"You are. You've been there for me since the moment we met."

"Since I'm not good at being subtle, I'll just ask. But you don't have to answer. Do you still love her?"

He stayed still for a few seconds.

"Mano?"

Keeping the phone to his ear, he laid on his bed, put his arm behind his head then stared at the empty ceiling. "I don't know."

"Wrong question?" Eden asked.

"No. I just don't know."

After a few seconds, Eden spoke again, her voice gentler. "Feelings just don't disappear, you know. They change. For example, there's still a lot of love between Brandon and me."

"Because of Aidan."

"Aidan's a big part of it, but we created a new relationship in order to parent Aidan. And part of it is based on a kind of love. I think it's a mix of friendship and common interests and history. Feelings don't end just because a relationship does. And because we both love Aidan, it only made sense we learn to include each other in our lives. Not saying it's easy. I'm not sure if I want him back in my swimming. He can be a fathead about stuff. I'm babbling, aren't I?"

Mano smiled. "Yes."

"But no, I haven't made a decision about taking his help. Why is it so hard to turn away from a sport? I thought I was done. But the questions are still popping up. Could I? Should I?"

"Your times say you're not quite done yet, Eden." Mano's eyes settled on the shadow box on his wall. The gold medal it protected was barely visible in the dark. Rieann had put it up, horrified when she found the medal in a kitchen drawer a week after the World Championship.

"My times aren't quite what's needed."

"But they can be. We all know how close you are." Mano's gaze dropped to the framed photo of the National Team, taken moments after Mitch had lifted rugby's most famous silverware in victory. "You know, at one point, Mitch was supposed to quit international rugby. A lot of people didn't believe he was the one to lead us. And if he had retired, no one would have thought much about it. He was still a legend. But he couldn't until he delivered the World title to New Zealand."

"It's a good thing he won then. Not all of us make it up the podium."

"He wouldn't have quit until his body gave out. That's just who it is."

"Would you? Have kept going until you reached your goal?"

"I never had to make that decision. I won the title. Twice. Not much more to win after that."

"Over achiever."

Mano laughed. "Eden, follow your own advice. You know deep down what's the right decision. You're a competitor. Trust that instinct. Trust your heart. There are people waiting to help you get there. Including me."

* * *

A few hours later, Eden threw her bag on the bleachers and began to stretch. She hadn't planned to be back at the pool that afternoon. But her dads insisted she get out of the house while they spend some time with Aidan.

The water was where it always made sense.

This time, however, Eden took some time to watch the lines of silicone-capped heads swimming back and forth. It must be a type of insanity that drives people to do the same thing over and over again. What is it about competitive athletes that propels them to carve time from full, busy lives in pursuit of an elusive, often changing goal? The greats kept going, until their bodies screamed in protest. It was no longer about the titles, the money, or even the recognition.

Am I brave enough to think of myself like them? They do it because they want to know if they can.

Eden reached for her swim cap and pulled it over her head. Making it to the National Championships was supposed to be in honor of her mother, an accomplishment they would both share though achieved decades apart.

That couldn't be the only reason anymore.

"Why, Eden?" she whispered to herself. "Why set yourself up for heartache again?"

Why not?

CHAPTER EIGHTEEN

Mano spent the next few mornings with Antoinette and Michael; then he'd drive to either Mitch's or Connor's homes, his friends having returned from Los Angeles soon after him. There was a day out at sea with Uncle Malcolm and his cousins. What was supposed to be a free morning to catch up with work was spent at the gym with Neela and her teammates.

In all that time, no one brought up Margot's name. Not even Antoinette. So, he didn't either.

Only Eden would ask if he heard from her. But she never pushed for more, satisfied with his simple answer of 'no.'

Thousands of miles away, her voice in his ear was how he ended his days.

"He can be such an ass," Eden said.

"Brandon?" Mano asked.

"I should never have agreed to work with him."

Mano decided not to make a comment. She'd hear his amusement immediately.

Instead, she picked on his silence. "And this is the part where you go 'You're right honey-bunny. He's an ass. Don't work with him, blah, blah, blah'."

"Honey-bunny?"

"Too much?"

"You're no one's bunny."

Eden's laugh released his smile.

* * *

Michael passed away exactly a week after Mano returned home. This time Corrine came with him to fetch Margot. No one was able to get hold of her directly.

"Do you think she knows?" Corrine asked on the way to Tekapo.

"I think she would've guessed what had happened after you, me, and Antoinette tried to phone her in the space of one hour," Mano said.

Corrine looked out of the window. "Why can't she say good-bye, Mano? Not to you, not to me, not to her father. The girl I grew up with would have stayed by his side twenty-four-seven."

"We know she's changed. All we can do is learn who this 'new' Margot is."

"Well, I'm not sure if I like this new Margot. I want our old one back."

Mano glanced at his passenger. Her face remained averted, but a flush had crept up a straining neck. He carefully reached for her hand and hoped she felt his support. He, as the jilted fiancé, garnered a lot of sympathy. He doubted Corrine received much words of comfort at her friend's disappearance. "I think the Margot we knew is gone forever, Corrine."

Margot was outside the motel, a bag at her feet. Before Mano could turn off the engine, Margot reached for the handle and slid into the back of the car.

"Hi," Corrine said softly. "We didn't know if you got our messages—"

"Mum planned the funeral quickly," Margot said.

Mano caught her attention in the rear-view mirror. "Actually, it was all your father. He organized it as soon as he learned he had Alzheimer's."

Margot's shoulder deflated as she leaned deeper into the seat. "That would be dad, wouldn't it? Always thinking ahead."

Corrine tried to start a conversation with Margot, but after a couple of monosyllabic responses from the backseat, she, too, spent the rest of the drive back to Christchurch gazing out the window.

The funeral was held three days later. It was a quiet affair with mostly family and a few friends. Antoinette and Michael kept a small but tight social group. Mano sat with Corrine during the service, in the church where Margot had been baptized, and where they were to have married.

Neela and Blake sat behind them, as did Connor and Mitch. The latter two had never met Michael. They were there for him.

Neither Antoinette nor Margot said anything. Only the pastor spoke, a short but thoughtful eulogy.

This was definitely Michael all the way: no fuss and no fanfare.

As the church emptied, Mano's gaze lingered on Margot's kneeling figure. Neela looped her arm around Mano's neck from the back then kissed him on the cheek. "We'll take Corrine with us to help set things up at the house. See you back there?"

He nodded. When he slid into Margot's pew, she rose from her knees and sat back on the seat. "Are you okay?" he asked.

"Mum's giving me a few minutes," Margot said. "She's tired, you know. I hope she'll go back to Auckland now that he's dead. She never did anything for herself while she lived here. Did I tell you I found an old album of hers? Full of newspaper clippings and photos of her dancing days. She was good. Could have been a professional."

"I'm sure she was really good."

"Can you imagine spending so much of your life looking at what you had to give up?"

"She also has an album of her life with you and your dad. It's a big album."

Margot angled her body slightly to face him. "What about you, Mano? Do you have a collection of all the articles that say how great you were?"

"No."

"Do you still love me?"

The sharpness of her tone rather than the meaning of the question caused his frown. Was that a flash of anger in her eyes? Was this a test? "You're the second person to ask me that. Why do you want to know?"

"I'm not sure. Maybe because there's a part of me that still feels guilty for leaving you the way I did." She looked around. "You wouldn't lie in church, would you?"

"I've never lied to you."

She smiled. "You're right. But you don't owe me the truth anymore."

"Someone told me that feelings evolve," he began slowly. "And I've been trying to understand what I feel for you since you left. It's not the same kind of love, but it is a type of love. You were the first woman I ever felt I could spend my life with. And you will always hold that position – as the first."

Margot lowered her head, the earlier sassiness now gone. Her body slouched in her seat. She clasped and unclasped her hands nervously. "I'm sorry I changed. The future we were planning could have been a good one."

"Maybe. But don't be sorry. I'll never regret us."

She wiped her cheeks swiftly then gave him a quick smile. "Nor I."

She stood up, rubbed her skirt flat then turned toward Mano. "Be safe, and thank you for loving my parents the way you did." She leaned forward and placed a soft kiss on his cheek. "Another man would have stopped caring."

The next day, Mano flew to Auckland and followed the route he took almost a year ago. This time, however, there was no overnight stay at the pub despite an invitation from the owners who welcomed him back with open arms and lots of winking-and-nudging.

Mano spent the afternoon at Jay's grave before stopping in to see Jay's widow, Kelly, and their daughter, Maile. Curly hair-ed with big brown eyes, Mano saw a lot of his late friend in his little girl: her spirit, her smile, and especially with a rugby ball always in her hands.

When he reached the bach, the final light of the day was giving way to the coolness of the night. A stale scent hung in the air when he entered, but other than being a little dusty, the bach looked pretty much as he left it. He immediately opened the door to the deck and the rush of sea air slapped his face. He didn't feel its chill; he embraced its raw and unreserved welcome.

A couple of days later, as he watched the surfers while eating a sandwich, the last thing he expected to see were four familiar bodies walking up the beach towards the bach. There was some friendly jostling from the younger two, with one nearly getting dumped in the waves. The group moved casually, no urgency in their strides. At one point, the largest of the four put his hand to shield the sun from his face. Mano raised his hand up, recognizing his friends would want a signal from him.

They were uninvited guests, but they were never going to be turned away from his door.

When Mitch reached the top of the hill, Mano threw a can at him. "What are you lot doing here? I left a message this time."

Connor came up behind him and opened his hand to receive the next can tossed. "Yeah, but we had such a good time when we here last, we thought we'd do it again. We did make the mistake of telling these two, and they decided they wanted to come along as well."

"Who's taking care of my house, Tim?" Mano asked.

"Nothing's going to happen to it if it's empty for a couple of days. Hey, where's my drink?" Tim said.

"Get it yourself, mate. Only the captains get service," Mano replied.

Tim looked at Mitch. "We're pulling rugby rank this week, are we?"

"Don't look at me. You wanted to come along," Mitch said.

The deck became crowded very quickly as bar stools were moved from the kitchen to outside. "There's only one bed here, and it's mine," Mano said.

"It'll stay yours," Connor said. "We rented a place not too far from here. We thought you could use both company and some privacy, this time around."

"Basically, we don't think you're going to kill yourself this year," Blake added.

Mano glared at him. "Why are you even here?"

"Neela's training in Wellington for the week. I rather be with my rugby-brothers than alone," Blake said.

The next few days felt like deja-vu. They indulged in a lot of physical activity, cooked, went fishing, borrowed some boards and gave surfing a go. Eventually, they were going to ask, and the questions came on the last night of their stay as they gathered round the makeshift fire pit Tim put together.

"You staying there or she coming over?" Mitch asked.

Just like that. No fuss; no build-up. Straight to the point in typical Molloy fashion.

Mano took a drink from his beer. "Who do you mean?"

Mitch simply raised his eyebrows. Blake laughed so loud he almost fell of his stool. Timothy hollered. "Yes! A showdown between Molloy and Palua. I knew being put through physical torture this week was going to have its rewards!"

Connor, dressed in a cashmere sweater, his neck protected by a woolen scarf, was seated in a foldup chair, next to Mitch. "Come on, mate. We saw the way you looked at her," he said, tapping his fingers expectantly on the metal armrest. "She's come to mean a lot to you."

"True," Mano said.

"And?" Mitch asked.

"Nothing to add. I'll go back to California in a couple of days. Finish up my contract. But she lives there; my home is here. That's it. End of story."

"Why should it be the end of a story?" Blake asked. "From what everyone has said, she's been looking out for you almost since the day you landed in California. You've come home more like yourself."

"Do you love her? This Eden Pak?"

Mitch's quiet question hung between them. Even the wind died down then, as if the universe was waiting for his public declaration. Once it was said for others to hear, it could never be taken back. It would reach the ears of the past, the present, and the future. His future; her future.

Their future.

"I...do."

Even he heard the anguish in his voice. He finished his bottle abruptly, got up and walked towards the recycling bin hidden in the dark corner of the small garden. He ran his hand through his hair.

"What's she like, Mano?" Tim asked.

He emerged from the shadows and returned to his seat. His heart warmed at the memories that came with her name. He smiled. "She's a single mum juggling everything. The kids at uni really like working with her; she gets them, being an athlete herself. She forgets her keys a lot, loves to cook and hates talking to her son's teachers. She makes do with what she has; doesn't like hand-outs. Aidan – her son – has her smile. It's all smiles or none. And she said she'd wait for me until I'm ready to love her back."

"What?!" "Shit!" "No way!"

"Why the hell are you still here?" Blake asked.

"Stanton..."

Blake glanced at Mitch. "What? You're thinking the same thing!"

"Not everyone has been in love with their wife since they were twelve-years old, Stanton," Mitch shot back.

Mano smiled. He had been in France when Blake reacquainted himself with his cousin, who also happened to be Blake's childhood crush. Neela and Blake—or "NeeLake"—were last summer's feel-good story, but he knew behind the media blitz about the romance were two people who were always meant for each other.

"As a member of your family—"

Mano stared at Blake. "As the *younger* member of my family, you'll know better than to say more."

Connor laughed then. "Well, since I'm not, I'll say what I think Blake was going to say. You love her. There's nothing holding you here right now, mate. Come on, even her name is perfect for you. She shares the name with your favorite place in the world."

Mano tapped his temple. "I'm not quite right yet in here. There are still days…" He glanced at the faces around the fire place, and tried again. "There are still days I can't let anyone in. It wouldn't be right."

"What does she say about this?"

"What do you mean?" Mano turned to Mitch.

"Liana said Eden is fully aware of what you're going through. When Liana went through postpartum depression, I had never felt so helpless in my life. But the only place I wanted to be was by her side. Eden has seen a lot of life. And she's choosing you."

"Yeah, but—"

"If Eden is willing to wait until you are ready to love her like you can, then the man I know would fight for that," Connor said.

Mano heard the words and understood the message. He had learned to live with loss, to shelve another life under "what-could-have-been," but was he ready to consider himself the right partner to a beautiful American swimmer whose kisses took him to a different place?

It'd be a future of sunshine and chlorine and teenager-hood.

Tim cleared his throat. "If the words of a single, gay man have any weight on this topic, here's my input—"

"Oh god, here he goes…please, no rugby metaphors," Blake moaned.

Tim ignored him. "The bigger regret would be not knowing if you two could make it work. You're not the type of man to stand on the sidelines wishing for anything. None of you are. You were born to take calculated risks. Those instincts have been fine-tuned on the pitch. It's what made you lot world champions."

"And there it is…just couldn't help himself…associating our love lives with rugby," Blake muttered.

"Hey, I was right about you and Neela, wasn't I?" Tim retorted, smugly.

The fellas left just after midnight.

Mano doused the already dying fire with water: a soft sizzle followed by a light plume of smoke rose. The crashing waves promised his night wasn't going to be quiet. He appreciated the white noise.

Once inside, he shut the sliding doors and drew the curtains. A quick glance at the kitchen clock suggested a call to California might be a little early. Eden could be up but probably in bed, mentally planning out her day. She emanated a quiet strength from the first moment they met. She'd already shown that she didn't need him in her life.

But she wanted him.

Being with her would be a "calculated risk". Was it one he was willing to take again?

CHAPTER NINETEEN

THE BART RIDE FROM THE AIRPORT TO SEVEN HILLS WAS EMPTY
and on time. He was returning a day early, unconcerned at the
last-minute cost of his flight change. There was nothing waiting
for him in New Zealand anymore. Not alone, anyway.

He smiled at the blue skies that welcomed him after the train
emerged from the final tunnel before his stop. Cloudless; higher;
wider; bright. It was now familiar and welcoming.

Normally, especially unburdened by a suitcase, he would
have considered the three mile walk home from the station. But
not today. He headed straight for the taxi stand.

"The swimming pool at St. Anne's, please."

Fifteen minutes later, Mano walked through the glass doors
to hear a familiar voice…yelling.

"I don't think so, Bran-don!"

"That's not how this works, E-den. You listen to what your
coach says; then you do what he asks you to."

"And Lisa doesn't argue back when she's ordered around
like this?"

"This has nothing to do with Lisa and me. We're talking about *you* taking my advice about swimming seriously."

"My. Turns. Are. Fine." Eden then dove under water as Brandon threw his clipboard on the floor.

Aidan's giggle grabbed Mano's attention from the pool. He climbed onto the metal bleachers and walked toward the seated Robert Pak and Aidan.

"You're back!" Aidan climbed over a row and reached Mano within seconds, giving him a big hug. "Mom said you were coming back tomorrow. We were going to bake you something."

"Just took an earlier flight." Mano looked over Aidan. "How are you doing?"

"Good." Aidan looked to the pool. "It's kinda weird having dad and Lisa nearby. But since I'm homeschooling for the rest of the semester, I like having someplace else to go."

"How's Matthew?"

Aidan pursed his lips. "Okay, I guess. We text every day. But I'm not sure."

Mano squeezed Aidan's shoulder. "You being there for him is all you can do. You're a good friend."

"Matt's my best friend. He says he might want to come back next year but doesn't know if his mom is up for it. Mano? Uh… rugby tryouts are in January. Mom and dad say I can still go out for it. Will you help me even though it's just me?"

"Of course, mate."

Mano reached over to shake Robert's hand. "How are you, sir?"

"Very good, but I'm glad you're back. She's been giving Brandon hell. He may need your help. She's on edge a little."

"She's cussing a lot more," Aidan added.

Mano returned his attention to the pool. "Will it work? Them working together?"

Robert grinned. "They just need some time to settle into their new roles. I will say this about Brandon: he knows his stuff, and he will give her all he's got. They're both equally stubborn, though. Should be a good time for us on the sidelines!"

Mano smiled then turned to Aidan. "I want to say something to you, and it's okay if this is something you don't like."

Aidan tensed. He glanced at Robert then met Mano's gaze. "Okay."

"I love your mother. And I've decided I want to love her forever. I'd like to very much be part of your life. And you to be part of mine. How does that sound?"

Aidan didn't say anything. Mano felt all he needed to know in the hug they shared, a tight embrace Mano knew he'd remember forever. When he looked up, Robert Pak had removed his glasses and was wiping his eyes.

Mano began. "Sir—"

Robert waved dismissively. "There's nothing for you to say to or ask of me. Eden's her own woman. But if it's helpful, both Don and I like you very much. I hope this works out for the three of you. I really do."

Mano took the offered hand and shook it. "Thank you. I do appreciate knowing that." He looked up. "Do you think she'll mind if I interrupt her training for a while?"

Aidan shook his head. Amusement now danced in his eyes. "Dad would love you for it."

Mano climbed down the metal bleachers effortlessly, his focus now on the fast-moving figure in the pool. Despite her earlier anger, Eden swam in controlled, clean, seemingly effortless strokes. She turned with stealth-like precision when she reached the far end of the pool and was now headed towards him.

Brandon didn't hide his surprise at Mano's presence. "What are you doing here? Aren't you supposed to be in New Zealand? Aidan and the girls were planning to bake cupcakes for you tonight."

"They still can. Mind if I talk to your star swimmer?"

He didn't wait for Brandon's permission; he quickly discarded his shoes then jumped into the pool.

Mere seconds later, a befuddled figured emerged from the water. "What the he…" Shock turned to surprise. Eden gasped and pulled off her goggles. "Mano? When did you get back?"

He met her halfway, one arm over the pool divider while the other reached for her waist, drawing her close. "I didn't want to be away from you one more day."

"You really need to stop jumping into pools fully clothed, it's danger…" Her next words were lost when his lips claimed hers. He pulled her closed, uncaring that he no longer had the support of the buoys to stay afloat. Even as they began to sink, he felt her complete and utter commitment to their kiss. To him.

When their feet touched the ground, they both opened their eyes simultaneously and pushed up, hands entwined.

"I love you," Mano said when they both broke the surface.

She smiled. "I love you, too, Mano."

"You made me realize all I need, I have it with you. With Aidan. Here. But," he was compelled to warn her again, "…there will be days I may not be what you need."

She hugged him tight. "We'll take this day by day. But I'll be here for you. All of you. Always. Forever. Promise."

EPILOGUE

Four months later, Mesa, Arizona

She should be feeling some kind of pressure now that she was at the Aquatic Center. But a Masters meet was different that way; it was a celebration of the swimming community as a whole. Brandon had suggested she start watching some of the earlier races, especially those in the most senior categories.

"Be inspired again," he suggested. And this time she didn't argue.

She cheered loudly when eighty-year-old Maureen Holden finished her Fifty free, out-touching her nearest rival and twin sister, Molly.

She laughed when she caught the likes of Liana Murphy and Cat Dane starting a stadium wave in the stands, somehow getting their hands on poms-poms. Their husbands, Eden noted, weren't around when it happened.

She still couldn't believe they were here in support of her goal.

"Eden!"

Eden pulled out her earbuds. "Jordan! Congratulations! A national record!"

Jordan shrugged. "Thanks. Yeah, that was a surprise. But it's a fast pool. Perfect conditions today. I have a good feeling about your chances."

"Thanks. The team's doing really well."

"Yeah, but you are missed. Tommy still has you in his notebook, you know."

Eden smiled. "He's been gracious to talk to Brandon."

"Well, you're the one person everyone wants to see make it."

Eden had to know. "I appreciate all your support, even after I left the club. I've asked you once, but you didn't give me an answer. Why? We're friendly but not really friends."

A look of vulnerability settled on Jordan's face. "I don't expect you to remember this because it was so long ago. And you didn't ask my name back then, but at my first state meet, I got DQ-ed for a bad start. You were one of the biggest swimmers there, and you looked for me. You then told me to just focus on the next race. That there will always be another race. Another chance. It was the kindest thing anyone said to me that day, that week. It kept me going. Still does."

"Are you sure that was me?"

Jordan smiled. "Oh yes. You're pretty unforgettable, Eden Pak. And part of the reason I'm so passionate about building the Berkeley team up is because of what you'd said. We all deserve second chances, to try one more time."

She reached to give him a hug. "Why didn't you just tell me?"

"I've never shared it with anyone," Jordan said. "But if you must know, I wasn't sure if you were still that nice now that I'm an adult."

Eden laughed as she pulled back.

"But you are, and more," Jordan said. "Some angels are also meant to be fighters. You're going to make it. I know it."

"Thanks," Eden said. "And when we're back at St Anne's, let's have lunch. I'd like to know the person and not just the swimmer."

"Deal." Jordan looked passed Eden. "I'd better go. There's an ex-rugby player staring me down." Jordan held out his hand. "Good luck. I'll be cheering in the stands."

Mano's arm snuck around her waist, drawing her close. His head nuzzled into her neck. "Did I hear you make a date with Jordan Kennedy?"

"He called me an angel. Why not?"

She felt his smile on her skin, eliciting goose bumps on the back of her neck. "That you are, Eden. That you are." He turned her around. "You're ready, aren't you?"

She nodded, breathing deeply. "I have to get into my zone."

"I know. Whatever happens…"

"… will happen. I'll have no regrets after this swim. Whether I make it or not, being here, at this moment, with everyone who means the most to me, is all I need."

"I love you, Eden Pak."

"I love you, Mano Palua."

* * *

Mano watched Eden pick up her bag and walk towards the waiting area, tall and confident. Her earbuds were now in place, and he suspected her music of choice was going to be Aretha. He took one more look at his love before finding his way back to the crowded bleachers.

"I still can't believe all of you are here," Mano muttered, stepping over Connor's legs.

"Hey, when one of our own is about to make history, we're going to be here," Connor said. He held out a big tub. "Why's American popcorn so good? Even the microwave stuff is really good."

"Where's Aidan?" Mano said.

"Brandon took him to meet some of his former teammates," Cat said. "You got the ring?"

Mano stared at Connor. "Couldn't keep your mouth shut, could you?"

"I didn't say a word," Connor said. "She heard the message from the jeweler about the new setting. She guessed right away."

Mano rolled his eyes. "You're not very good at keeping these things a secret."

Connor stopped midway from putting the next handful of popcorn in his mouth. "Have *you* ever been successful at keeping something secret from Cat?"

"I admit to nothing."

Connor resumed eating. "Yeah, I thought so. I can't either. I don't know which is worse: when Cat thinks I'm hiding something, or when Liana finds out Cat is mad at me. Ouch! Cat! That hurt!"

Liana climbed into the row behind them, carrying a cardboard tray. "Where did you get that popcorn, Con? Cat, have you tried these? Corndogs! It's the mustard! And they have these incredible pretzels with jalapenos. Good, yeah? Who knew swim meets could be so social? Did you remember the ring, Mano?"

Mano shook his head. "None of you will be there when I propose. None of you. It's meant to be a private moment. Bad enough you lot know all about it."

Liana grinned. "Don't make me take out the binder we have for your wedding!"

Cat burst out laughing, and despite all intentions to maintain his straight face, Mano smiled. Liana, Cat, and their girlfriends were notorious for planning events before any of it happened.

From behind him, Liana looped an arm around Mano's neck and whispered into his ear. "Mitch said you're enrolling at St Anne's as a student? To study psychology?"

Mano nodded. "I've come a long way. There's still a long way for me to go. And I think I'd like to eventually work with other former professional athletes, to help them deal with what happens after our careers are over."

"Yeah. There hasn't been enough done to help us transition to a life after sport. You'll be great at it."

Mano squeezed Liana's forearm. "Thanks."

"And, if it makes *any* difference, we all love Eden. She's a good fit for our family. For you. Whether the ring is in your pocket or not, it doesn't matter. We just want you to be happy."

"I am happy."

Thirty minutes later, their comfortable chatter ceased as eyes focused on the eight bodies now on the block. Aidan and Brandon were back; the latter kept clenching and unclenching his hands nervously. Donald preferred to stare at the ground; Robert had his phone up, providing a quiet narrative while FaceTiming the event to Eden's maternal grandparents.

Eden rolled her shoulders, slapped her thighs and took the block. She looked poised and primed. And ready.

"Swimmers! On your marks!"

At the starter's buzzer, everything around Mano disappeared. He may have been in the stands, but he felt her strength, her precision, her power.

Just over twenty seconds later, she emerged at the other side of the pool. She didn't look at the board for her time; it was his eyes she sought first. Voices around him erupted. He was unaware of the time she'd clocked. He didn't bother checking.

Her smile said all he needed to know.

ACKNOWLEDGEMENTS

To my friends and family, for being my greatest cheerleaders. I so appreciate your constant enthusiasm and encouragement.

To Giana Sikora and Supicha Castro for their insights into the swim world.

To the ladies of my book club who keep me laughing about all things to do about reading. I couldn't be a writer without first being a reader, and my monthly meetings with you help feed the writing muse.

To my beta readers, critique partners and faithful readers who, through your feedback, help grow and form this story.

* * *

If you enjoyed this book, a review is always appreciated! Thank you!

www.ingramcontent.com/pod-product-compliance
Lightning Source LLC
Chambersburg PA
CBHW050338190726
48284CB00007BB/2055